Pride Publishing books by Jason Wrench

Single Books
Twelve Days of Murder

TWELVE DAYS OF MURDER

JASON WRENCH

Twelve Days of Murder
ISBN # 978-1-83943-757-1
©Copyright Jason Wrench 2021
Cover Art by Kelly Martin ©Copyright November 2021
Interior text design by Claire Siemaszkiewicz
Pride Publishing

TWELVE DAYS OF MURDER

Dedication

This book is dedicated to my NaNoWriMo buddies.

Acknowledgements

I want to thank everyone at the Office of Letters and Lights for their continued support to budding novelists everywhere through National Novel Writing Month—NaNoWriMo, https://nanowrimo.org/. Without your continued support, this novel never would have happened. And to my NaNoWriMo buddies, thanks for the help, the write-ins and the great memories.

Foreword

Every November is National Novel Writing Month or NaNoWriMo. I set out to write a mystery based on an initial image I had of a Christmas pageant and a murder. As often happens, the last story took a direction of its own, which I am justly proud of. One of my favorite television shows, *Castle*, starts with a voice-over where a mystery writer says, "There are two kinds of folks who sit around thinking about how to kill people — psychopaths and mystery writers." I'm proud to consider myself among the numerous novelists who spend their days thinking up atrocious and exciting new ways of solving them. I just hope my vision is enjoyed by those who read this novel.

On the twelfth day of Christmas,
My true love sent to me
Twelve drummers drumming,
Eleven pipers piping,
Ten lords a-leaping,
Nine ladies dancing,
Eight maids a-milking,
Seven swans a-swimming,
Six geese a-laying,
Five golden rings,
Four calling birds,
Three French hens,
Two turtle doves,
And a partridge in a pear tree!

Prologue

Five years prior

Frank busied himself clearing the table as Adam unloaded the recently cleaned dishes back into their places in the apartment's kitchen cabinets. Christmas dinner had been a huge success, and now their friends Logan and Ben were sitting on the couch watching *It's a Wonderful Life*.

"I always love this part," chirped Logan.

"Why am I not surprised? You always like the sappy parts," replied Ben.

"You know, there are some days where I wonder how the hell I've put up with you for this long."

Frank peeked into the living room and caught a glimpse of the two snuggled on the couch. "Well, Logan, you know there's a reason I got rid of Ben a long time ago."

"Hey!" Ben responded, picking up one of the throw pillows on the couch and tossing it at Frank, barely missing him. "Besides, you seem to have a revisionist version of the story. I do believe it was me who dropped your sorry ass and started dating your best friend instead."

"Keep telling yourself that, Ben and maybe one day the rest of us will finally believe it." Ben looked at Frank with a jaw-drop and an overly dramatic stare as he turned back to the movie. Logan was playing with his ear as Ben rested his head on his shoulder. Frank smiled and chuckled to himself. He went back into the kitchen to see if Adam needed any help.

"Anything I can do?"

"Nah, just enjoy the night, honey."

"Ahh, you're too damn good to me, Adam."

"I know I am. Now, go finish clearing the table."

"Aye-aye, Captain."

Frank leaned in, gave Adam a quick kiss on the cheek and hurried back to his domestic duties. Despite Ben's fictionalized version of their history, Frank realized that his and Ben's breakup three years before in November had been amicable. Within a month of the breakup, Ben had been seeing Logan and Frank had been dating Adam. All-in-all, everything had turned out for the best. Adam and Ben had met in the lobby of *Wicked* on a Saturday matinee. Ben had been pulling a six-month stint as Fiyero while his soap-opera day job was on hiatus, so Frank had agreed to be Logan's plus-one on his day off.

During the intermission, Frank had headed down to the bar area and was getting a glass of red wine. The bartender had handed him his wine in a plastic sippy cup that he could take back to his seat for the second act. Frank had cracked some kind of joke about feeling like he was three again, when he'd heard someone chuckle to the right. He'd turned his head and stared into the most amazing green eyes he'd ever seen.

"*Adam Bosque.*" He'd just stuck out his hand and introduced himself. Normally, Frank would have been a little annoyed by the ballsiness of it all. Still, there had just been something innately charming about the blond man standing in front of him.

"*François... Frank Schultt.*"

"*You aren't Detective Frank Schultt, the NYPD detective who busted that crystal meth ring over in SoHo last month?*"

"*Depends — are you a relative or a lawyer of one of the accused?*"

"*No, I'm just a concerned citizen and gay rights advocate who tries to get dangerous drugs out of the hands of club kids.*"

Before long, the second act had started, and Adam and Frank had spent the rest of the evening just talking. Adam had later admitted he'd recognized Frank from a newspaper article printed in the *Village Voice* about the bust and that he'd been taken aback when the newspaper article had quoted Frank as being concerned about the cooking and distribution of illegal drugs in the gay community. Something about the way the newspaper had written up the quotation had showed that Frank was a member of the tribe.

Before long, the two had started dating and ended up moving in with each other, purchasing a condo in Greenwich Village two blocks from Logan and Ben. Ever since that fateful encounter at *Wicked*, Adam and Frank had been inseparable, and had married before the end of the year.

"Oh shit!" Frank heard Adam exclaim from the kitchen.

"Did you hurt yourself?"

"No, I just realized I forgot to pick up the rum for the eggnog."

"It's not a big deal. We'll just drink virgin nog. No biggie."

"Speak for yourself. The lushes in the living room want their rum," Logan yelled toward the kitchen.

"It's not a big deal. I'll just run down to Village Liquor at the end of the block," replied Adam. "Besides, I'm sure Mr. Faroq's business is quite dead tonight, so I'll go give him a little Christmas cheer."

"You do realize that he's a Muslim?" questioned Frank.

"Really, and I thought 'Faroq' was an English surname."

"Jackass." Frank grabbed Adam and spun him around in a giant bear hug. He smiled at Adam, looking him in the eyes, and Adam smiled back. Frank leaned in and brushed his lips against Adam's. Pulling away for a brief second, he whispered, "God, I love you," then pulled him in closer for a deeper kiss.

After a minute, Adam pulled away. "I won't be gone long. Store. Rum. Back. I promise."

"Okay," Frank replied.

As Adam went to grab his coat from the bedroom, Frank slapped his ass with the back of his hand. Adam looked at Frank over his shoulder, "Not while the children are in the room."

Adam grabbed his coat and wallet and left the apartment.

Frank went into the living room and sat on the other side of the couch to watch the movie with Ben and Logan. After a few minutes of watching Jimmy Stewart trying to earn his angel wings, Frank headed to the bathroom. On the way, he stopped in his bedroom to make sure his police scanner was on. *Quiet night. Thank God!* He checked his cell phone just to make sure no calls had come in from the precinct. Frank had drawn the short stick that year and subsequently had become the detective on call in case of an emergency. He'd been on call for Christmas Eve a couple of times before, but the night usually ended up being a quiet evening, since most people were either at home with their families or generally staying out of trouble.

Frank walked back into the kitchen to see if anything else needed to be done. Adam had already taken down the special Christmas glasses for the eggnog toast to follow the annual showing of *It's a Wonderful Life*, so he was ready to go.

Frank walked in the living room to see that Ben had fallen asleep on Logan's shoulder. Frank was about to say something, but Logan held a finger to his lips and mouthed, "Don't wake the baby."

Frank's pocket started buzzing, and almost simultaneously, the police scanner in his room went off. "There's a 10-31 at the corner of West Ninth Street and Fifth Avenue."

Frank phoned in to his command. "This is Detective Frank Schultt. I just heard the 10-31. Is it a store or residence being burglarized?"

"Just a second, Detective," responded the dispatch operator. "The first car just arrived on the scene. The 10-31 is at Village Liquor. A silent alarm was tripped, and we're still getting more information."

"Did you say Village Liquor?"

"Yes, Detective, Village Liquor. 10-6 for more information."

Frank walked toward the door, his mind racing with a million anxious thoughts, his cellphone still pressed to his ear.

"Frank, what's up?" Logan questioned.

"Stay here. Village Liquor was just burglarized."

"Isn't that where...?"

"Yes, I'm on my way there now."

The voice on the other end of Frank's cell began talking in his ear. "Thank you for standing by, Detective. The first responders just informed me the suspect is in custody, but there are two bodies at the scene. Ambulances have been dispatched, but the officers on the scene said the bodies are DOA."

Frank said nothing. The cellphone slipped from his hand and crashed to the floor as he ran from his condo into the cold, dark winter outside.

Chapter One

December 15, 6 a.m.

Mornings were never something Frank looked forward to. His usual routine consisted of waking up at around six a.m. and heading over to Club H, a couple of blocks from his walkup apartment in Hell's Kitchen. Club H had all the trappings of a top-notch gay bar — pumping rhythms commonly heard at circuit parties, guys cruising each other left and right, hot, fit men as far as the eye could see. But Frank wasn't interested in any of those. Frank came to Club H for its intended purpose — to work out. This particular morning would have to be cut short, as Frank was meeting his best friend Logan for breakfast before heading over to the precinct.

Frank arrived at the gym and stored his stuff in an available locker, noting the locker number in his head. *101… That shouldn't be too hard to remember.* He grabbed his iPhone, found the first free treadmill and started jogging. Frank found the early morning ritual a great way to clear his head. He increased the speed and incline, losing himself in his workout. He looked around at some of the younger guys in the gym. Many were over in the free-weight section, lifting weights with partners in an erotic exchange of muscle and steel. Frank had long ago realized that being ripped was less important than being healthy.

When Frank had been in the academy, one of his classmates—a tall, brutish guy named Theo—had stood out because of his bulging muscles and neck thicker than a Christmas ham. Unfortunately, the guy had ended up having a heart attack during his second week, due to having no cardiovascular ability at all. Sure, he may have made the Incredible Hulk a little jealous, but, as a cop, Frank had become aware that brawn didn't get anyone very far if it wasn't equally matched with stamina.

Frank looked around the room and nodded politely to some guys he'd known over the years. Jerry was over in the corner with his new boyfriend, Seth. Frank had met Jerry about three years ago in a back room at The Eagle, an NYC bar that catered to people looking for edgier sexual experiences. After Adam had been murdered in the liquor-store burglary almost five years earlier, Frank had tried to find solace in a range of sexual fetishes. As each one failed to make him feel whole, he'd moved on to something even edgier. He'd also started doing some light drugs and graduated to crystal meth, fearing each day he'd be randomly drug tested. He was good at keeping up appearances at work and never did drugs that required a needle.

His wake-up call had happened while sitting in a trailer getting ready for a porn shoot he'd impulsively agreed to do. He'd caught a glimpse of himself in the mirror and just hadn't liked what was looking back. His body, while still in shape, had just looked worn down. His eyes were sunken into his head and his cheekbones were visible. He'd looked like a slightly healthier version of an Egyptian mummy. In that one glimpse, he'd seen more than his physical appearance. He'd seen his future. The one porn shoot could easily get him censured or thrown out of the NYPD altogether. Frank had grabbed his duffle bag and headed home. He'd told no one he was leaving. He'd just left.

He'd gone right from the porn set to his Chief's office and admitted he had a problem with drugs. Since Frank had come in voluntarily, the NYPD had allowed him to enter rehab and he'd never been disciplined. Still, he'd been required to receive random drug tests regularly for a year to ensure he wasn't relapsing. That had been a year and a half ago, and Frank had thrown himself into getting straightened out physically.

After finishing his six-mile run, he grabbed his towel and iPhone and hit the showers. Although showers in most gyms took on a certain homoerotic quality, Club H's were notorious for hookups. Frank had learned long ago to just go in, shower and pay no attention to anyone around him. He toweled off and got dressed, throwing his dirty gym clothes into his duffle bag. As he was leaving, he heard two guys having sex in the steam room. He thought about warning them that Club H was a public space and that sex was technically illegal there but decided it wasn't worth his time.

As Frank exited Club H, the cold morning air hit his warm face like a thousand little icicles. Frank pulled out his cell phone and dialed Logan's number. "You up and at 'em yet?"

"As a matter of fact, I'm already at the Midtown Diner."

"Great. I just got out of the gym, so I should be there in ten minutes. Order me the usual."

"Sure thing."

Frank hung up his cell phone, putting his AirPods in his ears. "Siri, check messages." A female electronic voice informed him that he had zero new messages. Frank had Siri play his favorite podcast as he continued trekking down East Forty-Third Street, crossing Broadway and heading toward Central Park. Frank liked it when he was by himself, alone in his head, taking in the early morning rush that was Midtown at eight a.m. Midtown had more foot traffic by that time than most cities did in an entire day.

Ahead, Frank recognized the yellow-and-purple awning, the entryway to the Midtown Diner. Frank and Logan often met there for breakfast, as it was near both Frank's precinct and Logan's law office. Logan and Frank had been friends at the Leysin American School in Switzerland. It was a boarding high school. Frank's parents owned Schultt Pharmaceuticals and had sent Frank there since both of them had been too busy with their own lives to worry about their son. When he'd graduated from high school, Frank had come back to the States and gone to Yale, where he'd majored in business, the heir apparent to the Schultt empire. Instead, Frank had come out right after graduation and his family had disowned him. The blowup had happened when Frank had told his father he was gay. Those had been the last words Frank had ever spoken to his folks. He'd dropped off the map for a while, moved to New York, got a master's degree in Criminal

Justice from New York University, joined the academy and the rest was history.

Frank took off his coat and hung it on a peg inside the door as he entered the diner. He looked around and found Logan sitting at a table reading *The New York Times*.

"How's my favorite useless attorney?"

"I'm not useless. Real-estate law is an important branch of law in this town, mister."

"Oh yes, helping all those fat cats who own this city get richer and richer while the lower and middle classes end up committing crimes just to make it by."

"Dear God, what a sob story. Just because you think everything is a matter of who's getting screwed and who's screwing, don't bring my job into it." Logan looked at Frank and smiled, likely knowing full well that this would hardly be the last time this little conversation would occur. "So, any hot guys at the gym today?"

"Remember Jerry?"

"The leather dude?"

"That's the one. Well, he was there with his newest 'thing'." Frank always told Logan everything that was going on in his life, even the seedier parts. Unlike most people, Logan never outwardly judged. Frank could tell when Logan wasn't happy with him, and Frank never wanted to hurt or disappoint him. So, when he did, he knew he'd screwed up royally.

The waitress arrived at the table and put a plate with two pieces of bacon, two eggs and two sausage links in front of Frank. She came back a minute later and freshened Logan's cup of coffee.

"So, Frank, how are you doing? I know you don't want to talk about it, but dammit, I'm your best friend and have the right to be concerned."

"Logan, I'm fine. Don't worry."

"Well, we're creeping up on the fifth anniv—"

"I know, so drop it." Ever since Adam's murder, Frank had kept that part of his past bottled inside, refusing to release it. Once or twice a year, Logan would check in and see if Frank was ready to open up, but he never was.

"Oh, I was watching *It's a Wonderful Life* last night with Ben. He says 'hi', by the way."

"How's that new show of his going?"

"Well, the soap is officially canceled. Apparently, America wasn't ready for a daytime science-fiction soap opera."

"Even hearing you talk about it sounds like a bad idea."

"I know... Tell me about it. But Ben was so proud of being on another soap. Anyway, he has been cast in the off-Broadway revival of Arthur Bicknell's *Moose Murders*."

"Now, I'm not exactly a Broadway aficionado, but what the hell is that?"

"Yeah, that was my response. Apparently, it was some play from the 1990s that was a huge flop. I googled it. The story sucks and should never have been revived, but I've got to be supportive, nonetheless."

Frank laughed and choked on his coffee. "So, why'd you bring up *It's a Wonderful Life*?"

"Oh, Ben and I always watch it a couple of times each Christmas season and again on Christmas..." He realized what he'd just said to Frank. "Oh God, I'm so sorry. I totally forgot for a moment..."

"It's okay. I hate that film. It's so fucking sappy. Every time a bell rings an angel has its wings ripped off and is bludgeoned to death."

"Well, hello, Scrooge McScrooge. Talk about jaded."

Frank was about to make a comeback when his pants pocket vibrated. He pulled out his phone. "I've got to get this," he told Logan. "Detective Schultt... Oh, hey, Jasika... There's a *what*? At FAO Schwarz? Okay, I'll be there in about ten minutes, depending on how many tourists get in my way."

"What was that about?" questioned Logan.

"They've found a body part over at FAO Schwarz, hung like a Christmas ornament. You call me jaded. I may hate this fucking holiday, but at least I'm not hiding body parts in a toy store." Frank took out his wallet and threw down enough cash to cover his meal and coffee. "I'll talk to you later." With that, Frank turned and headed toward the door, grabbing his coat as he walked back outside into the December cold.

* * * *

Frank rounded the corner of Fiftieth Street and Rockefeller Place and saw the patrol cars out front as he made his way toward FAO Schwarz at its newer home in Rockefeller Center. A crowd had gathered on the other side of the street, trying to see what was going on inside the famous toy store. Frank got to the yellow police tape and flashed the officer the shield on his belt. The young woman lifted the tape and he walked under. He then located a female crime scene tech getting out of the van with a digital camera.

"Hi...Detective Schultt," he said, flashing his badge once again. "Will you please get some shots of the crowd? You never know when you're going to need them." The tech complied, and Frank eyed the gathering throng. Often killers liked to stick around and watch what was happening from a distance, while others wanted to be closer to the center of the action. He opened the door to FAO Schwarz and was immediately greeted by his partner Jasika Torv, a twenty-eight-year-old half-Black, half-Latina with a short haircut of tightly wound black curls on the top of her head.

Jasika had joined the NYPD because, like so many, she wanted to do something for the city she loved so much. Jasika had earned her BS in psychology before joining the force at twenty-one. She'd spent the requisite two years on probation, primarily working in and around Grand Central Station. Out of nowhere, she'd been approached by the Organized Crime Control Bureau to work an undercover job in narcotics. A narcotics gang had been purposefully recruiting young women as traffickers in the city, and Jasika had fit the profile perfectly. She'd worked that case for two years before they'd brought down the two men who ran the gang.

One joy of working in OCCB-Narcotics was that it was considered an investigative unit. And as long as someone could last for eighteen months, they automatically got their detective shield. Jasika had gotten her shield three years before and had since been a detective third grade. In the back of Frank's mind, he knew she needed a big case if she was going to make it past the three-year probationary period. January first would mark the completion. *In the next three weeks, she'll either be up for promotion to a detective second grade, or the brass will have to kick her back to patrol before the probation ends.* Overall, Frank thought Jasika was still a little green at times, but she had a good mind on her, so making a second-grade detective shouldn't be a problem—as long as she stayed under Chief Hays' radar.

"Hey, Frank. How's Logan?"

"Logan was fine. What have you got for us today?"

"This one is definitely a new one—even for you, Frank." Jasika went on to explain exactly what had happened.

An international charity organization that helped provide food, shelter and medical services for needy children, Children's Welfare International, had a mitten tree set up in the store's lobby. Inside each of the mittens was information about a child in NYC who wouldn't have Christmas if it weren't for the generosity of people visiting the toy store. People interested in helping children would ask a volunteer for a mitten and go find the toy that the child had asked Santa for at Christmas.

"It's a way for wealthy New Yorkers to feel good about spending countless thousands of dollars on toys and other gifts for their own brats?" Frank questioned.

"Pretty much. Gotta love altruism in the name of capitalism."

"God, I hate this holiday. So why are we here?"

"One volunteer went to grab a mitten off the tree, and instead of finding a kid's name and the toys he wants, she found a human hand."

"Well, with all those mittens up there, I guess a cold hand has to go somewhere."

"Frank, that's sick...even for you," Jasika responded. She led him through the maze of toys, store employees, shoppers and police personnel to where the city medical examiner, Mariella Ramos, was working. When Frank approached Mariella, she spun on her heels, her mouth shaped as if she were about to yell.

"Oh, Frank. It's about time you got here. I don't know why I was called. Without a whole body, there's not much I can do at a crime scene. I mean, come on... This is a waste of my time."

"Good morning to you too. Someone hasn't gotten her morning coffee."

"And someone took a nice stroll through the city before getting his ass to work this morning," Mariella responded sarcastically.

"So, what have you got for me?" Mariella took Frank over to where Al-Rashid Nasab and Colin Richardson, two forensic criminalists, were working. She laid out the basic findings. The hand had been cut post-mortem, so somewhere there was a dead body that had once been attached to the hand. Other than that, the only thing she could tell for sure was that the body had been frozen before the hand had been removed.

"The removal process wasn't very clean, so you're probably looking at some kind of over-the-counter power saw. Notice here." She bent down and pointed at the part of the bone sticking out from the bottom of the hand. "You can see how the cut wasn't smooth. Instead, it's jumpy. If it were a surgical saw, the cut would have been smoother, because those blades are designed for clean cuts through bone."

"Your knowledge of the macabre is always impressive, Mar. Anything else?"

"I'll run some tests when I get it back to my lab, but as of right now, there isn't anything else I can tell you."

"Thanks. Maybe the geek twins can spread some light on this for me." Nasab and Richardson had been commonly assigned to Frank's cases over the years, so the three of them often joked with each other. Frank had even tried referring to them as 'NabyRich' at one point, but that nickname had never quite seemed to stick, so he'd just started calling them the geek twins.

"Just remember, the geeks will inherit the earth," Nasab said from underneath a table draped in a Christmas cloth.

"That's only because you geeks and your tinfoil hats won't drink the magic Kool-Aid when the man finally ends it for the rest of us."

"Maybe so," Colin said, "but we'll have a good time when the rest of you are gone." Nasab popped his head out from under the table, grabbed a small evidence bag and placed what looked to be a cloth fiber inside.

"What can you two tell me?"

They both hesitated for a second, looking at each other before Nasab took the reins. "It's more like what we didn't find that's interesting. Colin, you finished photographing the hand?" Richardson grunted something that sounded like a 'yes' before Nasab picked up the hand and pulled off the mitten completely. "Notice the fingerprints have been burned off. Whoever did this didn't want anyone to know who the victim was. Other than that, we're not finding any trace evidence."

"We're collecting anything and everything near, above and underneath the crime scene, but nothing looks out of the ordinary as of right now. Admittedly, once we get back to the lab, something may jump. But for now, nada, zilch, zip."

"I get the idea, Richardson. Just email your report when you get back to the precinct and process the evidence."

"Sure thing," the geeks replied simultaneously.

Frank turned around and almost ran into Jasika. "Umm, sorry. Didn't realize you were still behind me."

"The wonder twins were waiting until you got here to tell me anything. I swear, they see me like your pet or something."

"They treat all third degrees that way. Don't take it personally. Okay, so I'm guessing you have the employees, shoppers and charity people lined up to be interviewed?"

"Yeah, a couple of patrolmen are keeping the three groups separated. The employees and the charity people are still okay, but the shoppers are getting a little indignant."

"Get the contact information from the shoppers and cut them loose. Chances are they aren't responsible. They wouldn't have been able to approach the tree without someone seeing them." The tree was between two tables against a blank wall, so someone tampering with it would have been seen by one of the attendants standing there. Shoppers who approached the tree would be immediately helped by one of the charity employees, so the likelihood of one of them slipping anything onto it was slim. "When you get a chance, cross-reference the security tape with the shoppers, just to make sure nothing stands out as suspicious. I'll take the charity people, because they had the most access, and I'll let you interview employees. Gather information on them, but don't worry about the ones working on other floors. Focus on the employees who work on this floor or have access to this area easily."

"Got it." With that, Jasika turned on her heels, approached the patrolman keeping the shoppers in line and asked him to get their information and let them all go. She then strolled over to the employees and started asking questions.

Frank scoured the room and found where the third patrolman was keeping a small group of people, and he assumed these were the workers and volunteers for CWI. Most of them were wearing appropriate holiday clothing, but one of them was wearing a suit.

The man in charge. Let's start with him.

Chapter Two

December 15, 10:30 a.m.

Frank approached the man in the suit. *Damn smug rich fucks think they're better than everyone else. This should be fun.* Frank pulled out his pad and asked the man his name.

"Aaron, Aaron Johnson. I'm the assistant executive director for CWI. Anything I or my staff can do to help you, please just let me know."

Frank eyed the guy, jotting down his name in his notebook. He looked the part of a spoiled rich kid turned executive. Mr. Johnson's shoes went for several hundred dollars in most men's specialty shops, and the suit had probably set him back two grand. Frank made a note in his book about the expensive tastes the man had. *So much for child welfare. These nonprofit types are some of the biggest crooks I've met.* "So, Mr. Johnston."

"Johnson, there's no 't' in the name."

"Thanks, I'll make a note of it." Instead, Frank noted that the guy was both rich and egotistical and definitely appeared to feel a little superior to those around him.

"So, tell me what happened in your own words."

"Sure thing." Aaron began by explaining that he'd been talking to the store manager when the incident happened. He'd heard one of his office workers scream, so he'd rushed back to the table to find out why. When he got to the table, he'd noticed that everyone was staring at something on the floor. He'd then leaned over the table, seeing one of the mittens on the ground with what looked like a wrist sticking out of the open end.

"Did you touch the mitten? Did you see anyone else touch the mitten?"

"I know I didn't. I mean, I watch enough police procedural shows on TV to know better than to touch something that may be evidence at a crime scene."

"Okay, good to know. So, should I expect to find any trace evidence from you on or near the glove?"

"Well, I was behind the table earlier this morning when the store opened, but other than something that fell off me and was on the ground, there shouldn't be anything. I mean, I may have dropped a candy wrapper earlier. We're handing out candy canes to potential benefactors." He gestured over toward a large bowl of candy canes sitting on the table surrounded by a ring of holly. "Please, take one. You look like you could suck on something," he finished with a mischievous grin.

Great, is this dude trying to hit on me while I'm interviewing him? That's the last thing I need. Keep it professional, Frank. "Thanks, but no thanks," he responded flatly. "So, who was the woman in your group who found the hand?"

"That would be Shelia — the one in the Santa Claus sweater," Aaron responded. "And too bad about the candy cane. They're not going to lick themselves."

Frank groaned and rolled his eyes on that one. "Are you flirting with me...at a crime scene...where you're a suspect?"

"Oh, I'm a suspect, am I?"

"Everyone's a suspect. If you've seen so many cop shows, you should know that already."

"Touché. Can't blame a guy for trying. Finding stable hot guys is hard these days."

"Try Grindr. Oh, and one more question... How does someone working for a nonprofit, such as yourself, afford a two-thousand-dollar suit and five-hundred-dollar loafers to match? In fact, I've estimated your whole outfit, Rolex included, is probably worth nine to ten thousand." Frank noticed that three of Mr. Johnson's colleagues were eavesdropping on their conversation.

"Umm-m... Well, uhh-h...that's a little uncomfortable." Mr. Johnson eyed Frank but didn't exactly make eye contact. Frank wasn't entirely sure how to interpret Mr. Johnson's clear desire not to discuss the issue in front of his employees.

Then he looked Frank directly in his eyes. "Well, if you must know..." He hesitated for a second before continuing. "I have some family money that not only supports my richer tastes, but it also allows me to give back to the needy. So no, I don't have a sugar daddy, if that's what you were thinking, but if you're looking for a boy toy..." Aaron said with a smirk. Frank overheard one of the man's colleagues snicker at that one.

The balls on this guy, Frank thought as his entire body stiffened tightly. *Don't react. Don't give him the satisfaction of a reaction.* "Once again, no thanks," he said. "If I need to talk to you again, how can I find you?"

Aaron reached into his suit pocket, pulled out a business card and handed it to Frank. "And, Detective, I hope you'll be seeing me again...sooner, rather than later. I bet we have more in common than you can imagine," Aaron responded, raising his eyebrows on the last word.

Frank took the card by the edges and slipped it back into his coat pocket. Frank inclined his head, turning to leave. *Thanks for the fingerprint, douchebag. Let's see who you really are.* Frank walked over to Shelia, where she retold the event in her own words. The version of the story she told was like Mr. Johnson's, but something just didn't sit right with Frank.

After finishing the interviews with the other employees, Frank headed back to check in with the geek twins to see if they'd found anything else. As he approached, Richardson and Nasab were taking off their gloves, which was a good sign that the two were wrapping things up on their end. Frank inquired if anything new had popped out, but it was more of the same. Lots of possible evidence, but they doubted any of it would lead to anything helpful.

Frank took a step back and looked at the larger picture. He eyed the various mittens on the tree and tried to determine whether any of them looked out of place. The tree looked perfectly spaced. He started at the top of the tree and looked at every part, hoping some clue would jump off the blasted thing. When he got to the base, he noticed something half-hidden in the folds of the rug, which blanketed the bottom. "Hey, Nasab, what's that thing sticking up in the back there?"

"Where?"

"Look toward the base of the tree behind the stump. There's just something that looks like it's tucked in." Nasab grabbed his camera and took a few pictures of where Frank had indicated before pulling a pair of latex gloves back on to ruffle through the tree curtain. After unveiling a small card roughly the size of a postcard, he took a couple more photos before picking it up.

"Bring it here," Frank said.

Frank slipped on a pair of latex gloves, then took the card from Nasab. On one side, the card was blank. The other side was a picture of two birds. Frank brought the card over to the charity people and asked if anyone recognized it. One woman in the group piped up that she had seen that postcard set at Hallmark the previous Christmas.

"That's two turtle doves," she stated. Frank gave the woman a blank look. "You know, as in 'two turtle doves and a partridge in a pear tree'." She sang the last bit to Frank, who just stared at her and thanked her for her help.

Frank walked back over to Nasab and explained what he'd learned from the woman. "Might as well bag it and see if there are any prints on it when you get back to the lab. Hey, have either of you seen Jasika?"

"The last time I saw her was when you sent her to talk to the employees, so I guess she's probably still over there interviewing her little heart out," Colin informed Frank.

"Thanks — and call me once you've found anything on the evidence. And start with that card. It's the only thing here that seems out of place beside the hand itself." Frank started to walk away before he remembered the card from Mr. Johnson sitting in his pocket. "Oh, and one more thing... Can you dust and check this business card for prints?" Colin used one of his gloves as a barrier and accepted the card from Frank, placing it into an evidence bag. Then Frank set off to find his partner.

He found Jasika talking to the store manager. Frank overheard his version of the story, which meshed with Mr. Johnson's, but Frank still wondered why his stomach said that something about Aaron Johnson was off—way off. Frank became so lost in his own thoughts that he didn't hear Jasika approach.

"Earth to Frank," Jasika playfully chided as she snapped her fingers.

"Oh, sorry... I was just mulling over the details."

The two spent the next few minutes trading information about what they'd learned from the suspects. Frank filled her in on the card and his feeling that something was odd about Mr. Johnson.

"You mean the really hot, rich guy who hasn't taken his eyes off you since the moment you got here?"

"Really?" Frank responded with a hint of excitement in his voice. *What the hell was that? Did I just squeak like a schoolgirl with a crush? Get it together.* Frank started to swivel his head to see where Jasika had pointed but stopped himself. "See what I mean? Something just seems off with him. I can't put my finger on it, but the rich tastes and the nonprofit thing just don't seem to go together to me. Anyway, I gave the geek twins his business card to pull a print. Hopefully, something will turn up as a result of that fun little test."

"Well then, I guess our work here is done. Shall we head back to the precinct?"

"Sounds like a plan. Did you come here via car or did you hoof it?"

"I hoofed it myself. Besides, it's maybe a ten-minute walk from here to the precinct, so let's go."

* * * *

After the quick walk back, Jasika and Frank started on the paperwork. Sadly, until the forensic evidence was processed, they didn't have a lot to do, so they started a whiteboard and tossed around a couple of possibilities. There was the obvious question that needed to be answered — prank or murder? From the way the hand had been displayed at the crime scene, the situation could easily be a college student prank from students at NYU or Hofstra. For all Frank knew, the hand could have been taken from one of the many anatomy labs at any of the area colleges and universities.

If the hand *was* part of a prank, then Frank and Jasika's job would be to determine how someone had gotten the hand. But without clear prints, it would be hard to determine where the hand came from unless one of the medical schools in the area admitted that someone had stolen one. The hand had been severed by someone using nonmedical tools, which could indicate that the body was at a mortuary or possibly even from a medical examiner's office. However, each of those different scenarios contained massive flaws and made little sense based on the perpetrator's desire to display it.

"Why would someone want to publicly display a hand in that fashion?" Jasika questioned, looking to Frank for a possible theory.

"Sorry, Jas, but this one even has me beat at the moment. This is the part of a case that drives me crazy.

36

We have no real evidence and no indication something has been done to warrant a murder investigation. Still, at the same time, I can't exactly rule it out."

After putting their wild theories on the board, Jasika and Frank went down the street to an Indian restaurant for a quick lunch. They continued tossing around outrageous theories, but both of them knew the 'out there' ideas would never make it to the board.

After lunch, they got coffee and headed back to the precinct. Frank glanced at his watch. *Almost two o'clock. Hopefully the geek twins will have something for me.*

Frank sat down at his desk and checked his messages. He had one from Mariella, informing him that she had just received the hand from the geek twins and she hoped to have a preliminary analysis done within the hour. Frank picked up the phone and called down to the geek lab. "Is either Colin or Al-Rashid in? Yeah, thanks."

"Richardson."

"Hey, Colin, it's Frank. Any luck on the items we sent down to the lab from the scene?"

"As a matter of fact, we just got some results from the fingerprint analysis. First..." Colin's voice trailed off as Frank heard rustling papers in the background. "Okay, the business card you gave us came back clean. Very clean. I also ran the guy's name and even the agency's name, and everything came back so squeaky clean it's almost strange. He hasn't as much as had a parking summons, but he does have two cars listed in his name. I sent everything to one of our cyber guys who may know some back channels to see if anything else is going on that we can't see on the surface."

"I had the same reaction. The guy just seemed too polished. Sure, he talked the part, but there was something innately off about his demeanor. Everything about him screamed 'out of place'." *And this is why I don't date anymore. Can't trust any of the men in this town to be who they say they are.* "Anything else?"

"As for the two turtle doves, the card is part of a postcard set sold by Hallmark and several other stationery stores across the city, so trying to figure out who bought the cards is virtually impossible."

"That leaves us absolutely nowhere." Frank sighed.

Jasika looked up from her desk, probably to see what Frank was sighing about. He reached down and hit the speaker button so Jasika could listen in.

"There's something that popped out. I dusted the card, and lo and behold, there was a print."

"Ahh, you saved the best for last," Jasika said, loud enough to be picked up by the speaker.

"Ahh, thanks for joining us, Jasika. Wouldn't want Frank to have all the fun. Okay, so I found the print, ran it locally first and we had a hit. The print—drum roll, please—connects to a former case of Frank's. It belongs to Damian Savage."

"Refresh my memory?" Frank asked.

"Last Christmas Eve, the subway suicide. Damian Savage was the operator of the train the girl jumped in front of."

"Oh God, I totally forgot about that. It was pretty much an open-and-shut case. The girl jumped in front of the moving train, but there was nothing the guy could have done to stop it. Either way, the media had a field day labeling him as an irresponsible driver. Jenny Mace, that hack of a reporter on WNTV, called him the Subway Suicide Driver and all but called the guy a terrorist behind the wheel of the train." Frank thought back to the case. The investigation had cleared Savage

38

emphatically, but the media never seemed to care about reality and had done everything but crucify the guy. Ultimately, Savage had lost his job due to political pressure. The whole affair was upsetting, and Frank thought the Metropolitan Transportation Authority had dropped the ball on that one.

"Well, that's all that we have here. Hopefully, this will give you some kind of direction."

"Thanks, Colin." Frank hung up the phone. "Let's go ahead and call Mariella. Maybe she'll have something for us by now." Frank dialed the number for the ME's office.

"Dr. Ramos."

"Mariella, it's Frank. Any news?"

"For you, dear heart, I've got some dirty details. What have you got for me?"

"Hey, Doc, this is probably the point I tell you that you're on speakerphone and the whole squad room is listening to our dirty talk. Shall we continue?"

"Oh, baby, keep talking to me like that. You know I like it orally infused and in public."

"Umm, Mariella, please refrain from that kind of language. The children are listening." Frank winked at Jasika, who giggled. "Okay, enough innuendos for one afternoon. What ya got for me?"

"Not much." Mariella shared that her original hypothesis had proved to be pretty damn accurate, that the body had been killed, frozen and cut. Other than that, she was still testing saw cuts, but there was nothing unique about the saw blade, so she explained it was probably a pointless direction to take in the case. "If you find me a saw, I can probably match the cut, assuming the blade hasn't degraded. The fact is, saw blades wear down pretty fast with use. Hence, unless there's a unique nick in the blade that doesn't get altered by subsequent sawing, blade comparisons are definitely hit and miss."

"Well, thanks for the information. We'll take it from here." Frank hung up the phone and walked over to the board, writing the fresh information about Savage and confirming the evidence list.

Jasika glanced down at her watch. "Frank, it's almost five. I've got to get back to Queens. Ginny's ballet recital is tonight." After working in narcotics, Jasika had met a guy who she thought was on the up-and-up, until months after their daughter's birth, she'd caught him during a drugstore snatch and grab. He was now doing time at an upstate minimum-security prison and Jasika's mother was helping her raise Ginny.

"Sounds like a plan. We'll pick up where we left off in the morning. I'll have dispatch check in on Savage tomorrow. At least this way, we can get some eyes on him."

Jasika gathered her coat and purse and took off for the night. Frank continued staring at the whiteboard, uncertain where the case was going. *At this point, we have a lot of questions and no answers.* Frank stared at the board, trying to make some connections, until six o'clock rolled around and he called it a day. *Twelve hours until my wake-up call.*

Chapter Three

December 16, 9 a.m.

Aaron had done a little homework of his own the previous night. After his run-in with Detective Schultt, he couldn't quit thinking about the man. Had his gaydar been off? The guy who had questioned him yesterday was fucking hot. Something about the six-foot-two-inch physically fit man with hazel eyes and brown hair kept short and tight, almost military but not quite, was a huge turn-on.

A quick search on Google gave him all kinds of information on the infamous Detective François Schultt. Schultt was a decorated first-grade detective in the NYPD with an impressive ability to close cases. One journalist put his case closure rate at over ninety-five percent, but then there were some questions about him as well. Apparently, there had been a scuffle about seven months prior where he'd unloaded his clip into someone. Aaron also found many pictures taken — and even a few video clips — of him at various crime scenes.

In many of the photos or clips, Aaron saw him holding a paper cup that contained some kind of coffee. He enhanced one picture and immediately recognized the label, Viva La Coffee. Again, thanks to Google, Aaron was able to pinpoint the most likely franchise near Frank's office and did an 'accidental' run-in the next morning.

God, I'm such a stalker. I can't believe I flirted with him so unabashedly. Aaron stood in line at Viva La Coffee at around eight-twenty, a few people ahead of Frank. He didn't want to turn around because he wasn't quite ready to have his run-in. *Gotta make it look accidental.* When it was his turn, Aaron ordered a supreme café mocha with peppermint. *Something to get my Christmas juices going.* He went over to the counter and waited to get his cup. Out of the corner of his eye, he took in Frank's position. *Perfect, he's standing a little out of the line.* The timing of the run-in had to be just right or it would look incredibly obvious.

Aaron was happy with the life he made for himself. Now, he just wanted to find the right man to share it with. And right now, his eyes were set on a smoking hot detective.

Aaron got his cup and conveniently placed it in his left hand. *This way, when I accidentally bump into him, I'll get a little on him.* Aaron walked past the detective, who was conveniently looking in the other direction. His plan was perfectly executed. Aaron brushed his shoulder slightly into Frank's, and his cup discharged the perfect amount onto Frank's jacket — not too much that it would soak him, but just enough so he would need to offer his help.

"Hey, watch it." Frank looked down at the wet spot on his jacket and didn't even notice who was in front of him.

"Oh my God, I am so sorry. I'm such a klutz. Let me help." Aaron grabbed the extra napkins from one of his suit's pockets and dabbed at Frank's torso. *Firm. God, I can't believe I just did that.* Aaron then casually looked at the guy's face. "Oh, hi," Aaron exclaimed as if he'd just realized who was standing in front of him.

"Mr. Johnson... I think I can handle this," Frank said through gritted teeth. "Can I have those napkins?" Aaron gave Frank the napkins, and he subsequently finished blotting away the coffee but still left a spot running down the side of his trench coat.

"Please, let me get that dry cleaned for you."

"Unnecessary. Trust me... This coat has seen worse things on it than coffee." Aaron looked at Frank questioningly, but Frank just muttered, "Never mind."

"So, how are things going with your investigation from yesterday?" Aaron asked, trying to sound casual.

"I'm not at liberty to discuss this matter with anyone, let alone any of the possible suspects."

"Oh, I'm still a suspect, am I?" Aaron flirtatiously glanced down at Frank's belt and asked him, "Got your cuffs on you? I would love to see you use them." Frank's face was an unmasked image of shock at Aaron's obvious and over-the-top pickup line. *Why did I just go there? What the actual fuck am I thinking?* When it came to dating, Aaron had a tendency to be a little pushy. He saw it as seeing what he liked and going after it with a vengeance. So occasionally, he pushed the boundaries. His friends, on the other hand, informed him that it wasn't like he went over the line a little. It was more like he'd river-danced right the hell over it. "I'm sorry. That was completely unprofessional. Sometimes my inner monologue has a tendency of rushing out of my mouth before my brain intervenes," Aaron said rapidly while blushing. "I'm going to stop talking now. That was awkward."

Frank just kept staring. Aaron felt like an insect being examined under a high-powered microscope, and he realized there was probably at least a seven-year age difference between him and Schultt. But at that moment, Aaron might as well have been a nine-year-old. *God, open mouth, insert foot.*

"Well, this was an interesting and very awkward conversation, Mr. Johnson."

"Again, I'm so sorry about the coffee. If you want your coat dry cleaned, don't hesitate to call my office." *God, what do I say? 'Hey, I'm sorry about the crazy flirting. I'm not normally so in-your-face. Please accept my apology for acting like a complete jackass.'* Aaron stood there awkwardly, waiting for Frank to say something, anything.

"Don't worry about it."

Aaron walked away, kicking himself for blowing the opportunity and making a horrible impression. Frank grabbed him by the shoulder. "I do have one question for you. How was it living in University?"

"University?"

"As in University, Mississippi, the town?"

"Oh, uh, umm," Aaron's mind went blank, then he remembered. "When I was attending Ole' Miss?"

"Yeah."

"University was a pleasant place to live. A little quiet for my taste. I was glad when I finished my degree and got out of there. Well, have a great day, detective. I hope I accidentally bump into you again, preferably without coffee next time."

Frank just looked at Aaron and nodded sideways in a noncommittal fashion. *God, he must think I'm the biggest ass in Manhattan.* With that, Aaron hurried from the coffee shop.

Frank watched Aaron leave Viva La Coffee. Despite the awkwardness of the conversation, Frank had found Aaron likable at the end. *Maybe he's not a complete douchebag after all.*

"Can I help you, sir?" Frank realized he was now at the front of the line.

"Yeah, umm, two supreme coffees to go."

"What blend, sir?"

"Whatever you have today that's fair trade."

"That would be our Ethiopian."

"Perfect." Frank paid for the two coffees and walked down to the end of the counter, where he placed thermal sleeves and lids on the cups. Frank liked his coffee hot and black, whereas Jasika liked the coffee doctored — but she could do that herself at the station.

Frank left Viva La Coffee and started walking toward the precinct, mulling over his run-in with Aaron. *Any way he planned that?* Frank pondered the possible ways Mr. Johnson could have planned their 'accidental' meeting. Still, all of them would be difficult for even a good detective, let alone some rich schmuck running a nonprofit. He also questioned Aaron's response to the Ole' Miss question. *I mean, he seemed to genuinely have no clue at first and suddenly remembered the answer.*

As he rounded the corner near his precinct, another thought popped into his head. *What is up with the crazy-ass flirting? I may be out of the saddle when it comes to dating, but this guy is a bigger klutz than me.* Frank replayed the whole scene again in his head. *Yesterday, he seemed so cock-sure of himself, but today he was almost adorkable. And, dear God, when he touched my chest... That is a rabbit hole not to jump down. Get it together. He's a suspect. He knows he's a suspect. Nothing about this seemed accidental. That's the behavior of someone who has something to hide.*

Before Frank realized it, he was walking up the steps at the precinct. Two uniformed officers were walking out. One of them held the door for him, calling him by his name. Frank muttered a polite hello. Frank sucked at names, and the constant turnstile of uniforms in the building prevented Frank from ever trying to get to know any of them, let alone their names.

He walked into the building and headed toward the bullpen, but Jasika had her coat in hand and was walking toward him, her purse slung over her shoulder. He handed the coffee to her. "Thanks, no point in sitting down. Just got off the phone with Mariella. We've got new body parts out in the Bronx."

Frank and Jasika checked out a Lincoln town car from the carpool. Jasika volunteered to drive, so Frank tossed her the keys and told her to go gently this time. As a native New Yorker, Jasika hadn't grown up driving at all. So when she got a chance, she seemed to think she was a NASCAR driver. Often, Frank just closed his eyes and hoped for the best.

"So, why did Mariella call us? Did she say?"

"Something about the cutting and presentation of the body parts seeming eerily familiar, so she figured these were tied to our case."

"Or, she just wants to see her tall, sexy gay lover," Frank replied, to which they both laughed. Frank then described the run-in he'd had with Aaron Johnson at the coffee shop. He concluded by saying, "If I didn't know better, I would swear the encounter wasn't exactly accidental. But how could he possibly have known I'd be in that store at that time?"

"Ah, Frank has his own personal stalker. Maybe he just sees you for the hot stud muffin you are?"

"Stud muffin, really? God, I feel so objectified by you when you say it like that. Don't make me run to human resources and file a sexual harassment complaint," Frank jested.

Frank's cellphone started blaring a song from the Broadway musical *Wicked*.

"It's Logan."

"Tell him I said hi and will definitely come to Ben's opening next week."

"He told you about that?"

"Ben emailed everyone in the city, inviting them."

Frank chuckled as he answered the phone. "Hey, Logan, what's up?"

"Not much. Just wanted to see if you wanted to join Ben and me at La Bella's at seven?"

"Sure, sounds like a plan. Oh, and Jasika said to tell Ben she'd be honored to attend his opening next week."

"Oh God, she got the email too? Apparently, Ben emailed half the city with that invitation. If just an eighth of the people who Ben contacted about next week's show attend, he could fill the sixty-seat theater like ten times over."

"Well, you'd better save two tickets for Jasika and me. We'll sit with you and smile broadly, then critique privately later. Anyway, heading to a crime scene, so I'll talk to you tonight." The rest of the drive was relatively uneventful. They sat in quiet, Frank wondering what new clues the crime scene would offer.

Chapter Four

Jasika tried pulling into the small parking lot at the Bronx Botanical Gardens, but a large white delivery van blocked the entranceway. Frank opened his door and proceeded around to the driver's side to find the van door open, with no one inside. The logo on the side of the van read 'Delicious Delights', with an array of pastries, cupcakes and other foods cushioning the words like a pillow of calories. Frank walked around to the front of the van and yelled, "Hey, does anyone belong to this thing?"

A man in a white delivery suit appeared from around the corner of the building and said, "Yeah, who's asking?"

"NYPD. You're interfering with our ability to get to a crime scene."

The young man walked over to Frank and apologized. "I am so sorry, officer. I'm supposed to be meeting a client at the service entrance. I hadn't

Jason Wrench

realized this was the main entrance. Never gotten out here before. Most of my deliveries are in Midtown."

"Not a problem," Frank reassured him. "Just move your van out of here." In a few short moments, Jasika was pulling in the town car and parking close to the main entrance. They hiked up the steps.

As Frank reached out for the door, it flew open, almost knocking him over.

"Hey, watch it!" he bellowed.

"Well, if it isn't detective sexy pants. 'Bout time you showed up. If you keep waiting for engraved invitations to my crime scenes, you're never going to solve anything."

"And good morning to you, Mariella," Jasika chirped as she placed a hand to the middle of Frank's back to ensure he caught his balance.

"So, what have you got for us this morning?" Frank asked, throwing his arm out to his side as if waving on royalty and saying, "Your majesty."

"Got that right. Walk with me. I left something in the medical examiner's van." Frank and Jasika followed behind Mariella as she walked to the ME van and filled them in on the basic scene. The call had come in around seven that morning, but no one had put two-and-two together until the geek twins had gotten there and discovered a connection to yesterday's scene.

"Since you two were already on the case, the brass played push-and-pull with precinct jurisdiction, and it was decided you guys could take the lead. You have more experience and a higher rate of solved crimes. Although I was not involved in that conversation, from what Chief Hays told me at your precinct, it was very much a measuring match between lead detectives. Thankfully, baby, you came out ahead." She shot a quick glance down toward Frank's crotch and sighed to herself.

"I'm not just a piece of meat. I do have a brain."

"I know, Chico, but you can't help a married woman from enjoying the package," she said, shooting Frank a flirtatious smile. Mariella likely loved to flirt with Frank because nothing would ever come of it. "Once the decision was made, I got the go-ahead to bring you in and deal with the scene. There are a few bruised egos out here in the Bronx, but overall, everything's well with the world." She then started delivering information about the current crime scene.

One janitor had been dusting the various model trains in the Botanical Garden's annual Christmas Train Show and had found two feet hacked off at the ankles. "Our killer took both feet, turned them over and using some kind of wire—probably a craft wire, but nothing that couldn't be found in hundreds of places in the city—fashioned them into a bridge." Mariella opened the passenger side door as she climbed into the ME van and started rifling around for something.

"A what?" Jasika questioned, raising her eyebrows.

"A bridge, as in the ankle was the part of the bridge going down into the Hudson, and the bottoms of the feet were used to lay train tracks over," Mariella said from within the van, without looking.

"As in, there is a train running over the bottoms of the guy's feet," Jasika said.

"Trust me... The geek twins are having a field day. At one point, I caught them running the train just to see if the feet would function as a full bridge."

"Did it work?" Jasika and Frank asked almost in unison.

"You two twisted fucks... But I won twenty dollars off each of them, predicting that it would." With that, she found what she was looking for in her van, closed the doors and headed back to the building with Frank and Jasika. "As for the body parts, I haven't had a real good look at the ankles because we were waiting for the jurisdictional pissing match to end, but the cuts seem similar. I'll know more once you give us the go-ahead to dissect the scene in there a little closer."

Mariella, Jasika and Frank walked up the steps into the building to investigate what was going on with the twins. Once inside, Frank glanced to his right to see another detective standing in the room. *Must have taken this one from his division.* He nodded toward the other detective—a Detective O'Brien—in a professional manner. Frank gave the guy a 'whatcha gonna do' look, indicating that traipsing on the other detective's crime scene hadn't been his idea.

Mariella walked them through a maze of different toy trains of every shape and size, until they reached the backmost corner of the wall. Frank and Jasika gazed at the display table and the twenty-foot virtual mountain and wonderland before them. The display had schools, restaurants, parks, skating rinks and dozens upon dozens of miniature figurines scattered about, inhabiting the world that lay before them. Frank walked around the entire display, taking in all the details—a kid playing with a dog on the side of the mountain, a mother and father chopping down a Christmas tree with their little child, a woman hanging a wreath on the front of a building with a clock tower that read 'Town Hall'. When he came to the side where the geek twins were working, he noticed the feet had a brown—almost wooden—quality to them against the backdrop of the mountain.

"I'm impressed that the janitor even had the wherewithal to see the feet in this maze of small pieces." Frank bent down and examined the foot. He could tell that the foot was from a Black person. *Probably size ten shoes, so the guy is probably in his upper fives, maybe lower sixes, height-wise.* "Jasika, what do you see here?" he asked, motioning toward the feet.

"The victim was a Black male."

"Why male?"

"Size and shape of the foot is way more likely to be a male than female," she responded.

Listening to the conversation, Richardson responded, "The female foot is also less dense when it comes to muscle mass."

Frank shot the two a look that said 'shut up'. Then he asked Jasika, "What else?"

"I would put the feet at around a size ten, maybe ten-and-a-half? Hmmm, which would probably make the vic around five-foot-eight, maybe just over six foot, but I wouldn't put him much taller than that."

"Pretty much what I was thinking as well. Why don't you go talk to Detective O'Brien and find out what happened before we got the case? Oh, and he's a good guy. Just be polite and friendly. But watch his hands. He has a thing for your type."

"Thanks," Jasika said sarcastically as she rolled her eyes. "I guess it's true what they say, 'You win more flies with honey.'" Jasika headed off in the direction of the front door.

Frank continued to stare at the display in front of him as Richardson and Nasab stood off to the side, watching. "Okay, guys, I give. Why did you believe this case was related to my other one? Beyond the requisite body parts, I do not see any similarity between this case and the other one at all."

Richardson smiled coyly, "Well, maybe it's not because of what you do see, but what you don't." Richardson got down on his hands and knees, lifted the tablecloth covering the table immediately below the feet and motioned for Frank to bend over, so Frank got down in front of the lifted cloth. Richardson pulled out a small flashlight, shining its light in a little way under the table. Against a table leg somewhere in the middle of the mountain was a card with three French hens.

"Ahhh, the light goes on?" Nasab questioned. "When Richardson was first processing the scene under the table, he didn't even notice the card. We were more concerned with the table the foot bridge was on. Get it? Foot bridge?" When Frank didn't laugh, Nasab continued, "We started doing a more thorough investigation of the area, and Colin accidentally found the card."

"It wasn't accidental. I just found it in an appropriately timely manner based on the grid search I was conducting."

Nasab continued, "Anyway, once we realized what we had, we talked to Mariella, who put in the call to get you reassigned to the case. You can thank us later."

"Preferably with beer and Doritos for the lab," Richardson said as he stood from the ground and lowered the tablecloth back into place.

Frank just rolled his eyes. "Well, I've seen the scene. You two can now process at your will. I'll go find Mariella and let her know she's good to examine the feet." Frank started walking toward the door, pausing every few seconds to see if he could hear Mariella in the room. The space was fairly cavernous, so sound carried pretty well. When he finally caught her voice, he headed in her direction. As he approached, a thin, wiry guy around forty-five years of age sat fidgeting. The little man had a small and slightly upturned nose where his black-rimmed glasses sat.

"I'm sorry, no. I will *not* be patient anymore. I want answers, *now!*"

Frank positioned himself behind Mariella and touched her shoulder before interrupting the conversation. "Mariella, the body — well, the parts — are now ready for processing."

"Thank you, Jesus. I'm so sorry for your loss, Mr. Hyde, but Detective Schultt here will be more than happy to help you with your problem. Detective, this is…" her voice trailed off as she tried to remember the guy's name.

"Harvey Hyde."

"That's right, Harvey Hyde. He's the creator of the table where the feet were found." After the introduction, she bolted.

"So, Mr. Hyde, tell me about your 'Winter Wonderland'."

"Puhlease… 'Winter Wonderland' is a boring name. Who does alliteration anymore? No, that display, which took over two hundred hours of planning and development, is called Nestled Village at the Mountain's Base. Or NVMB for short."

"Okay," Frank responded, not sure how to interpret the squirrely little man in front of him. "Tell me about NVMB. I'm assuming the feet weren't part of your original plans."

"Heavens no." Mr. Hyde reached into his back pocket, took out a small folded-up rectangle of paper, bent down to the floor and started spreading it out to show an elaborate blueprint of the entire design. The design covered everything from where trees and bushes would be placed to the exact locations of the depicted scenes. Mr. Hyde turned the paper around and pointed at a section of the paper, "See this right here? This is where the Lionel Train Trestle Bridge was located."

"The wha...?"

Mr. Hyde repeated himself, and added for further clarification, "This bridge alone sells for five to eight hundred dollars at auction."

"You're telling me... that a toy train bridge..."

"Model train bridge," Mr. Hyde said, emphatically sounding out each of the different syllables as if Frank were deaf.

"Okay then, *model* train bridge," Frank said, adding as much sarcasm to his voice as he could muster, "is worth five to eight hundred dollars."

"But of course." Hyde responded single-mindedly. "You and your people must make this your first priority. You must find the bridge."

"Okay, well, thanks for the information. If we find anything, we will make sure that you are called first thing." *After I accidentally step on the damn thing!* Frank didn't even wait for a response or for the guy to realize he hadn't taken any information down before turning on his heels and heading back to the crime scene. "Hey, Biatch," Frank playfully said when he saw Mariella, a big grin already spreading across her face. "I owe you one."

"Hey, Frank," Jasika started as he approached from behind. "I finished with O'Brien, and he interviewed the two staff who were here at the time the feet were found. The place was locked tight all night, so no one knows how or when the feet were placed. I was told the guy who built the model closes the place every night and arrives first thing every morning, so we may want to find him and talk to him."

Mariella started laughing, and Frank shot her a sideways grimace. "Done...and a complete waste of time. Guess that was O'Brien's idea of payback for them taking the case from him. Anything else the employees have to offer?"

"Not really... O'Brien phoned them in this morning, and both came up clean, so he doubts either of them were involved."

"He's probably right. We'll double-check just to make sure, but the two employees and the Winter Wonderland guy," Frank said with extra emphasis as he gestured to the display, "are highly unlikely suspects. We must start with the one lead we got yesterday from the fingerprint when we get back to the station."

* * * *

That afternoon was filled with lots of phone calls, but no leads panned out. Frank had a patrol car go pick up Damian Savage, but he couldn't be found. Savage's apartment was vacant, he hadn't been to work and no one in his building had seen him for at least a week. Jasika had ordered an APB on the guy, but nothing had come in on him yet.

Frank had called the geek twins, where more problematic information had appeared. Although the feet hadn't provided any additional information, the card had a fingerprint on it, just like the last one had.

The only problem was that the fingerprint was in the exact same location as the previous one and looked to be the same finger as the last one — the right index. The geek twins had thought this was almost a little too coincidental for their tastes. They'd run the print through the FBI's Integrated Automated Fingerprinting Identification System, or AIFIS, but nothing had popped. They'd followed protocol, sending the prints to the Department of Defense and Department of Justice databases, but had expected nothing there either.

After that phone call ended, Frank had received a phone call from Mariella. He had put the phone on speaker so Jasika could hear the details. Mariella had explained that the cut marks had come from the same bladed saw, but without a comparison blade, she still couldn't give them much more information. After getting nowhere with either the hand or the foot, she'd extracted DNA samples and sent them to the DOJ for DNA testing, but she had explained that the processing could take weeks, depending on how backlogged they were. Obviously sensing Frank's increasing frustration with not having identified victims, she'd asked for a speedy return on the DNA results, as they were desperate for direction. She had hoped that the DOJ could turn around her request quickly, but Frank was still looking at three to four days, at the earliest.

Around five p.m., Frank and Jasika had gazed at their increasingly filled whiteboard. Still, the information provided hadn't gotten them anywhere, so he sent Jasika home, and he'd gone back to his apartment to shower and change before heading to his dinner date with Logan and Ben.

* * * *

Frank, along with his friends, was shown to the table shortly after arriving. They were seated at a small table in the back, near one of the side windows. They looked at their menus intently for a few minutes before the waitress returned to take their orders. Logan ordered a bottle of Shiraz for the table and they each ordered a pasta dish, all asking for wholewheat pasta.

The bottle of Shiraz arrived at the same time as a breadbasket, to Frank's delight. The sommelier showed Logan the label, opened the bottle and poured him a small amount of wine using an aerator. Logan grabbed the wide-mouthed wine glass and took a deep inhale through his nose to experience the different scents of the specific vintage. He then swallowed the wine and nodded his approval to the server, who then poured wine for everyone at the table, still using the aerator. By the time they all had glasses of wine, the bottle was completely empty.

"Would you care to keep the label, sir?" the Sommelier asked.

"No, thank you," Logan responded.

The server placed the breadbasket and a small plate in the center of the table. She then filled the plate with olive oil and a couple of herbs for the group to dip the bread into and left.

"So, I got hit on by a suspect today," Frank said, finally breaking the group's silence.

"You *what?*" Logan and Ben replied almost simultaneously. Frank then went into the details of how he'd been getting his morning coffee at Viva La Coffee and how he'd run into Aaron Johnson, a suspect from the previous day's mitten case.

"Well, if the glove fits, you must acquit," Ben joked.

"Dear God, how long did it take you to come up with that one?" Frank questioned.

"Umm…he spent most of last night coming up with mitten slash glove jokes," Logan responded. "I told him not to, but he just can't help himself." Logan then reached and tussled Ben's hair. Ben had the kind of hair that just hung from his head perfectly styled. Even though Logan had given his mop a rigorous shake, Ben's hair just immediately fell back to frame his face.

"So, is he hot? Did he have a ring on his finger? Are we sure he's even gay?" Logan started shooting off rapid-fire questions.

Frank put his hands up in surrender while saying, "I give up. To answer your questions, I guess he's attractive." He then described Aaron as being, "approximately six feet tall, light-skinned, blue eyes, brown hair with a short, intentionally messy haircut. He wore a pair of black-rimmed Gucci glasses, and his taste in clothing and jewelry came to approximately ten grand, plus or minus a thousand dollars."

"Wow, that was…clinical-sounding," Ben remarked.

"Would you prefer for me just to just say he's fucking hot? He has a smaller frame than me, and I could probably bounce a quarter off his ass?"

"Now you're speaking my language," Ben said with a smile as he leaned in for more juicy details.

"Well, I'm sure he's all those things, but remember that word 'suspect'. Even if I was inclined to go there, which I'm not, I couldn't."

"Well, at least you noticed when someone was hitting on you. That's a step in the right direction," Logan responded. "Let's face it. These past few years have been very rough on you."

It was moments like this when Frank's memory of Adam would come flooding back. Frank looked at Logan and Ben, sensing the awkwardness of the silence that had fallen on their table.

Oblivious to that, Ben kept going. "Yes, but how hot is he? Are we talking Jake Gyllenhaal-hot, Chris Pratt-hot or Chris Hemsworth-ass-up-feeding-a-baby-kangaroo-hot? Inquiring minds need to know."

"I had Mr. Johnson investigated," Frank choked out, trying not to let the Shiraz come spewing out of his nose. "As far as we can tell, he has two cars, no priors and very little information exists about the guy other than the fact that he went to Ole' Miss before moving to New York to work for a nonprofit."

Logan and Ben stared perplexedly at Frank for a few seconds before Frank asked, "What?"

Logan and Ben looked at each other before Logan finally talked, "Well, Ben asked you if he was hot, not whether the guy could be picked out of a lineup."

"I guess by conventional gay standards, he's an attractive guy."

"Come on, Frank. You keep talking about this guy like he's an object you're analyzing and not another human being who may or may not be fuckable," Ben responded.

"Ben! Leave Frank alone. You've got to remember this guy is a suspect in a murder investigation. The last thing we need is you" — gesturing to Frank — "getting involved with a killer, who will then hang you from a lamppost or worse, decide to eat you."

"*Come here, Frankie,*" Ben said in his best Hannibal Lecter voice.

"Both of you, I know you want what's best for me," Frank started hesitantly, "but I'm not in a position to think romantically or even sexually about anyone at this point. Besides, Logan's right. The dude's a suspect. Even if I thought he was 'fuckable', there's nothing I could do about it."

Before Logan could respond, the waitress came over with their dinners. The rest of the dinner conversation turned to Ben and his new play and how he was struggling to find his character Nelson Fay's motives for behaving within the story. Frank began tuning him out when he started talking about his wife and the problems the two had with their relationship, as if Ben were Nelson. Thankfully, the topic ended, turning to issues in the gay community, so Frank tuned back in.

After dinner, they put on their jackets and headed back out into the cold. Frank, Logan and Ben said their goodbyes, giving each other quick hugs before heading off in different directions.

There was a rumbling sound of a vehicle approaching from behind before Frank heard the squealing of tires next to him and the distinct sound of a van door being thrown open. Frank spun around, hovering his hand over his sidearm, releasing the strap that held the gun in place. He was blinded by the bright headlights of a television crew van and the distinct voice of Jenny Mace.

"Calm down, Detective Schultt. We're not here to capture you," she said as she jumped out of the van, followed by the cameraman. Jenny Mace was a five-foot-seven-inch thin Asian woman, who was quickly making a name for herself in NYC. Her winning smile and long brown hair cut to frame her face made her the perfect talking head for crime news. She'd broken several major stories through her rather confrontational method of quickly approaching and taking an interview subject off-guard. Many other detectives who had been the victims of one of her sneak attacks had started referring to her as 'the Macinator'. Although not exactly a robot sent back from the future to kill John Connor, she was definitely a formidable foe.

Frank re-latched his gun's safety strap as Mace stated, "Based on my confidential sources, I've heard that you have no leads on the Twelve-Day Killer."

"The who?" Frank asked, genuinely not understanding Mace's assertion.

"The Twelve-Day Killer," she responded, "The serial killer that's killing New York citizens and displaying their bodies in public spaces."

"I'm not sure where you're getting your information. I'm investigating two crimes that may or may not be related."

"Two?" Jenny said slowly.

"I'm working on two cases," Frank responded, attempting to hold his animosity toward the woman in check.

"What about the first? You know the Partridge in the Pear Tree? From what my sources have told me, you have body parts from three different victims, and the killer is leaving the same calling card at each of the crime scenes?" Jenny Mace asked the last statement in the form of a question, but it was meant to sound like an authoritative fact.

"As I said, I'm not at liberty to discuss ongoing investigations." With that, Frank turned on his heels and started walking away. *Three bodies? Partridge in a Pear Tree? What the hell is Mace talking about?*

The more Frank walked, the more concerned he became. He put his AirPods into his ears, called into dispatch and had them see if anything in the crime report system had the words 'partridge' and 'pear tree'.

"Are you pulling my leg?" the dispatcher laughed.

"I'm not. Please run the search." Frank waited a few moments until the dispatcher came on informed him that on the fourteenth of December, the head of a man had been found in the manger of an outdoor nativity at St. Patrick's Old Cathedral Church on the corner of Prince and Mulberry.

"When did that report show up in the system?"

"Umm-m, let me check. Uhh-h, it looks like it went into the system around six this evening."

"Great," Frank muttered to himself. "Hey, anything in the evidence log about a card found at the scene?"

"Checking... Yeah, a postcard with a bird and a pear tree... Oh, hey, there's your 'partridge in a pear tree', Detective."

"Thanks." Frank hung up on the operator and just started saying 'fuck' repeatedly as he continued walking down the street. *How the fuck did that woman get that information before I did? Fuck!* Frank knew what his next move had to be. He dialed Chief Hays.

"Hello, Hays' residence, Melanie speaking." A young girl's voice sounded in Frank's ear.

"Good evening, Melanie. Can I speak to your father?"

"Sure, may I ask who's calling?"

"Tell him it's Detective Schultt." Frank heard the little girl run through the house and tell her father that a 'detective shit' was on the phone. *How appropriate. That's what I will be after this conversation.*

"Detective, this had better be important," Chief Hays stated, ripping Frank back to the moment.

"Chief, I wouldn't call you at home unless it was serious." Frank then went into detail about being cornered after having dinner with friends and how Mace had asked precise questions about the two cases. He then explained how Mace had asked about the third murder, which Frank hadn't been aware of because the file hadn't even entered the system until after Frank had left the precinct that evening. "Chief, she caught me with my pants down, fiddling with my balls — or at least that's going to be how it looks once she airs the segment at ten."

"Fuck!" the chief muttered on the other end of the line. "I will call the police commissioner and try to get ahold of the mayor's office. I will stand behind you, Frank, but let's face it, shit rolls downhill." At this, the chief hung up the phone.

Frank then decided he should call Jasika and give her the full warning as well. Frank told her everything, from Mace to Hays and what the chief had planned on doing when he'd gotten off the phone minutes earlier.

"Frank, is there any way you think she won't get it edited in time? I mean, she accosted you around nine. Do you think she'll get it on air in an hour?"

"From what I hear about Mace, she can confront you one minute and have it on the air the next, so an hour probably will not be an issue for her."

Jasika and Frank continued to talk as Frank got home, slipped off his shoes and got himself more comfortable. He hung up with Jasika and promised to call her after the news, then he grabbed a beer from his refrigerator, sat down in his leather Lazy Boy and turned it on.

The screen went blue, and a shot of people walking around Times Square appeared as a voice-over narration read, *"WNTV… The number one source for news in New York City. Tonight in the news, is city hall purposefully preventing plans for building a new ice hockey arena for the Rangers? We'll also examine tomorrow's forecast, so you'll know how to dress during the morning commute. But first, we have a special report from our crime reporter, Jenny Mace."*

Mace appeared on screen. *"We are now in day three of the Twelve-Day Killer's murderous rampage through New York City. If you haven't heard of this serial killer yet, it's because even the police department hasn't completely put all the pieces together."* Frank's face was on the television saying that he was investigating two crimes and looking completely clueless about a third crime scene. *"The usual NYPD ineptness is preventing this crime spree from being solved quickly. When we can't trust our police force to know the actual evidence, we as a citizenry must stand up to city hall and tell them to get their act together or we'll have to clean house for them."* She went on to explain how she'd found out about the killing spree through a confidential source within the NYPD. She also explained how the cards were being left at the various crime scenes. *"It doesn't take a genius to realize that the killer is counting up and leaving one dead body each day leading to Christmas, which would be the Twelfth Day."* In the background, a demonic-sounding choir started singing the *Twelve Days of Christmas* as the station went to commercial break.

Frank picked up the phone and called Jasika, who answered saying, "Well, at least she didn't mention you by name."

"Yeah, true, but my mug is now out there for the world to see. There's no escaping this case now." They talked through the commercial break and said good night. The next segment talked about upcoming events for tourists in town for the Christmas holidays. Frank muted the television and walked into the kitchen to get another beer. When he came back in, he unmuted it.

"In a striking collaborative effort between the NYPD and the FBI, the largest child smuggling ring in history was brought to justice this evening." The story then explained how the NYPD, the FBI and Interpol had set up a joint task force to stop the Stapkovich Syndicate, which was known for smuggling children around the world. The video showed a number of FBI agents wearing black flak jackets with yellow lettering on the back perp-walking a group of people in handcuffs.

The picture jumped back to Jenny Mace as she read, *"Famed FBI profiler, Aaron Massey, is suspected of having been the chief architect of this task force. With his experience as both an FBI profiler and his work with Interpol, which led to his bestselling book,* Blood Money, *we're glad to know that Supervisory Special Agent Aaron Massey was on top of the case."* The camera then zoomed in and focused on a single agent bringing out a suspect with his hands cuffed behind his back. For a split second, the agent's face was on the screen before he was blocked by the perps's body.

It can't be, Frank thought.

"Calls to the FBI have not yet confirmed that Agent Massey worked the case, but the FBI has promised a press conference tomorrow morning at eleven in front of their office in Federal Plaza."

Frank rewound his DVR to get another shot of Supervisory Special Agent Aaron Massey. He watched the segment again and froze the DVR right when the camera caught a glimpse of the agent.

Aaron Johnson?

Chapter Five

December 17, 9 a.m.

Frank's morning routine went as it generally did. He got up, went to the gym, grabbed breakfast on the way to work and made it to the precinct by eight-forty-five. He avoided Viva La Coffee, as there were a half-dozen messages from Aaron Massey on his cell phone. He deleted them without bothering to listen. Frank wasn't even sure how Massey had gotten his cell phone number. *But then, what do I expect from a Fed?*

Frank sat at his desk and found another three messages from Massey on his work phone. Each call started with *"Detective Schultt, it's Aaron Massey..."* Frank deleted the message and went on to the next one. He was in no mood to deal with the man who was a suspect one minute and a Fed the next. The only credible lead they were working with had been flushed right down the drain. Frank opened his email to find a couple of messages from Massey there as well. *Dear*

God, stalker much? As Frank closed his email, he spotted Jasika coming toward their desks.

She didn't even hesitate before saying, "I saw. I almost called you last night but thought better of it."

"Good, I probably would have said a few things to you that could be misconstrued as unprofessional."

"Have you heard from him yet?"

"Nah, haven't heard from him," Frank lied.

"Schultt, Torv, my office *now*," bellowed an unseen voice. Frank didn't have to look to know who had beckoned them.

Chief Dennis Hays had worked his way through the department back when racial injustices had still been a common occurrence in the force. At sixty-four years old, Hays was one of the first Black police chiefs in the city. At the time when he'd been promoted, many suspected it had only been for affirmative action, but his skill and administrative adeptness had quickly won over anyone who'd doubted him within the Midtown Precinct. He was a portly man with graying hair—at least what was left of it—and his mustache sat on top of his upper lip like an extra appendage.

Frank and Jasika walked into the chief's office, where he motioned for them to sit in the chairs opposite his desk. He was already on the phone. From what Frank could tell from the one-sided conversation, he was trying to calm down a pissed-off aide from the mayor's office.

"Yes, I understand the gravity of the situation… Yes, I plan on making sure that the two detectives are reprimanded… No, I do not think it is necessary to remove them at this time… Yes, I understand that the mayor is considering bringing in a profiler… No, I don't think it's necessary for you to come down here and supervise the case yourself. Good day, sir." Chief Hays hung up the phone then cursed under his breath, "Punk-ass bitch." He then looked at them. "You see what position you've put me in. The mayor's office wants to see both of your heads on a spear. I've tried to explain the situation, but the mayor is only concerned with her image."

"Sir, it's not—" Frank tried to interject.

"Don't waste your breath. Everyone in this precinct knows it's not your fault, but that doesn't matter. You made the mayor look bad."

"Sir, what was I supposed to do?"

"You say nothing. You got that? Neither of you says a goddamn thing to anyone outside this office. Do you understand me?"

"Yes, sir," they said in unison.

"Good," Chief Hays picked up a manila folder and tossed it to Frank. "This is the information from those assholes over at the first precinct. How they're staying clean in all this is anyone's business... Go. Do police work!" He barked this last statement as he flicked his wrist toward the door.

Once at their desks, Frank let out a sigh of relief. The chief was pissed, but at least he knew it wasn't their fault. Frank understood the veiled threat beneath the chief's message—*I'm covering your asses now, but don't expect that for long.* Frank opened the folder and asked Jasika to write on the whiteboard.

The first murder had occurred on the fourteenth and had been found at approximately six in the evening. A group at St. Patrick's Old Cathedral Church had been holding an outdoor nativity. The girl who was playing Mary had bent down to pick up what she'd thought was the baby Jesus, only to find the bundle of joy was a human head—with its face peeled off. Frank held one picture for Jasika to see. The hair and ears had been left intact, but the skin normally covering the front of the face had been removed, revealing the musculature underneath. Frank made a note to call Mariella to see if she had any information about the head.

The detectives in the case—Hardy and Nord—believed it had been a hit from the Chinese mafia. Frank read their analysis of the crime aloud. "Because of the proximity of this crime to China Town, it's probably a warning to someone in that neighborhood, which is more Italian than Chinese."

"Wow, talk about jumping to conclusions based on no facts," Jasika said, still standing and scribbling away on the whiteboard.

"That's the kind of mistake even a rookie shouldn't make," Frank replied disgustedly. "How these two are even allowed to carry shields is beyond me."

"And because of their royal screw-up, we're the ones left looking inept."

Frank nodded in agreement. He kept flipping through the folder and finally found the picture of the 'partridge in a pear tree' postcard. "Here's what I can piece together," Frank said. "Apparently, the reason it hadn't raised a red flag in the system was that the detectives had written off the card as extraneous to the mafia hit. Thankfully, some lab tech had gone ahead and entered the card into evidence last evening. The card had one print located in the same place as the other two we have." Frank flipped through a few more pages in the folder before concluding, "The lab tech ran the print, but nothing showed up in AIFIS." *Once again, a dead end.*

"So, at least we have new evidence. It still doesn't get us anywhere, though," Jasika noted.

"Frank Schultt," a voice said from somewhere near the front of the bullpen, "I have a delivery for Frank Schultt."

"I'm Detective Schultt."

A delivery guy strolled over to his desk and delivered a package from Barnes and Noble. Frank opened the box after tipping the delivery guy and found a copy of *The Twelve Days of Christmas – A Pop-Up Book*. The book came with a card that read, *Here's some light detective reading, from The Geek Twins*. Frank handed the book to Jasika, who giggled while reading the card.

"Well, they may be twisted, but it's still pretty damn funny," Frank said with a slight smile on his lips. He picked up the phone to call the lab but got no reply. As soon as he lowered the phone to hang up, he received another call.

"This is Schultt."

"Did you get the present from the geek twins yet?" Mariella's voice asked from the other end.

"Were you part of this?"

"God no, but I wish I could have taken the credit for it."

"Bitch."

"I know. So anyway, I've got another body for you. I just got the call. We have 'four calling birds'."

Chapter Six

The five-thousand-dollar suits were gone, along with the rest of his ten-thousand-dollar wardrobe. The black Gucci glasses, on the other hand, still adorned his slender face, as those were his. Supervisory Special Agent Aaron Massey found himself back in the New York City field office of the FBI, located at Twenty-six Federal Plaza on the twenty-third floor of the building. Aaron swiveled in his chair and stared out of his window, trying to avoid the stack of paperwork that had accumulated while he had been working the case.

Aaron Massey wasn't exactly poor, but he didn't have the same income as his alter ego had for the child smuggling case. Aaron had gone undercover after the executive director of Child Welfare International had been caught with an underage prostitute. When the NYPD had interrogated the man, they'd realized the case was considerably larger than they'd originally suspected. When they'd entered the details of the case into the FBI's criminal database, the NYPD had received phone calls from the FBI within the hour and a phone call from Interpol shortly thereafter. Unbeknownst to the NYPD, they had just stumbled across the first inroad to a huge global child-smuggling operation. Interpol had been compiling data on the group behind the ring for years, but nothing had ever been able to stick. With the arrest of CWI's CEO on child prostitution charges, they'd had their first chance to stick someone else into the organization. The FBI had agreed to drop charges on the CEO if he would allow one of their agents to work with him directly and introduce the agent to the individuals working in the Stapkovich organization, a Russian-based crime syndicate suspected of running the trafficking ring.

Aaron Massey had been chosen for a couple of different reasons. First, he had been an FBI legal attaché working in Lyon, France, and had worked closely with people at Interpol for a couple of years, so he was adept at working with Interpol compiling a case with large amounts of international data. And second, he had been out of the field for a few years working as a forensic psychologist, treating agents after they'd gone undercover in fairly traumatic situations.

Aaron's father had worked for the United States embassy in London while Aaron grew up. After he'd graduated from an American high school for embassy kids, Aaron had attended the University of Buckingham for two years, earning a BA in history. During his undergraduate career, he'd become very interested in the criminal process after a close friend of his had died in a murder that had been investigated by Scotland Yard. When the killer had been brought to justice because of the work of a psychological investigator, Aaron had gone to Middlesex University in London to get his MSc in Forensic Psychology. While working on his masters, his dad had retired from embassy work. His mother, father and two sisters moved to Omaha, Nebraska, where his mother's family lived.

When Aaron had received his MSc, he decided it was time for him to move back to the States when his parents did. But Nebraska hadn't seemed to call to him, so he'd moved to NYC and finished his education by getting his PhD in Forensic Psychology from the CUNY John Jay College of Criminal Justice. When he graduated at twenty-four years of age, Aaron was highly sought-after by a number of law enforcement agencies in the United States and England.

Aaron had agreed to a job with the FBI under the condition that he would get to work at the Behavioral Analysis Unit or BAU at Quantico, the FBI's primary training ground. Aaron had advanced through his career, and by the time he was twenty-six, he'd worked closely with agents from Interpol. While there, Aaron had helped lead an investigation that had spread across four continents in eleven countries and had involved murder, money laundering and a large international organized crime syndicate. The arrest, which had finally been made in Washington, DC, had made news across the world. The case had skyrocketed Aaron's notoriety in the FBI, and he'd sometimes been called the 'profile kid', because the ultimate arrest had stemmed from the criminal profile Aaron had created, based on the data he'd sifted through.

He had gotten permission to publish his process, and at first, he'd intended the book to be an academic account of his data analysis, but his editor had realized that the book could be so much more. At twenty-nine, he'd published *Blood Money*, which had been a huge international bestseller. Unfortunately, the success of his book had meant that Aaron would have to take the back seat to active fieldwork for a few years. When the opportunity had arisen two years later to work with the CEO of CWI, Aaron had practically begged his bosses at Quantico to be sent to the NYC field office to work the case. Although Aaron enjoyed criminal profiling, his real heart was in the field, working with law enforcement personnel and FBI agents solving real crimes.

Although there had been some concern that his notoriety would be a detriment to the case, Aaron had promised them that if he ever thought his cover had been compromised, he would drop the case in an instant. Within six months, Aaron had ingratiated himself with the Stapkovich crime family by presenting himself as a very rich kid whose parents had cut him off and who was now looking for a quick way to keep up appearances. Shortly after his thirty-second birthday, Aaron had arranged a meeting where the whole crime family would meet at a fancy hotel for a summit on streamlining the business. Amazingly, the whole escapade had gone down without a hitch. The only real problem was the news reporter catching him on camera the previous evening and broadcasting his name and face in connection with the bust.

Aaron picked up his desk phone and tried calling Detective Schultt one more time. The call went immediately to voice mail. *God, I feel like a fucking schoolgirl, and the high school quarterback won't look at me.* He stared back at the stack of paperwork in front of him, sighed and looked back out of the window. His cellphone started chirping, so he glanced at the caller ID, which flashed 'Judith Wright' on the screen, so he answered.

"Hey, Judi, what's up?"

"Saw you on TV last night. Not the best shot, but at least it showed your pretty face."

"Thanks. I'm waiting for my boss to rip me another one about that."

"Why?"

"Well, the Bureau frowns upon it when our photos are in the news. We're supposed to support the bust, not become the focus of local television."

"How did Jenny Mace even know the bust was going down?"

"That's a very good question."

"So, any word on Detective Dreamy yet?"

"No, Detective Schultt hasn't returned any of my calls or emails."

"How many have you sent?"

"A few."

"God, Aaron, you've got it bad." Judith Wright was one of the first people Aaron had met when he'd started working on his PhD, and he always kept Judi in the loop on his life. She had a masters from Dartmouth in English Literature and had tried to write a great American novel. That pursuit had ended, and she'd gone to work for Scholastic Publishers as a book editor in their young adult fiction line. She'd had a few editing successes, so she was once again starting to think about the great American novel, but seemingly her job just kept her too busy.

"I do. But I know he watched TV last night. Why else wouldn't he call back?"

Bzzzz! His desk phone rang. "Gotta take this real fast," he told Judi as he picked up the other receiver, laying his cellphone on the desk.

"Agent Massey, Ms. Barling is ready for you," the voice on the other end said, not bothering to wait for a "hello."

"Thanks, Caroline," Aaron responded to his boss' secretary. He hung up the desk phone before putting his cell phone back up to his ear. "Well, Judi, time to face the reckoning. I'll call you later." After saying goodbye, Aaron picked up the case file in front of him and headed for Chief Barling's office.

Temperance Barling was the NYC field office's Bureau Chief, and Aaron could tell from the look on her face that she was pissed. Before he could shut the door, she flew off, talking about how in the past week he'd almost destroyed the case because of the damn mitten incident. "And what didn't you understand about Director Price's warning you to stay *out* of the media? After this one, we can't have you undercover anymore. Those days are officially over."

"I'm sorry. I had no idea a camera was there, let alone how Jenny Mace knew the bust was coming."

"Well, she did. And if it weren't for the NYC mayor, you'd be a permanent desk jockey."

"Huh?"

"Mayor Rinehart watched the little display last night and has officially asked Director Price for your immediate help on the Twelve-Day Killer. You're to report to the Midtown precinct and talk to Chief Hays immediately. You're now heading the task force with the NYPD. Play nice."

"Yes, ma'am," Aaron said, his head a whirlwind of emotions. *Did I just lose my job and get a promotion in one sentence?*

"Oh, and Agent Massey, this time, stay away from television cameras."

Aaron strolled back to his office to pick up his jacket and briefcase. When he exited the building, he hailed a cab and instructed the driver to take him to the assigned precinct. While the cab weaved in and out of traffic, he called Judi to let her in on what had transpired.

"Well, I guess Detective Dreamy can't avoid you now."

"Nope, he can't."

* * * *

Frank took one last sip of his coffee before putting it down in the cup holder and exiting the car. Le Parker Meridien Hotel was one of those uptown hotels trying to sell itself as the cutting edge of luxury for a city surrounded by dirt and decay. The exterior of the building was brick and could easily be mistaken for an office complex. Set in the brick were three bays of glass doors, creating a glass wall that ran some thirty-feet wide and twenty-four feet tall. All the glass allowed passersby to see directly into the lobby of the hotel. Although the exterior wasn't much to look at, the lobby was a mix of modern furniture and painted tile flooring, with marble walls, ornate Greek-inspired columns and Roman-inspired archways. All in all, the facade was modern, with a clear undertone of history and class.

As Frank and Jasika approached the hotel, Frank didn't see the lobby for its ornateness. He just took it all in as another crime scene. Instead of noticing its luxury, he focused on the layout of its entrance. Rather than absorbing how the glass walls showed off the lobby inside, he found the officers and crime scene investigators crowding the area. He and Jasika flashed their shields and the patrolman on the front door let them right in.

"I planned on coming here this weekend," Jasika informed Frank. "I promised Ginny I'd bring her here to see the Gingerbread Extravaganza." Although only a few years old, the Gingerbread Extravaganza was becoming one of the must-see events of the holiday season in the city. Local bakers and restaurants created intricate gingerbread houses that were then publicly displayed to raise money to feed the hungry.

Frank and Jasika were guided into a ballroom of the hotel, where hundreds of gingerbread houses of all shapes and sizes were displayed. Frank took in the ballroom's enormity. The sheer size of it made it surprising that anyone would have noticed something out of place.

"Mariella?" Frank bellowed, his voice reverberating around the large room.

"Back here," her voice echoed off the walls.

They passed dozens of gingerbread houses with a range of themes, from the New York Yankees to Disney characters. The number of different houses amazed Frank. Some were traditional gingerbread houses, barely larger than a shoebox. Other houses stood four or five feet tall and appeared almost like a child's play fort.

Frank and Jasika found Mariella and the geek twins examining a relatively modest gingerbread house. From a distance, the house appeared like the hundreds of others scattered around the room. But as Frank drew closer, he still wasn't sure what he was supposed to be noticing.

"Mariella, geek twins, what are we looking at?"

"Well, good morning to you, sunshine. Three bodies in three days... We've got to stop rendezvousing like this daily or my husband's going to get jealous."

"Mar, if your husband's threatened by a thirty-seven-year-old gay man, that's just sad. But really, what am I looking at?"

"Look closer," Nasab said, pointing to the house.

Frank and Jasika leaned in toward the candy-coated house.

Wait a second! Is that an ear?

Frank and Jasika stared at a gingerbread house entirely decorated with candy-covered body parts. Instead of gumdrops, candy-coated fingertips made up the edges of a pathway leading to the house. Replacing the wreath on the door were two ears forming a green heart-shaped decoration. The longer he stared at the house, the more body parts he discovered. Two candy canes decorated the front door. "Well, that's just gross," Frank said, shaking his head back and forth.

"What are the candy canes?" Jasika asked leaning in.

"Well..." Richardson paused for a second before continuing, "We think they're either tongues or possibly labia, but the candy coating is pretty thick, so we can't tell yet. Either way, it's not a complete part of the body."

"I had to ask," Jasika confessed, starting to look a little sick.

"Jasika, why don't you go talk to the staff. I'll finish up here," Frank suggested.

Jasika jumped on the reprieve and was gone within a blink of an eye.

"So, what can you three tell me?" Frank asked.

"I'll start." Mariella delved into her analysis. "Everything looks the same. It's hard to be sure what's going on because of the candy coatings. We can generally tell what the body parts are but identifying them definitively will be difficult until we can get all that candy off."

"Yeah, same on our end," Nasab said. Richardson nodded in agreement.

"I do have one thing I can tell you," Nasab said, using a pair of tweezers to lift one of the 'gumdrops' on the front pathway. Richardson then pulled out a magnifying glass and directed Frank's attention to the barely visible fingerprint that lay underneath the sugary coating. "Although we can't exactly print these yet—even pictures would be useless—there is one characteristic about this print which I find interesting."

"Spill."

"Gladly. Notice the type of print. In tech-speak, it's what we call a tented arch. That may not sound like much to you since arches, in general, account for only about five percent of fingerprints, and of that five percent, tented arches account for roughly forty percent. Tented arches exist in approximately two percent of people."

"Okay, and?" Frank questioned.

"And the print we got yesterday on the back of the three French hens was also a tented arch. It could be a coincidence, but the chances are not likely."

"So, what you're telling me is the print you found yesterday on the back of the card may correspond to the fingertip we see today?"

"Yes, and we'll know for sure once we get them all cleaned." Nasab then took the candied fingertip and placed it in a plastic bag before writing the location and number of the crime scene. "We are going to carefully deconstruct the house one piece at a time before transferring it back to the lab."

"Wait a second, do you think these decorations came from one vic?" Frank asked.

Richardson looked puzzled for a second before saying, "There could be multiple vic body parts in here, but we really can't say until we get them all cleaned off. But I will not discount the possibility. We should have some conclusive answers this afternoon."

"Well, Mariella, geek twins, I look forward to your reports later."

* * * *

Frank stared at the whiteboard once again from his desk at the precinct. He took out a small rubber ball and bounced it against the wall. This habit annoyed some in the bullpen, but most detectives had their little quirks when staring at a board full of evidence with no clear direction.

"Jasika, do you have anything?"

"Sorry, Frank. I just keep staring at it and nothing's popping," she replied in between bites of a sandwich.

"I hate doing this to you but go over it with me one more time. What do we know?"

Jasika started rattling off the basic facts within the case. First, they had body parts from multiple vics and no way to identify them. Second, the only person of interest, the MTA train conductor, was MIA and no one had seen him since before the killings had started. Third, the print on the previous day's card might be from one of the fingers from today's gingerbread house. Lastly, the locations weren't easily accessible, so someone had to have some kind of access to get in.

"Dammit, I'm just not seeing anything."

"Hey, Frank, the geek twins just sent over the crime scene photos from today. Want to see if anything jumps out?"

Frank circled around to Jasika's desk, and they began scrolling through pictures. They had been taken both outside and within the hotel, so Frank was able to get a larger view of the scene. First, they scrolled through the onlookers' photos to see if they recognized any of the faces from their previous crime scenes, but that got them nowhere. Frank asked Jasika to send them over to facial recognition to see if their software could scrub for anything Frank and Jasika couldn't notice with their naked eyes.

Next, they examined the pictures taken up and down the block and around the front of the hotel. Nothing seemed out of the ordinary at first glance, but a photograph of a white van caught Frank's attention.

"Wait a second! Back up." The white van photo flashed onto Jasika's screen once again. "I've seen this van somewhere. Zoom in on the side of the vehicle." Jasika moved her mouse and clicked on the location in the image Frank wanted to be enhanced. The decal on the side of the van filled the screen, *Delicious Delights*.

"Jasika—"

"I'm already calling FAO Schwarz," she responded before Frank could even speak his idea. Frank walked around to his side of the desk. He flipped open his detective notebook, where he'd jotted down Le Parker Meridien's main number. The operator connected him to the special events manager, who told Frank that Delicious Delights had been used for a high society tea on the premises. He thanked the manager for her help and hung up the phone. He stared at Jasika, waiting for her to finish her call.

"Well?" Frank questioned.

"FAO Schwarz used Delicious Delights for an employee holiday party earlier this week."

"So did Le Parker Meridien. Goddammit, finally, we get a break!"

Chapter Seven

December 17, 1 p.m.

Chief Dennis Hays' office was exactly what Aaron had expected to see — minimalist and simple. The office had a massive oak desk that was much too large for the room, but then, that was a phenomenon Aaron was quite used to in Manhattan. In the display case at the back of the room were various awards and accolades — a photo of Hays with the mayor, then with the President of the United States, a handful of plaques and some family pictures.

Aaron watched the chief, not paying attention to what came out of his mouth. He'd been in this position before. *The city is in a panic. The mayor is up-in-arms. The poor police officers are getting the shit kicked out of them by public opinion. Blah, blah, blah.* Aaron read his assignment to the NYPD as half a slap on the wrist by Director Price and half a slap from Temperance Barling. Neither of them was happy with him due to the notoriety of *Blood Money*. Still, Price had at least signed off on the project when it was initially underway. *For some reason, Price still believes I intended for the book to become an international bestseller. Oh well, shit happens.*

Aaron caught himself drifting, so he refocused on what the police chief was saying, "Agent Massey, I'm sure you're well aware that your presence here is not my idea, nor is it that of the detectives working the case."

"I am, Chief Hays. I am here to function in a support and advisory position only. Despite what you may have seen on the television, I am camera shy and don't like being in the spotlight."

"Good... Let's keep it that way." The chief took in a deep breath before continuing, "Now, I'm sure you realize that until yesterday you were considered a suspect— Well, a person of interest in this case."

"I do."

"I'm just warning you that the lead detective, Frank Schultt, is probably not going to be overly happy to see you becoming part of the investigation at this point."

For a number of reasons.

Aaron nodded, acknowledging the chief's point.

"Good... As long as we're both on the same page. So, you've seen the news reports and read the initial files. What's your take?"

"Chief Hays, at this point, the only thing I can tell you with accuracy is there's a fair chance we're looking for a white male between the ages of eighteen and thirty-five."

"That's it?" prodded Chief Hays, seemingly hoping for more information.

"Without more information on the actual victimology, I can't be sure about much. One problem with this case is the innate lack of knowledge about the actual victims. Until we know who the victims are, I'm kind of flying blind with a profile. Although there are some generalizations I can make, we still need detail before saying anything concrete."

"Well, hopefully, you can get that detail fast." The chief took in a long, heavy breath. "I guess it's time to meet your new team." He stood, and Aaron followed. They walked toward the bullpen to find Detectives Schultt and Torv putting on their coats.

"Where are you two heading off to in such a hurry?" Hays asked.

"We just had a break in the case, so we're off to follow a lead." It was then that Frank took notice of Aaron's presence in the room. "What's *he* doing here?"

"Supervisory Special Agent Aaron Massey has been asked by Mayor Olivia Rinehart to consult on this case as a special favor from Director Price at the FBI," the chief said matter-of-factly. From the tone in the chief's voice, Aaron could tell this was news to Frank.

"He's a suspect in a rash of killings," Frank pressed.

"He *was* a suspect," the chief stated. "I've been fully informed by the FBI and NYPD that during at least three of the four killings, Agent Massey was surrounded by Bureau officials and our own personnel. Furthermore, Agent Massey's unique experience in handling serial crimes is something this case can benefit from." His last statement sounded like a verbatim of what the mayor's office had said. "So, let's play nice and catch this motherfucker. Any questions?"

Not even waiting for a second to hear if there were questions, the chief turned on his heels and headed back toward his office.

"Detective Torv, it's nice to meet you in person. I've spent most of the morning going over your notes. Very impressive." Aaron extended his hand, and Jasika hesitantly took it, shooting Frank a quick glance.

"I see the expensive suits are gone," Frank stated while giving Aaron a quick once-over. From the original wardrobe Frank had noticed at FAO Schwarz, the only item still in Aaron's possession was the Gucci glasses.

"Yes, that wardrobe was all part of my cover. I needed to look like a spoiled little rich kid whose parents had cut him off and was desperately looking for a quick way to make money. Thankfully, no one saw through the facade, besides you."

"What do you mean?"

"Please, Detective Schultt. I may be a Fed, but I'm not an idiot." Frank continued to stare blankly at Aaron. "First, at the crime scene, I took in the way you watched me and my clothing. I also warned my handler you'd probably be checking into me, so they needed to make sure the cover was airtight. Apparently, it wasn't tight enough, which leads me to how you caught me off guard with the Ole' Miss question. I had all the basic answers about the campus ready to go, but you threw me off, and I could tell you realized you'd thrown me off. I was almost nervous about it, but my case was heading into the end game that evening, so I wasn't worried you'd blow it."

"Well, all that may be true, but you Feds do a decent job of creating a cover. One thing for next time... Don't make yourself so squeaky clean."

"What do you mean?"

"When our lab guys ran your cover, everything came back so squeaky clean you looked like a fucking choir boy. That in its own right made you look suspicious."

"Good to know, so…where are we off to?"

"Torv will explain everything to you in the car."

Frank took off in the direction of the precinct's motor pool. Jasika got the keys for the 2005 beige sedan. As the two approached the car, Jasika motioned for Aaron to sit in the front seat, but Frank just said, "Nah, let the boy wonder sit in the back seat. Maybe he can learn a thing or two about how police work is really done."

"That's what I've heard about you, Detective Schultt. You prefer it when a guy takes you from behind," Aaron quipped without skipping a beat.

"Uh-oh," Jasika said, climbing into the passenger seat, her eyes widening, looking from Aaron to Frank.

"So, that's how you want to play this, Agent Massey?"

"Supervisory Special Agent Massey."

Every muscle on Frank's face clenched. He closed his eyes, took a breath and looked straight at Aaron and said, "Fuck you!" in what came out as almost a whisper. With that, Frank raised himself away from the car door and started walking toward the garage entrance with Aaron close at his heels.

"What's your fucking problem? It was just a joke. I mean, come on. I was trying to break the ice," Aaron yelled halfway across the garage.

"You. You're my fucking problem," Frank said as he spun on his heels when Massey approached him dead-on. "We were doing just fine before you had to come and stick your nose into my investigation."

"Fine? Ha! If you were doing so fine, then why did I see your face splattered across the television last night looking like a lunatic with a badge?"

"Lunatic, eh? You're the stalker trying to get into my pants. What the hell was that at the coffee shop?"

"That was called protecting my cover, dipshit. And please, don't flatter yourself. I tend not to go after guys known for trolling the back lounge at The Eagle." Aaron didn't see the fist or even know what happened until he ate asphalt. As he tried to get his bearings, he heard Jasika yell from the other side of the garage as two uniformed officers tackled Frank to the ground. Aaron got himself to his knees and shook out the fog that consumed his vision as he brushed dirt off his clothes. He could distantly hear Jasika scolding Frank. *For a short little woman, damn does she have a set of pipes.* He steadied himself and was turning around as Jasika approached him.

"Agent Massey."

"Supervisor Special —" he muttered.

"Are you okay? Please don't file a complaint," she blurted, looking at Aaron with eyes full of pity and fear.

Aaron ignored her, watching Frank, who was still being held by two officers. "Are we done now? We still have an investigation to complete. The faster we get done, the faster I'm back in my office." Aaron didn't wait for an answer. He walked over to the waiting car, opened the back door and climbed inside.

Aaron watched Frank shake off the cops and follow Jasika to the car. She started the engine, and they sat in silence for the entire drive.

* * * *

Delicious Delights was just off Washington Square Park in Greenwich Village and was at the heart of New York University. The park unofficially functioned as NYU's quad, so the place was rarely empty. Finding parking near the park at two in the afternoon was no small feat, so Jasika double-parked in a fire lane.

While they were searching for a parking space, Frank spoke to Aaron, explaining what had led them to Delicious Delights. He explained the van's appearance near three crime scenes.

Upon exiting the car, Frank noticed the small fleet of vans in an underground garage beneath the storefront to Delicious Delights. As they approached the building, he directed Jasika to take the lead on the interview. They then bounded up the stairs, opened the doors — which set off a set of chimes above the doorway — and entered the small display room. "I'll be right out," a voice called from somewhere in the back room.

"NYPD, ma'am," Jasika announced.

"Oh, just give me a second."

Frank glanced around the display room, examining pictures of a young brunette woman with a veritable who's-who of upper society New York. The woman was standing with the mayor, the head of the Broadway League, Chairwoman of the Board at Lincoln Center and a smattering of New York City's celebrities. It was then that the young woman from the photos appeared from the back.

"NYPD, did you say?"

"Yes, ma'am," Jasika replied. "I'm Detective Torv, this is Detective Schultt and the guy with the bruised chin is Supervisory Special Agent Massey from the FBI. He's helping us with a case."

"I'm Alexi Clegg, the owner of Delicious Delights." She smiled and nodded her head in each of their directions. "Wow, all that detective skill in my little storefront. What can I do for you?"

"Is there a place where we can talk, Ms. Clegg?" Frank asked.

"Oh sure, right this way." She led the trio into the back room, which led to four side-rooms — the kitchen, a small office, down a set of stairs — *probably toward the garage* — and a small tasting area, which was where Ms. Clegg led them. The room was filled with a variety of catering books and photo albums, probably of various events Delicious Delights had catered. "So, how can I help the NYPD and FBI?"

"Have you catered events at FAO Schwarz, the Botanical Gardens and Le Parker Meridien this week?" Jasika questioned.

"I think we have, but I'm not completely sure. Let me go grab my appointment book." Alexi stood and crossed the larger room into the small office. She emerged with a large, leather-bound appointment book. "Okay, we had a staff luncheon on the fourteenth at FAO Schwarz, a charity event in the evening of the sixteenth at the Botanical Gardens and a high tea for a group of society women this afternoon at Le Parker."

"Okay," Jasika said as she nodded and scribbled information into her notebook. "How many events do you have this week?"

"Oh, dear God, I'm sitting at around thirty events from now until Sunday. Christmas is always a huge time of year for me, so I'm always forced to hire extra hands to help with the rush."

"That's a good segue into my next question. How many employees do you have working for you?"

"Full-time, all year long, I run on a staff of twenty-seven. During the holidays... I'm running a staff of fifty-six right now. That includes cooks, drivers, cater-waiters, everything."

"Hmm-m, and how many vans do you own?"

"The company owns six full-time vans. And depending on the season, we also rent a couple of refrigerator trucks to help get food from here to various locations around the area. Oh my God, I have been so impolite. Can I get you three anything? Never mind, I'm sure you're not supposed to say yes, but I just created this new cherry-cheesecake cupcake, and I've been dying to get someone to try them. Stay right there." Before they could object, Alexi was out of her seat and heading toward the kitchen. From his seat, Frank could see Alexi the whole time as she walked into the kitchen, barked out some orders and headed back to the tasting room.

"Now, where were we?"

"Ms. Clegg, have you heard about the killings over the last three days?"

"You mean the Twelve-Day Killer? I saw the news report on it last night on WNTV." Staring right at Frank, the dawn of realization flooded her face. "Oh my God, you're the detective from the TV last night."

"Yes, that was me," Frank said flatly.

"Oh, don't worry. I take nothing Jenny Mace says on television seriously. An old friend of mine was crucified by Jenny a few years ago."

"Really? Who was that?" Jasika questioned.

"Maybe you've heard of her...Katie Simmons. She had a television cooking show on the Food Network for a few years. Then about six years ago, Katie had a case of food poisoning happen at one of her restaurants on Christmas Eve, and Jenny went after her with a vengeance, calling her a malevolent chef. Although the health inspector cleared Katie of all wrongdoing, the high-profile exposure from Jenny Mace caused all three of Katie's New York restaurants to go out of business, leading to Katie's bankruptcy."

"Sorry to hear that," Jasika cut in. "The reason we're here is that your catering vans have been seen near every crime scene."

"Oh, so you think there may be a connection between the Twelve-Day Killer and Delicious Delights? God, that's the last thing I need during the busiest season of the year. Anything I can do to help ease suspicion of my business, just ask. As for my whereabouts, I'm pretty much living here these days. I have round-the-clock help, so you can ask my employees about my whereabouts, and they can pretty much provide you with an alibi for any day."

"Thanks for your help, Ms. Clegg. Can we get a list of your current employees?"

"I don't think I should give you that list until I've spoken to my lawyer," Alexi said hesitantly. "I don't want to violate my employees' rights. Would you mind if I call his office really fast?"

"Sure, we'll wait," Jasika said.

Alexi stood and turned to head toward her office when one of her helpers walked into the room carrying a tray of cupcakes and a freshly brewed pot of coffee. Before leaving, Alexi acted like the perfect hostess and served the group. "I insist that you must try these and give me your honest opinion. I'm thinking of taking a batch of these to an office party I'm catering next week for the various Madison Square Gardens' groups. It's a new twist on an old family recipe. And by *old* family recipe, I'm sure my grandmother snipped it from *Lady's Home Journal* back in the 1950s."

Frank grabbed a cupcake and poured himself a cup of coffee, as did Jasika and Aaron. With that, Alexi headed into her office. From his seat, Frank could see her making a telephone call. Frank drew his attention back to Aaron, who was remaining quiet. *Fuck, I shouldn't have hit him.* They remained in awkward silence for what seemed like a year to Frank.

Aaron finally piped up, "I'm going to go find a bathroom." Aaron stood and left the small room, passing Alexi.

"Where's he going?" Alexi questioned.

"Restroom," Jasika responded.

"Thankfully, my attorney was in his office. He told me the decision to provide the information you requested was up to me. He recommended I ask for a warrant but still insisted the decision was mine. So, here you go." She handed Jasika a stack of papers. "I've separated the list into both part-time and full-time employees. I can generally vouch for my full-time people. They've all been with me for years. The seasonal help? They're all good folks, but I don't know them as well. I can't see any of them getting into the kind of trouble you're talking about, though."

Jasika glanced through the information, and Frank eyed the list from his seat. There was a massive amount on each employee. *Clegg is definitely a detail-oriented woman.*

"One last thing before we go for now. Can we see your van fleet?" Frank asked.

"Oh, sure, not a problem. You just go down the back set of stairs. At the bottom, you'll find the door that leads to the underground garage."

"Thank you for your time, Ms. Clegg," said Jasika.

"Again, anything you need from me, please ask," Alexi reassured them as she stood and followed them into the main room. "Just try to keep my name and

Delicious Delights out of the press if at all humanly possible."

Frank yelled for Massey, who came out of the kitchen carrying a box neatly decorated with the Delicious Delights logo. Together, they headed toward the garage. Jasika opened the door to a dimly lit garage with five vans. *Two of them must be out for deliveries.*

"Hello," Jasika called, entering the garage. To their left, a sudden crashing sound reverberated through the garage. A man then bolted for the garage's exit.

"Halt, NYPD," Frank yelled as the man continued to run.

Frank was off in a sprint. Aaron dropped the box of pastries and took off running behind him, with Jasika following closely on his heels. They rounded the top of the garage entrance ramp, and Frank yelled, "He's going toward Washington Square Park." Frank watched the runner take off through the archway of the park. "Jasika, cover the subway entrance on the other side of the central plaza. Aaron, you're with me," Frank yelled as they crossed traffic, holding their shields and darting among the cars. A few horns were blasting — and a few New Yorker mouths joined the loud chorus on the streets. Out of the corner of his eye, Frank watched a taxi almost run into Aaron, the driver shouting in one language or another and flipping Aaron off. If he hadn't been running at full tilt, he would have stopped to laugh. But Aaron kept running, keeping pace with Frank, which surprised him. *I guess Feds know how to run after all.*

Frank and Aaron ran through the famed archway while Jasika peeled to the right, likely hoping to outflank the man before he got lost in the subway. When Frank and Aaron got to the central plaza, they lost sight of him. At three in the afternoon, there were just too many people milling there. There were artists set up with their wares, and a group of fencers from nearby NYU was practicing on the grass. Frank spun his head from side-to-side, trying to get sight of the fleeing man again. "Aaron, go toward the subway entrance on this side. I'll see if I can get a better view of the park," Frank huffed. Frank noticed that Aaron didn't question him. He just turned and ran in the other direction.

Frank went to the highest point of the central plaza, staring in all directions to see if he could spot the runner. He spotted a foot patrol and ran toward the man. "Officer, I need to borrow your walkie-talkie," Frank said, holding out his shield.

"Sure thing, detective," the officer replied, handing over the walkie-talkie.

"All officers near Washington Park. We have a suspect fleeing. He's approximately five-foot-eight-inches, wearing a green hoodie, possibly of Italian or Latin descent," Frank said into the radio.

Frank caught sight of the green hoodie walking through the plaza heading right toward Aaron. Frank didn't think Aaron could see hoodie guy through the crowd of people going down the subway stairs. "Aaron, in front of you," Frank yelled. He took off running in that direction, watching as the hoodie guy picked up speed.

Frank watched Aaron spin to look at him. Frank pushed his muscles even harder, trying to catch up to the suspect. Aaron didn't have time to react before the runner crashed into him, knocking him to the ground as he fled down the stairs. Aaron was sent sprawling, but the guy barely skipped a beat as he headed for the subway entrance in the park. "He went down the stairs," Aaron barked, starting to pick himself up as Frank dashed past.

Frank didn't stop to make sure Aaron was okay. He ran full steam ahead. *I'm sure he's fine. He's a big boy.*

Jasika was their only hope at stopping the guy before he jumped on a train. Frank entered the MTA station and started down the steps. Halfway down, Jasika appeared at the bottom of the steps yelling, "*Freeze!*"

The runner swung his head toward Frank and ran toward Jasika instead. *Wrong move!* The runner tried to shove Jasika out of the way, but Jasika got a hold of his shoulder and shoved her elbow into his clavicle. The man yelled in pain and tried to push Jasika away, but she grabbed his arm and, in one swift move, yanked it behind his back, causing him to fall to his knees. Frank heard the distinct popping sound of the guy's shoulder being dislocated.

Frank ran toward her, holstering his gun. He lifted the guy from the ground, flinging him against the nearest wall while reading him his Miranda rights then cuffing his arms behind his back. "You have the right to remain silent. Anything you say can and will be used against you in a court of law. You have the right to speak to an attorney. If you cannot afford an attorney, one will be appointed to you. Do you understand these rights as they have been read to you?" The man said nothing, so Frank repeated himself, "Do you understand these rights as they have been read to you?"

"Yes. Yes, I do," was the man's pathetic response, with an obvious and heavy South American accent. Frank and Jasika flanked the guy and walked him out of the subway station. Aaron was hobbling over with the patrolman.

"Officer...?" Frank asked

"Haverly."

"Officer Haverly, can you please call central for a pickup to Midtown?"

"Sure thing, detective."

"Massey, what the hell happened to you?" Jasika asked.

"I think I sprained my fucking ankle when this guy tackled me." The runner turned sheepishly toward Aaron and said he was sorry.

"Now I understand why they don't let you Feds out of your tower. You guys tend to hurt yourselves, don't you?" Frank laughed.

When the car arrived, Jasika volunteered to return with the suspect.

For the first few minutes of the drive back to the precinct, Frank and Aaron rode in complete silence. Frank was replaying the entire afternoon from start to finish in his head. *I never even gave him a chance. I've been such a dick.*

"Aaron," Frank started, keeping his eyes forward while watching traffic, "I want to say I'm sorry for sucker-punching you earlier."

"If the shoes had been reversed, I probably would have done the same thing. I crossed the line."

"True, but I shouldn't have hit you. That was completely unprofessional of me. I know better. It's just you hit on a pretty raw nerve."

"I shouldn't have provoked you like that. I knew what I was saying. I knew it was going to cause a reaction, but it was out of my mouth before I stopped myself. If you haven't noticed yet, my mouth sometimes has a mind of its own."

"Really? I hadn't noticed," Frank said with a sly smile curling at his lips.

"So, can we start over?" Aaron asked.

"We're going to be working closely with each other, so I definitely think we need a do-over at this point. I'm Frank."

"I'm Aaron. It's nice to meet you, Frank."

Chapter Eight

December 17, 4 p.m.

Frank and Aaron watched the suspect, Geraldo Salvador, through the one-way mirror. Geraldo's hoodie, now pulled back, revealed a guy in his late twenties with a clean-shaven face. Frank had Jasika run Geraldo's information, and it had come up clean, but the last name still seemed a little off to him. Although it wasn't uncommon for a Latino to have a non-Latin-origin surname, this guy didn't look like a 'Salvador'.

Jasika entered the observation room and asked, "So, Frank, what are you thinking?"

"Not sure yet. Something definitely doesn't add up, but I doubt he's our perp." After a few more minutes, Frank decided it was time to interrogate the suspect. He had already made it very clear he wanted to be the only one in the box. If Aaron or Jasika wanted to say something, they were instructed to rap on the window twice and Frank would meet them outside.

Frank grabbed a legal tablet and walked into the room, Geraldo sat up straighter, his hands cuffed to the table in front of him. "Can I get you something to drink?"

"Nah, sir, I'm fine," Geraldo said, averting his eyes from Frank.

Frank turned the chair around and straddled it, leaning in toward Geraldo. "So, why'd you run?"

"I dunno, sir."

"Yeah, that answer doesn't fly with me."

"Okay, man. Uhh...I thought you were coming after me for parking tickets."

"Yeah, that still doesn't seem to fly with me."

"Don't know what to tell you." Geraldo raised his eyes for the first time, still keeping them slightly averted. Frank would usually have taken this as a bad sign, but he remembered that many South American cultures taught eye-aversion behavior in situations with authority figures.

"So, please, let's stop the bullshit. I know something's off, so why don't you just be straight with me?" The flatness in Frank's voice seemed to grab Geraldo's attention. He pressed on. "Let's start with your last name. When did you pick that last name?" Frank had an idea and figured he'd press Geraldo. *Let's see what happens.*

"What do you mean, man?"

"Last name... It's not yours, so when did you get it?"

"How'd you...?"

"I'm a detective. When we ran your name, it came back problematic."

"Fuck, dude! That guy said it was clean."

"Guy?"

"Fuck, I came to the US two years ago because… Ahh, *fuck*!" Geraldo then broke down and let it spill. He'd met a girl two years prior who had been on a tourist visa in Venezuela from the US. They'd become friends and had kept in touch through email. Three months later, Geraldo had found out she was pregnant, so he'd vowed to come to the US for her and their kid. Unfortunately, Geraldo had run up against some corrupt political forces at the US embassy who'd kept asking for more and more money to get a US visa. He'd finally gave up on going the legal route and found a coyote who had smuggled him all the way from Venezuela to the US for a fraction of the cost the crooks at the embassy were trying to charge him.

Frank stood up at the end of Geraldo's story and walked back into the observation room. "So, psych-boy, is he telling the truth?"

"Well, detective-boy," Aaron responded, "I'm not exactly a deception expert, but his facial movements rang true from what I understood. I had a seminar in micro-expressions in grad school, and his seemed contrite and sincere. I didn't detect any abnormal emotional tells except the disgust he showed when talking about the embassy workers." Aaron went on to explain the basic science behind micro-expressions, but Frank tuned him out.

"Works for me," Frank said, cutting Aaron off. Frank turned on his heels and walked back into the interrogation room. Once again, Geraldo sat a little taller at Frank's entry. "Well, Geraldo, I'm forced to call Immigration and Naturalization. Until they get here and you're handed over to them, you're going to be remanded to the custody of the NYPD."

Geraldo began to tear up. "I understand, sir, I understand. You just do your job." Geraldo wiped away the drop with his shoulder.

Frank felt bad for the guy, but he had to follow the law, whether or not he agreed with it. Frank removed Geraldo's cuffs and informed him that someone would be in shortly to take him to holding. Frank then left the box and returned to the observation room.

"Wow, that fucking sucks," Frank blurted as he entered the room. "All he wants to do is help raise his kid, and some crooked embassy twats tried to extort him. Fucking sucks!" Aaron and Jasika nodded in agreement. "I need some fresh air." Frank grabbed his coat and headed outside.

Aaron watched Frank walk through the front door of the precinct. He hesitated a second, looking to Jasika as if asking if he should follow. Jasika nodded, so Aaron grabbed his coat and went after Frank.

The briskness of the December cold hit Aaron the moment he stepped outside. He hadn't noticed the drop in temperature when they had been running earlier, but now that the sun was setting, the cold swept into the city like an icebox. Aaron pulled up his collar around his face to brace himself against the bitter frost. He looked up and down the street and didn't see Frank anywhere. *He must be at Viva La Coffee!*

Aaron started walking in the direction of the coffee shop. He was about to round the corner when he heard Frank's voice in the distance.

"Logan, hey, thanks for taking my call. I need your help." There was a pause in the conversation. Aaron assumed this Logan character was speaking on the other end. "Okay, here's the deal. Do you have anyone at your firm who does pro-bono work on immigration?" Again, Aaron listened as there was a pause when Logan spoke. A few seconds later, Frank began explaining Geraldo's plight and how Frank believed the dude was telling the truth about what had happened at Venezuela's embassy. After a few more back and forths, Frank hung up the phone and released a deep sigh of relief.

"That was a nice thing you did. I guess you're not as big of an ass as you try to present yourself to be," Aaron said, walking around the corner.

"You were spying on me?"

"Not intentionally. I came after you to make sure you were okay." Aaron gently touched Frank's shoulder and continued talking, "Hey, I'm with you. If I had the connections with a law firm in town, I would have done the same thing. So, what'd your friend Logan tell you?"

"Apparently this isn't the first time he's heard of problems with people trying to get visas out of Venezuela. But the head of immigration law has been looking for a good case to force the Feds to fix the Venezuelan embassy, so he has dispatched an associate to at least get Geraldo out of jail. He should be free in a couple of hours. Thank God the Cheeto-in-Chief still isn't President, or we'd already have ICE knocking down the door to haul Geraldo out of the country."

"That's good. It's a good thing you did, Frank. Sometimes the little guy needs help. So, wanna grab some coffee?"

"Sure. Why not?"

Frank and Aaron walked in silence down the block. They entered the shop, ordered two coffees and found a small table in the back.

"So, big-time FBI agent with a bestselling novel and everything?" Frank started.

"Oh God, not you, too." Aaron chuckled. "I was in the right place at the right time. I hadn't even thought about writing a book until my best friend made the suggestion. She put me in touch with a couple of her editor friends. Then the next thing you know, I'm on *The New York Times* Bestseller list."

"How did you keep your undercover work going after that?"

"I thought my career was sunk when the book became popular. I'd already resigned myself to a desk job or teaching position somewhere. Thankfully, it's amazing how you can go from being the toast of the town to a nobody. I lay low for a few years. When the child-trafficking case opened up, I practically begged my boss to let me go back into the field. Unfortunately, I was informed this morning that my undercover days are definitely over."

"What happened?" Frank asked.

"Jenny Mace happened."

"God, I know how that goes all too well."

"Yeah, I saw the ambush 'interview' last night. She's good at those."

The two spent the next half-hour talking about a range of topics, from Frank's decision to become a cop to Aaron's time as an FBI legal attaché.

On the walk back, Aaron admitted something to Frank. "I used the FBI database to find out where you worked. I also noticed the coffee cup you had brought into the last crime scene, and it didn't take much to figure out how to 'accidentally' run into you the other day."

"I wondered, but I couldn't figure out how you pulled it off."

"Yeah, I guess I was a little transparent."

"Ahh, my own personal federal stalker." They continued walking back toward the precinct. "Aaron, I'm sure you're a great guy, and I'm sure most people will say I'm an idiot for not responding to your advances. But I just want to make it clear... It's not going to happen." Aaron stopped in his tracks, seemingly weighing what Frank had said as Frank continued, "I think you're a nice guy and all. But if you've read up on me, which you have, you know about my past. I wish I could say that it's 'in the past' thing, but it's not." The words hung in the air like a lead balloon. "Anyway, I enjoyed getting coffee with you, but I'm going to call it a day. I have a five o'clock appointment, so I'll see you tomorrow."

Without waiting, Frank turned in the opposite direction and started walking away. Aaron stood in stunned silence. *Dude must be way more damaged than I thought. Well, fuck. No hot NYPD detective for me.*

* * * *

Frank had never taken himself as someone who needed serious amounts of therapy, but seven months ago that choice had been taken from him. Frank had stumbled upon a burglary in progress as he'd entered a deli. As he had headed toward the front to pay, he'd caught a glimpse of someone behind the counter with a gun aimed at the clerk. Frank had acted as if nothing was the matter and continued toward the checkout. From a distance, Frank had yelled to the clerk, asking if he could help him find a box of crackers. The clerk had looked down at the guy holding a gun on him. The burglar had then stood and faced Frank, gun in hand.

Frank had dropped to one knee and unloaded his clip into the guy, creating a bloody mess all over the wall.

After the police had come and secured the situation, internal affairs had showed up to check out the scene and make sure the shooting had been by the book. Overall, it was ruled within the confines of the law. But the fact that Frank had used his entire clip to take down the suspect had been unofficially ruled a little overkill. As a result, Frank was required to undergo weekly counseling with an NYPD staff psychologist until they deemed his counseling no longer necessary.

Every Tuesday at five p.m. on the dot, Frank would enter Dr. Samantha Weintraub's office and talk about a range of subjects, from the shooting to his personal life. Mostly, Frank didn't mind the weekly distraction, but he also didn't think it was necessary. Sure, the shooting had been overkill, but the security camera feed had clearly shown that the guy had aimed his gun at Frank before Frank had unloaded the clip. In the heat of the moment, Frank had been more worried about making sure the perp couldn't hurt anyone. Frank had rationalized the shooting many times during therapy with Dr. Weintraub and stuck with his story.

"So, Detective Schultt, how are you doing? I see you got the Twelve-Day Killer case."

"Yeah, the case is a real bitch. Right now, we're waiting on DNA and fingerprinting, but we're not getting anywhere."

"So, how are you handling this killer's very public and anti-Christmas displays?"

"Well, I don't know if they're anti-Christmas. He's just making a very public statement. I mean, maybe we'll have a better idea when we learn about the victims, and we can move forward."

Dr. Weintraub nodded her head and wrote something down on her legal pad. *God, I hate that legal pad. She's always writing.* Dr. Weintraub finished her written thought and resumed watching Frank. "Let me put it another way," she said, then read directly from her legal pad, "I know Christmas is an especially hard time of the year for you. How are you coping with the case and its thematic overtones?"

"So, I'm a little of a Grinch this time of year. I mean, you know my past. I'm not a Christmas junkie. Many people aren't, but people keep moving on, so I don't see why this case should be treated any differently from the other cases I've taken."

"Okay, Frank, I'm just making sure that you're all right. If I ever suspect you're not mentally handling a case because of your history, I'm required to inform your superiors about the situation."

"I know, but I'm fine with the Christmas nature of the case. My disdain for the holiday makes me a little less attached to its emotion. It enables me to look past the holiday themes for the perp who's killing people."

"Okay, so, let's talk about something else."

"Sure, why don't I tell you about the FBI agent who has been assigned to me." Frank then went on for twenty minutes, spelling out everything that was 'Aaron Massey'. He talked about how they'd first met and the coffee shop incident. He then talked about seeing the agent on TV and having him show up at the precinct that afternoon. "I mean, I feel like I can't go anywhere without having this guy following me."

Dr. Weintraub wrote something down on her legal pad and glanced up at Frank. "Do you think you may have feelings for Agent Massey?"

"Am I attracted to him? Sure. But I also made it very clear to him it's strictly a professional relationship," Frank said, somewhat trying to convince himself.

"You don't sound like you believe your own words, Frank. Why?"

"I... Uhh... I'm not ready to consider dating someone after Adam."

"That's a door that has been sealed shut during our meetings. This is the first time you've mentioned Adam by name."

"That's not true. I talk about him in here all the time."

"You've never said his name. You've alluded to him. You've alluded to his murder. But you've never said Adam's name during a session."

Frank thought about that comment for a second. His mind and eyes drifted, not looking at anything but looking at everything at the same time. "I miss him. Every day, I miss him."

"I would be worried if you didn't. You suffered a traumatic loss. People don't get over that kind of loss easily."

"See? So you get why I can't just jump into a relationship with the first hot FBI agent who comes knocking."

Dr. Weintraub wrote something down on her pad before asking, "Do you ever think you'll be ready to have a relationship with another man?"

"I honestly don't know. There are days when I wish I had one, but those are few and far between. I don't feel like I need a relationship to make myself complete."

"Good, because relationships should accentuate the best part of ourselves and not fill gaps we feel are missing. When we put that kind of baggage on a relationship, we set ourselves up for failure every time."

"So, what do you think I should do, doc?"

"Frank, you know I will not answer that question. I'm here to listen and help, but I will not give you relationship advice. I will ask you, 'what do you think's holding you back?'"

"You know what's holding me back," Frank responded while rolling his eyes.

"I know what you *think* is holding you back, but you've been grieving for five years. Now, you'll probably grieve your loss for the rest of your life, and that's natural, but when do you think you'll allow yourself to move on?"

"I've moved on. I really have."

"Really?" Weintraub questioned once again, making a note on her pad.

The silence between them could be cut with a knife. Frank glanced down at his watch and noticed that his hour was up. "Well, it looks like it's that time again."

Glancing down at her own watch, the counselor said, "Well, I guess you're right. Saved by the bell, so to speak. Before you go, I just want you to think about something. I've been waiting a long time for you to broach the subject of Adam. I want you to think about whether you're ready to have that discussion next week. I also want you to question what's holding you back from having a serious romantic relationship."

Frank mumbled something but avoided the question.

"Oh, and Frank, I need to switch our date next week. I'm taking off the twenty-fourth and twenty-fifth, so can you come in on the twenty-third instead?"

"Yeah, that works for me."

"Great. And, Frank, think about what I said."

Chapter Nine

December 18, 5:30 a.m.

Frank was dreaming about running after a perp. He'd just discovered the perp was Chief Hays dressed as a clown when the incessant iPhone ringing jostled him from his dream. *This better be good.* He picked up his phone to see that the caller ID read 'Mariella Ramos'. *Fuck, I know this isn't a fun chat at o'dark-thirty.*

"You woke me up, and it's not even light outside."

"What are you wearing? This is a dirty little phone call."

"Dear God." Frank yawned then he continued to speak. "I would laugh if my eyes were open."

"Well, get your cute ass out of bed, sugar-tits."

"Huh?"

"Well, at least that got a rise out of you. Anyway, get up, get dressed and get to Bloomingdale's. Our new friend has left us another present."

"Which store?"

"Broadway."

Frank got out of bed, feeling the cold wooden floor beneath his feet as headed toward the bathroom. Dressed in a pair of pajama bottoms, Frank looked at himself in the mirror, took a couple of blinks, rubbed his eyes and started about his morning routine. In a normal situation, he would rush to the body as quickly as possible, but he figured the dead body wasn't going anywhere at this time of the morning. *Besides, I'm not awake until I've had a shower.* His body just wanted to crawl back into bed and pretend the phone call was a nightmare. Still, twenty-five minutes later, Frank was freshly showered in a new set of clothes, standing outside his walk-up and hailing a cab.

The cabbie tried talking to Frank on the short ride to SoHo, but Frank was only half paying attention to the guy. He wasn't sure what new surprise his foe had left behind at Bloomingdale's. However, since it was still early, Frank was sure it would be another front-page story in *The New York Times* and the lead story on WNTV tomorrow morning. The cabbie had to drop off Frank a half-block away because of the police cars blocking the street. *Great, let's do this subtly.* Although the city was just waking up, there were still a handful of passersby hanging outside the perimeter, which was roped off by the police tape. *Ahh…the city that never sleeps. Always a crowd twenty-four hours a day.*

Frank approached the police tape and recognized the patrolman standing guard, who then ushered him into the crime scene. *Why can't killers do things in the middle of the day like normal people?* The front part of the SoHo Bloomingdale's location was adorned with Corinthian-style columns. In the middle of the series of columns was a set of double doors with display windows on either side. Over the doors, all-lowercase letters read 'bloomingdale's' in black metal. Frank noticed even more people gathered around the southernmost display window, where police were attempting to erect a barricade. As the final piece was being put in place, Frank noticed Mariella and Aaron standing in the case. Frank headed to the main entrance and flashed his shield at the police officer who was stationed just inside. He paused for a second to ask the officer how to find Aaron and Mariella. With information in hand, Frank headed toward the entrance of the outside display case. When he found it, the door was already open, so he took a second to take in the tableau in front of him.

Mariella was as put together as she always was — wearing a navy-blue pantsuit with a pair of red heels sticking out from underneath the cuffs. She was currently lying on her back on a white tarp, examining the Christmas tree. Aaron, on the other hand, was wearing a dark navy sweatshirt with 'John Jay College' arcing across his chest, dark blue jeans over a pair of white tennis shoes and topped off with a black trench coat, which Frank found quite 'fed-y'.

"Good morning, everyone," Frank said stepping into the display window as he pulled out a pair of gloves from his coat pocket and put them on.

"Hey, Frank," Aaron responded.

"About fucking time," Mariella said, glancing out from underneath the side of the Christmas tree.

"So, pray tell, why the fuck am I here this damn early?" Frank asked as he let out a huge yawn. He promptly covered his mouth with his latex-encased hand.

Aaron talked Frank through the display case, explaining what they knew. Around three in the morning, a cleaner had gone out the back way for a smoke. While outside, the cleaner had been approached from behind and rendered unconscious. By the time he'd regained consciousness at around four-thirty, the killer had used the guy's key card to enter the facility and erect his own window display.

The display contained Mrs. Claus knitting in a rocking chair next to a roaring fire in front of a Christmas tree, only the formerly fake hands had been replaced with real ones. The tree had been decorated with a range of different body parts designed to resemble ornaments.

"Oh, and one more detail that's different here... None of the body parts were disguised this time. The fingers are just fingers, no candy-coated shell, no taking off the prints to prevent identification. It's almost as if the killer wants us to know what's going on this time."

"Did you talk to the geek twins?"

"Yeah, they were here earlier. They're processing the custodian and the alleyway to see if there's anything back there. One tidbit from yesterday panned out, they told me. Remember how Nasab—or was it Richardson?"

"Doesn't really matter, I always see them as interchangeable myself."

"Anyway, one of them said they had mentioned something about tented arches?"

"Yeah, the card left at the scene from two days ago had a tented arch print on it."

"Yeah, sounds right. One twin mentioned that after de-candying... God, is that even a word?" Aaron thought for a second and shook his head as if he were attempting to refocus. "Anyway, umm, one of the fingers found at the crime scene yesterday was the finger in question."

"Wait a second, the killer purposely placed the fingerprint of his next victim at the crime scene the previous day?"

"Yep, of course, the question is whether the unsub —"

"Unsub?"

"Profiling speak for 'unknown subject'. So, the question is whether the unsub is capturing his victims, getting their prints, killing them and putting them on display or if the unsub is stealing the print ahead of time in an effort to give us a shot at catching him before he kills again."

"And this matters how?"

"Well, case A — the prints are designed as a complete red herring and he's toying with us. Case B — this is a killer who has some level of remorse and wants us to stop him."

"Case C — he's just a fucking psychopath with a Christmas fetish," Mariella offered.

Frank tried not to laugh, but smiled, turning his attention back to Aaron as he continued, "Hopefully, today's scene will give us a much clearer picture of the unsub we're dealing with here, because right now I'm flying blind on a complete profile. There are just too many possibilities at this point."

Frank was taking in Aaron's opinion when his thoughts were interrupted by Jasika finally entering the scene.

"Sorry, guys. I had a bitch of a time finding a cab at this hour out in Queens that would come into Midtown."

"We understand," Aaron replied.

Frank motioned for Aaron to follow him into the hallway behind the window display because things were getting a bit crowded in the show window.

Richardson then tapped Frank on the shoulder. "Hey, Frank, I wanted to let you know that we got nothing outside. Whoever this guy is, he's either amazing at cleaning his tracks or is damn lucky."

"How did the scumbag take down the janitor?" Frank asked, before looking at Aaron and saying, "'Scumbag' — that's a term detectives use when talking about killers."

"As for how?" Richardson jumped in. "Taser. The guy came up behind the janitor while he was smoking and tased him in the neck. Very crude, but it's a very effective way of taking someone down."

"Jasika, go interview the security guard and see if he remembers anything else."

"On it. Umm-m, where am I going?"

"Follow me" Richardson offered. "I need to gather up my kit back there."

"Frank, I have something for you back in here," Mariella yelled from inside the window display.

Frank headed to Mariella with Aaron following on his heels. "What do you have for me?" Frank asked, stepping inside.

"Although we haven't started printing any of the fingers in the display, I have a theory we're seeing body parts from multiple victims in this room." Mariella walked over and unhooked one ornament hanging on the tree, showing it to Frank. "Notice the fingernail."

"What about it?"

"Well, it's a red nail with a white snowflake painted on it. The fingernails we found at yesterday's scene had the same pattern."

"Yea, we didn't notice it until after we got all the candy coating off last night," Nasab said, from the other side of the tree before poking his head out and giving Frank a nod. "Speaking of which, de-candying a human body part takes time. We thought about melting it, but that could have harmed the fingerprints underneath. We soaked all the pieces and periodically rubbed off small layers of candy."

"Were you always in there?" Frank asked. "I didn't see you earlier."

"I'm sneaky like a ninja that way."

Frank rolled his eyes and motioned for Nasab to finish up his point but heard a small commotion behind him. A blinding bright light shone through the window. From the corner of his eye, Frank could make out a microphone-wielding Jenny Mace accosting a patrolman who was trying to get her to stop filming the closed crime scene.

Frank flew out of the window and back into the store like a banshee on the warpath. In that moment, all the frustration he was experiencing related to the case was about to explode in a nuclear reaction, and his target was Jenny Mace. Frank grabbed the brass handle on the front door, noticing its coldness under his hand as he yanked it open with a violent thrust. He was about to take a step outside when a hand gripped his upper arm tightly, preventing him from going.

Frank glanced behind him to see Aaron's stern face. "Calm the fuck down," Aaron whispered into Frank's ear. The television news camera turned on the two of them, and Jenny raced forward, already blurting out a series of questions. Aaron took a deep breath and flashed Jenny his winning smile.

"Jenny, long time no see. It's been years since that interview about my book," Aaron said, smiling as if he'd just seen his long-lost best friend. Frank noticed Aaron's arm around his lower back, tightly pulling him closer to Aaron's side. *What cologne is he wearing? Wow, I can't believe my mind just went there. This is the first time I've been touched since he laid his hand on my chest in the coffee shop... Don't go there, Frank. Don't fucking go there.* Frank tried to focus his attention back to Aaron and the Macinator, but his head was swimming with the kinds of thoughts he wouldn't want aired on television. Frank unsuccessfully tried to wriggle out of Aaron's grasp, but each time he tried, Aaron's grip tightened. *For a small guy, he's strong.*

"So, Agent Massey," Frank heard Jenny say as he focused on the conversation before him "Is this crime scene related to the infamous Twelve-Day Killer?"

"Oh, Jenny," Aaron said, just flashing Jenny his sparkling white teeth, "you know I can't confirm or deny any part of an ongoing investigation. I wish I could tell you everything, but you know I've got to follow protocol here."

"So, are you officially helping the NYPD on this investigation?"

"Mayor Rinehart asked for some consulting help with your Twelve-Day Killer, which I believe she said yesterday in her press conference. I've been asked to help the NYPD build a comprehensive profile of your Twelve-Day Killer. A catchy name, I might add."

Frank noticed how Aaron kept referring to the suspect as Mace's 'Twelve-Day Killer', like she'd birthed the killer somehow.

"Thanks," Jenny responded, almost blushing.

"As I said, as a forensic psychologist with the FBI's BAU, we are often brought in to help local law enforcement agencies like the NYPD with their investigations. It's not that the NYPD was handling the case poorly — "

"Then why has the NYPD had so many mishandlings of the case, Agent Massey?"

"Ms. Mace, the NYPD has done a phenomenal job handling the case. Although I cannot discuss case specifics, I can say there have been problems with evidence analysis outside the control of the NYPD. Heck, even the FBI, Interpol or Scotland Yard would be in the same place as the NYPD."

"So back to my original question then, Agent Massey. Is this crime scene related to Detective Schultt's case?" Mace motioned to Frank for the first time.

"Again, if I were at liberty to say one way or another, I would gladly do so. Unfortunately, both the NYPD and FBI policies state that detectives and agents should not publicly comment about a case on which they are currently working. You know, we don't want to show our cards just yet. The Twelve-Day Killer may be watching you on television right now. If the killer determines we have information, he or she may alter their modus operandi or signature."

"Thanks," Jenny said and motioned for the camera guy to stop filming, clearly realizing that the interview was going to get her nothing more. "It's so good to see you again, Aaron — and you too, Detective." Aaron released Frank, leaning in to give Jenny a hug while kissing her on the cheek.

"Anything for you, doll," Aaron said, pulling away and flashing her another one of his winning grins. "Oh, hey, do you think you could avoid airing what you recorded in the window? I'd hate for some poor family member to see those images and recognize a birthmark or a tattoo before we get the opportunity to inform them personally and provide them with all the help the NYPD and FBI can during their grieving?" As he said those words, Aaron looked more sincere than those guys asking the public to send money to help feed African orphans.

"I guess I could edit the hell out of the piece this morning. But it will most definitely go on air by five."

"Thanks, you're amazing." Aaron once again slipped his arm around Frank and ushered him back into Bloomingdale's. Frank watched Aaron glancing back over his shoulder to see if Jenny was leaving. Frank caught Mace mouthing to Aaron, "Are you two dating?" Aaron just smiled a little bigger at her and winked.

Once inside Bloomingdale's, Aaron ushered Frank away from the front doors and other offices. He gently steered Frank down a hall and away from the crime scene techs in the building. Suddenly, Aaron spun on his heels and got right up in Frank's face, "Listen up, Detective. If you ever pull a fucking stunt like that again, I will make sure your shield is taken. You can hit me. You can yell at me. I don't give a flying fuck. But if you ever go after someone like that again, I will take you down."

Frank wasn't expecting the tirade and stared at Aaron blankly, trying to fumble some words together. After a moment, Aaron continued, "You don't know what I just did for you, so let me spell it out. I was expressly forbidden from showing my face on television by both the Director of the FBI and the NYC

Bureau Chief. Although that may not sound like a huge deal to you, trust me. It's a huge fucking deal. I will spend most of this morning trying to smooth things over and hoping I'm not yanked from this case."

"I... I'm sorry," Frank mumbled.

"Don't be sorry. Don't let it fucking happen again."

"I didn't realize you two were friends."

"Please, no one's friends with a piranha like that. But I've learned over the years that it's best to play nice with annoying reporters rather than screaming at them, hitting them or, God forbid, drawing my gun on them like you started to do the other night when she cornered you."

"Hey, that's not fair. I didn't know it was a reporter at first. And I didn't completely draw my gun on her."

"True, but you did go for it right on television. Now, I'm going to go make some phone calls and play triage on my own career for the rest of the morning. Assuming I'm not pulled back to Quantico, I'll try to come by the precinct later."

"Again, Aaron, I'm so sorry." Frank reached out, grabbed the back of Aaron's head and drew him in for a kiss.

Aaron was suddenly pressing against Frank as he leaned into it. Before Frank knew what was happening, Aaron wrapped his hands around him and was pulling him even closer. A sudden push on his chest brought Frank back to the moment before Aaron slapped Frank. Frank instinctively reached up to touch his cheek as the look of shock filled Aaron's face. He wasn't sure, but Frank thought Aaron looked as surprised by his slap as Frank was.

"Wrong time. Wrong man. Wrong place," Aaron bit out through clenched teeth. Frank watched as Aaron turned on his heels and headed toward the main entrance of Bloomingdale's.

* * * *

Frank spent most of the morning back at the precinct going over what had happened with Aaron—the dressing-down, the kiss and the slap. When he wasn't mulling things over in his head, he tried to focus. Thankfully, this was a day of breaks in the case. First, the geek twins had been correct. The fingertip with the red nail polish and the white snowflake was identical to the one received the day before. In fact, several body parts came from bodies that had been found at the various earlier crime scenes. Only this time, the perp had left the prints intact. Frank couldn't exactly figure out why the perp was purposefully giving the cops clues, but he remembered Aaron saying something about why that kept coming back into his head.

Of course, with the thoughts of what Aaron had said, also came thoughts of Aaron—how Frank had attempted to kiss him, how Aaron had reacted to Frank's attempt. Throughout this, Jasika kept dropping hints that if Frank needed to talk, she was there for him. She hadn't witnessed either blowup—the Mace or the Aaron one—but Frank could tell that she knew something was off. Even though she tried to talk to him, he remained tight-lipped.

Aaron showed up around two, informing Jasika that he had been busy putting some final touches on the Stapkovich human-trafficking case. Of course, Frank could tell Aaron was lying, but was glad to see that the agent hadn't been removed from the case.

Shortly after Aaron's arrival, Frank received a phone call from Mariella, which he put on speaker, and asked Mariella to repeat what she had just told him.

"Agent Massey, Jasika, Frank, we finally got the DNA results back for the first four victims from AIFIS. I've been on the phone most of the afternoon with Nasab and Richardson, and we've been piecing together some interesting tidbits about these murders."

"How so?" Jasika questioned.

"Well, let me get Richardson and Nasab on the line, and we can all talk." Frank heard Mariella put them on hold, and a few seconds later there was a clicking sound followed by ringing.

"Crime lab."

"Richardson?" Mariella asked hesitantly.

"No, but I'll get him… Yo, Colin, ME's office on the phone." They heard a voice in the distance, but Frank couldn't make out what was said. "He'll be right here."

About a minute went by as they sat in silence, waiting for the grand unveiling. Finally, a voice came on the other end of the line, "This is Richardson."

"Hey, Colin, it's Mariella. I also have Frank, Jasika and Agent Massey on the line."

"Everyone, please just call me Aaron. There's no need to be formal."

"Okay," Mariella said. "Then we have Frank, Jasika and *Aaron* on the line. Tell them what you found earlier."

"AIFIS really came through for us this time. The first four victims were listed by family members as missing persons within the previous week."

"We'd already assumed they were missing persons. This also ensures we aren't just looking at a prank using bodies from a medical school or the morgue," Frank noted as he strolled over to the whiteboard and wiped off a segment that questioned whether the murders had been a prank.

"Ah, Frank, but that's just the beginning of the story." There was a clear hint of gleefulness behind Richardson's voice. "This one is definitely turning into a screwball case." Richardson took a deep breath and explained how some assumptions they had been tossing around about the case were panning out. "First, based on the fingerprints lifted today, we are fairly certain the first four victims were all represented in the Bloomingdale's display. On top of that, the working theory is that the perp was leaving the cards to help the police identify the next victim. However, the cards themselves cannot be used to help the police stop the killer. And for more on that, Mariella."

Without skipping a beat, Mariella started talking. "The cards are not foreshadowing as much as they are advertisements, in my opinion. The lab tests we've been running to determine how the perp is killing and freezing the bodies would indicate that the bodies are frozen for at least forty-eight to seventy-two hours, depending on the size of the vic. In essence, the vic is dead before the cards are ever placed."

"Can you tell us when the vics are dying?" Aaron questioned.

"Agent Massey... Aaron, I mean... At this point, with the freezing, it's hard to get a definitive time of death. Freezing always fucks up our time schedules because it delays decomposition. And without a full body, we can't exactly determine the liver temperature and try to mathematically work our way backward from there."

"Okay, so there's no way to know when the victims were killed," Frank said.

"Yep. But, I can…well, *we* can tell you who the victims are. Richardson."

"Thank you, Mariella. This feels like a newscast."

"A very fucked-up newscast," Frank replied dryly.

Richardson continued, "Okay, based on the information newly received from AIFIS, the four victims, one of whom Frank knows, are Timothy Bishop, Penelope Vasquez, Damian Savage and Katie Simmons."

"Wait a second." Jasika appeared puzzled before continuing. "Frank, didn't the owner of Delicious Delights know Katie Simmons? I remember her saying something about her when we talked about Jenny Mace."

Frank rolled his eyes at the mention of Jenny Mace.

Aaron quickly jumped in, "I think you're right. If I remember correctly, Katie Simmons was a TV chef whose career Mace destroyed."

"Hey, umm, guys," Nasab joined in. "You are correct. Katie Simmons was the head chef at La Bette, a French bistro that was accused of killing people a few years ago. According to our good friend Google, the alleged food-poisoning incident happened three years ago on Christmas Eve."

"We already knew that, Nasab," Frank stated matter-of-factly.

"Yes, but what you don't know is that all four of the victims have a common theme. Listen to this. Victim number one was Reverend Timothy Bishop. He was defrocked by the Roman Catholic Church for breaking his vow of chastity. The ruling came down two days before Christmas. Next, our victim from the mitten tree is a Ms. Penelope Vasquez..."

Jasika said, "I remember her from high school. She was a computer programming genius turned game designer who lost everything after her Christmas-themed game, Elf Shot, was found to have pornographic images."

"Elf Shot, a game where you shoot elves?" questioned Mariella.

"Actually, Elf Shot was like a slingshot game where you shot elves at various targets," Aaron noted. Frank and Jasika just turned and looked at him. "What? It was a fun game."

"Anyway," interrupted Nasab, "you are correct, Jasika. Ultimately, her whole gaming company went under as a result of the lawsuit and boycott that ensued. Lastly, we have Frank's old friend Damian Savage, who had the unfortunate run-in with one Natalie Miller after she threw herself in front of his subway on Christmas Eve."

"Hmm-m... I think I'm seeing a pattern in the victims," Frank noted as he finished writing the new details on the whiteboard. "All our victims are associated with problems that occurred around Christmas."

"Frank," Aaron interrupted, "I think we can go a step farther and say all our victims are being chosen because of their Christmas-related problems."

"What do you mean?" Jasika questioned.

"Think about it. Our unsub is picking people who he feels have been burned by Christmas. The priest was defrocked before Christmas, the game designer was ruined by a Christmas video game, the train driver's career was ended because of a Christmas Eve suicide and the television chef's business went bankrupt as a result of the food poisoning on Christmas Eve. Based on this information, I think I can build a fairly reliable profile now."

Chapter Ten

December 18, 3:30 p.m.

The conference room at the Midtown precinct was full. Chief Hays sat in front of Aaron as he prepared to present the initial profile for the Twelve-Day Killer. Various detectives, police officers and a few top-brass filled the room to capacity before he began.

"For those of you who don't know me, I'm Supervisory Special Agent Aaron Massey, a criminal psychologist from the FBI's Behavioral Analysis Unit working with the NYPD on the Twelve-Day Killer case. I've brought us all together because we've had a break in the case this afternoon, and as a result of this break, I am ready to provide you a preliminary profile of the person who is probably our unsub—or unknown subject."

Suddenly, a hand shot up in the back of the room. Aaron nodded, acknowledging the cop. "Umm, I heard this psycho-babble stuff is bullshit, pardon my French."

"Well, I'm glad you put that out there. There are a lot of mis-conceptualizations about criminal profiling. We're hardly perfect. I can say that from 1974 to 1994, the Behavioral Analysis Unit was accurate in our profiles about ninety-two percent of the time. We wish this number were higher, but we are definitely dealing with a good chunk of science with a little bit of art. I won't lie to you or sugarcoat this. At any given time in the United States, we estimate there are approximately fifty serial killers who could be responsible for as many as six thousand victims each year. Thankfully, through our efforts and the efforts of local law enforcement, such as yourself, only eighteen percent of serial killer cases remain unsolved. Again, we wish this statistic were lower. But all things considered, we're definitely doing a decent job of bringing these people to justice."

"Why is this happening here?" someone in the back of the room spouted out.

"I'm not sure what you mean but let me tackle a related question. The United States accounts for around seventy-eight percent of the serial murders that happen in the world. Of the rest of the world, our next closest cousin is England, which accounts for four percent of the other serial murders. Now, it's possible that some of the numbers around the world are skewed by state-run media, but the US is still way out in front on this issue. And if you think it's based on population, nope. India, which has a population of one point two billion people, compared to the US's three hundred eleven million, only accounted for about one point eight percent of the number of serial murders.

"As for why the US has more serial murders, I wish I could say. We have a ton of theories ranging from the openness of our media and the sensationalism of these cases, to higher incidents of drug use during pregnancy, to the fact that our forensic science has grown faster than other countries and allows us to link murders together over a larger geographical range than in the past. Whatever the reason, serial murder is an issue in the US."

"Excuse me," a female detective said as she raised her hand. "You keep saying 'serial murder'. What do you mean by that?"

"Good question. Serial murder, as defined by the FBI, is the unlawful killing of two or more victims by the same offender or offenders in separate events. Notice that we are looking for an unsub who kills multiple victims at multiple times. The reason we prefer this term is that it helps us differentiate between serial murderers and spree killers, who kill a lot of people in a single event. Ultimately, over forty years of research has shown us that these two types of killers don't have the same psychological issues." Aaron paused for a second, picked up a bottle of water, unscrewed the cap and took a drink. "Before I delve into the profile, are there any other questions?"

Finally, one officer raised his hand and asked if serial killers were just psychopaths. Aaron then had to explain what scientists perceived psychopathy to be. Aaron started by explaining how famed criminal psychologist, Robert Hare, had defined psychopathy as a personality disorder manifested in people who use a mixture of charm, manipulation, intimidation and occasionally violence to control others. Aaron then explained that when examining psychopathy, psychologists discussed four distinct areas — interpersonal, affective, lifestyle and antisocial characteristics.

"By interpersonal, we mean these people can charm people, but the charm is always superficial. Furthermore, these people have a grandiose sense of self-worth and are probably pathological liars. Lastly, psychopaths are amazing manipulators. In many ways, it's these interpersonal characteristics that enable psychopaths to get away with their crimes for as long as they do." Aaron then explained that the affective component of psychopathy related to the unsub's lack of remorse or guilt, a lack of empathy and a failure to accept responsibility for what he or she did.

"You keep saying 'he or she'. I thought all serial killers were male?" a young officer in uniform asked.

"Eighty-five percent of serial murderers are male. But there are a healthy eight percent of serial murders that are female, so we try not to make a general discussion of serial murder male-specific. I will say that in the current case, I'm ninety-nine percent sure our unsub is male. Female serial killers are more unorganized than males, which I'll talk about more in a minute." Aaron then finished discussing psychopathy by talking about the fourth factor, lifestyle. "Psychopaths seek stimulation that gives them a high. They are more impulsive, but they also lack clear, realistic life goals. Lastly, psychopaths are antisocial, so they have poor behavioral controls, higher rates of a juvenile record and may have been in and out of the penal system multiple times."

Aaron continued fielding various questions from the officers and detectives in the room. Finally, once everyone was on the same page, he broke into the profile itself. "As already mentioned, a profile is part-science and part-art. As for science, we've conducted hundreds of interviews with a range of convicted serial murderers as part of the daily functioning of the BAU. These in-depth interviews allow us, as psychologists, to get a much clearer picture of how serial murderers think and behave. Right off the bat, I can pretty certainly tell you we're looking for a lone white male between the ages of eighteen and fifty-five. This is based on decades of statistics about who generally perpetrates these types of crimes."

Aaron took a second to glance around the room to make sure everyone was keeping up with him. "I can also tell you that the Twelve-Day Killer falls into a category of perpetrator which we call *organized*. We call them 'organized' because the process of the murder is thought-out and intelligently enacted. Although not all serial murderers are highly intelligent, organized murderers tend to have IQs over 135. They are socially and sexually competent. They often have romantic partners and are quite likely to be living with their sexual partner. The partners are generally clueless about their loved one's behavior. In fact, the partners are generally the last ones to suspect that their loved one could be a serial murderer.

"Any questions so far?" Aaron asked. He gazed around the room, but no one raised their hands. *I hope they're getting this and not just placating me.* He continued, "As for their family situations, chances are they were an only child or at least the most-favored child, which is probably where their inflated egos come from. They probably experienced some kind of serious abuse or harsh discipline during their childhoods. Most of their teen acting-out is attributed to the harsh environment of their youth. When you meet them, they are generally very charming and want to be perceived as highly masculine.

"Before the crime, the unsub spends a good deal of time preparing and planning. As we have seen from the current case, this guy is methodical and has spent a good deal of time fantasizing and preparing for these murders. For this reason, he probably does not know the victims he's picking personally, because it's easier to target strangers. When committing the murder, he wants to control the crime scene, so he needs a place where he can work uninterrupted by nosy neighbors. Often, they use warehouses or condemned buildings because they don't have regular occupants. Our murderer is killing the victims in this location and somehow refrigerating the bodies, which means there is probably a refrigeration unit in or near where the unsub is acting. Where the killings occur, we will find a ton of evidence, but where the unsub displays the bodies, there is generally no evidence left at all.

"Lastly, organized serial murderers want to be known. They want us, as law enforcement, to see what they've done. I'm suspecting that the unsub was getting a little annoyed at our inability to find out who the victims were and release that information to the public, which is why he left us the crime scene he did this morning. He wanted us to know who these people are. He cannot get his jollies until the public knows what's going on."

"Don't these guys generally revisit their crime scenes?" Chief Hays questioned.

"It's definitely possible. Thankfully, Detective Schultt has a running photo archive of bystanders from each of the crime scenes. We've been putting them through facial recognition, but nothing has popped. This person may be a police groupie or even volunteer information, so we should start a hotline and get it to the media. Although most of the calls that we will get are cranks, we've got to at least put it out there.

"Overall, our killer is goal-oriented. He is targeting people who have had what he deems as horrible experiences in and around Christmas. He may even see himself as freeing the victims from their pain and suffering. He has an obsessive-compulsive mindset that stems from deep-rooted psychosexual issues, but this man is not delusional. No voices are telling him to do this.

"So, where does this leave us? We need to be focusing our energy on finding people who fit the general profile and who have the means. Any questions?" Aaron spent another fifteen minutes fielding questions related to the profile.

* * * *

After the meeting, Frank watched as Aaron had a couple of one-on-one conversations with officers who had questions about the profiling process. Jasika went back to her desk to follow-up on a couple of leads. Frank was surprised to see how authoritative Aaron became while in his element. *Maybe this guy isn't a stupid Fed after all?* Frank was mesmerized, watching how Aaron commanded the room. Aaron was smart, witty and captivating. *God, just watching him turns me on. Oh, don't go there, Frank. He made it very clear last night that ship has sailed. It figures, me and my own stupidity getting in the way of the first decent guy I've met in a long time.* Frank waited for Aaron to be free then ushered him back to the bullpen.

"Good job back there," Frank said with a smile.

"Well, thank you, Detective. Just doing my job. So, what did you think?"

"I think a lot of what you said sounds on target, but a lot of it is just generalities at this point."

"You're right, the profiling process is about generalities. We weed out possible suspects through generalities. Are they always correct? Nope. But we have a pretty good track record."

Frank gave Aaron a half-smile as if to say, "We'll see." He returned to his desk to find a manila envelope laying there. He picked it up and read through the document.

"What's that, Frank?" Jasika asked.

"It's the report on the employees of Delicious Delights. At each of the three crime scenes, we had different delivery people with the van. Furthermore, everyone alibis out."

"Everyone?" Jasika and Aaron said at the same time.

"Yeah, two-thirds of the staff were either working at the shop or were on delivery at every time of the murder. In fact, their schedules crossed paths so much that no one could have been responsible for more than one of the murders. It's an absolute dead end."

"Dammit," Aaron exclaimed. "I thought someone who worked for Delicious Delights would have been a great suspect. I mean, you can transport bodies plus refrigeration."

"True," Frank said as he flipped through the rest of the report. "I sent the crime lab to check out the place, and they came back empty-handed. They found lots of DNA evidence and fingerprints, but nothing ties back into the murders. Delicious Delights is officially off my radar."

"Well, Frank, don't get too upset just yet. I think I may have another idea," Jasika said as she motioned for Aaron and Frank to come around to see her computer monitor. "I typed in the four names of our victims and I found this website." She turned her screen so Frank and Aaron could see the website she was on.

"*HolidayHorrors.com*? Really?" Frank said looking at the website.

"Yep, take a look," Jasika said as she clicked through a few hyperlinks and showed Frank and Aaron a page that listed their first victim and his story. Over the next few minutes, Frank and Aaron went through all four of their victims' names and read detailed accounts of everything they'd been through.

"Wow, this guy is thorough. I mean, look at the detail he's given about each incident," Aaron said as he kept reading the screen.

"Jasika, don't you have a friend over at cybercrime?" Frank asked.

"Well, I don't know if I would call him a friend, but we dated for a while."

"Think you could call in a favor from him?"

"On it." Jasika picked up her phone, and within fifteen minutes and at least one promise to have coffee later that week, she came back with the name Connor Gordon. "My friend in cybercrime was also nice enough to let me know that Gordon has a record both as an adult and a sealed juvenile one. On his adult record, he has a battery charge that was eventually dropped. But on the surface, he definitely fits Aaron's profile."

"Then let's get moving," Frank said, grabbing his coat.

* * * *

Connor Gordon lived in an apartment near the corner of Avenue C and Loisaida, commonly referred to as either Alphabet City or the Lower East Side. The street where Connor lived had been part of the city's gentrification during the 1990s, so the once-Bohemian neighborhood was now a fairly nice part of town. However, many of the residents were hold-outs because of their rent-controlled apartments, and developers were just waiting for them to die off one by one so they could finish developing the area to charge premium prices for decent real-estate.

Jasika found a parking space near the apartment building, and the three exited the sedan and headed up the street. Sitting on the doorstep was an elderly woman who, going by her deep wrinkles, seemed to be pushing ninety.

"Excuse me, ma'am," Frank asked.

"Yes," the woman responded hesitantly.

"Detective Frank Schultt, Detective Jasika Torv and Supervisory Special Agent Aaron Massey," Frank started as they all flashed their badges. "We're looking for Connor Gordon."

"What's that little douchebag gotten into this time?"

"I really can't say," Frank said as he tried to muffle his laugh.

"Apartment C-12, third floor," the old woman said as she went back to watching over the neighborhood.

They entered the building and found a maintenance man who agreed to lead them to Connor's apartment with the master key. The four of them then made their way up the hallway and stopped on the third floor before apartment C-12, where they found a sign which read, 'Beware of Attack Dog'.

"Ahh fuck, I hate dealing with dogs," Jasika muttered as she unholstered her gun and pulled out her bottle of pepper spray.

Jasika and Aaron stood on either side of the door as Frank rapped on it saying, "Connor Gordon, NYPD, open up." Instantly, there was the distinct sound of yipping.

"Attack dog, my ass," Jasika said. "That's gotta be a ten- or maybe a twenty-pound dog in there." She put away the pepper spray as Frank rapped on the door again.

Nothing. Frank motioned for the maintenance man to open the apartment, which he did hesitantly. The door clicked as it unlocked. Aaron took the lead and entered first, followed by Jasika. As they opened the door, they were greeted by a small Chihuahua who continued to yap. *Well, if Connor's inside, he knows we're here.* They continued the sweep of the apartment, Frank and the others taking one room at a time — their guns drawn, scanning the room in an arcing motion.

"He's in here!" Aaron bellowed from the living room. "He's got a pulse, but I'm calling 9-1-1." Aaron took out his phone and started dialing.

Frank ran to find a man in his early forties passed out in an overstuffed chair. His remote control was still sitting on the arm. A small TV tray next to him contained a plastic mug with some kind of beverage in it. Franked sniffed, discovering the deep stench of alcohol. The face that Frank made after smelling the cup must have been amusing, because Aaron stopped to chuckle. Also on the table was a prescription for codeine. Frank picked up the bottle and shook it to hear only a single pill inside. Frank read the label to see that Connor had received a prescription for fifteen pills on the previous day. Underneath the bottle, he noticed a sheet that said '*Post-Op Instructions*'.

"Great, our suspect had surgery yesterday morning. He was supposed to take one tablet every six hours for pain. From what I can tell, he took fourteen pills, plus he took them with alcohol. Dumb schmuck," Frank informed the group.

"Well, when he wakes up, he may not feel pain from the surgery, but he's going to have one massive headache. His pulse is strong, so he's in no imminent danger of dying, but he still needs to be taken to a hospital," Aaron reassured the group. "Well, there goes our suspect. He would have been in a drug-induced haze at the time the Bloomingdale's display was created."

"Since we're already in here and had probable cause for entering his residence, I say we poke around," Jasika said, giving Frank a little wink. Jasika strolled over to a computer desk in the corner of the room. She booted up the system and was quickly faced with the need for a password. "Hey, Frank, read the name on the dog's tag for me."

Frank scooped up the little guy and read, "Whopper. There's irony for you."

Jasika plugged *whopper* in for the password and was granted access to the computer. "People who need passwords should be more careful when they pick them. The guy I dated in cybercrime once told me that the two most common passwords are the words 'password' and 'god'. Talk about idiots and ego trips."

After the computer booted, and at Frank's request, Jasika ran a search for the victims' names. In a matter of seconds, she found the folder containing the research and website development. "Dear God," she exclaimed.

"What's wrong, Jasika?" Frank asked, walking over to see what she'd found.

"There are over a hundred names listed in here. And, oh my God, you're on the list." Jasika pointed to a folder icon next to his name and quickly double-clicked the icon to reveal a wealth of information on Frank.

"What the fuck?" Frank scanned through the titles of some of the files. He had Jasika open them to get a better picture. The file contained information about Adam's death, Frank's involvement as the lead detective on the Savage case and a video clip of the incident with Jenny Mace earlier that week. "Dear God, he's my own personal cyberstalker."

"But not just you, Frank," Jasika explained. "There are at least one hundred named folders in here. I guess we didn't spend enough time looking at the guy's website before we came over. Too excited for the lead, I guess"

"Can you pull up the section of the website that deals with me?"

"Let me see. Apparently, he hadn't added you to the overall site yet. But here's what he has."

Frank read the full in-depth description of the night Adam had died and how it had impacted Frank's life. There was a description of his shooting seven months before, with clear speculation that the shooting was overkill as a result of the similarities to his husband's death. He even had copies of the photos that had been taken of Frank before he'd almost shot his porno video. *Holy fuck! I was told all those images were destroyed. The* more Frank read and saw what Connor had compiled about him, the more enraged he became.

"Delete it."

"Frank, you know I can't."

"Jas, for me, please delete it."

Jasika glanced at Frank then over her shoulder, obviously ensuring Aaron wasn't paying attention, but he was still checking on Connor's vital signs. In a few keystrokes, Frank's folder was gone. As Frank watched, she also downloaded a program from the Internet that would enable her to delete the file using sixty-four layers of encryption, which she quietly explained to him as she worked. The downloaded file would also self-delete, which would make it almost impossible for a cyber-criminalist to know something had been removed unless they were specifically searching for it and the program she'd used.

"Thanks, Jas. I think I need to go outside and wait for the paramedics." Frank then went out as he fought the combination of rage and tears that was building inside him. He wasn't sure where the overwhelming emotions were coming from, but he had an internal mantra. *I can't cry. I can't cry. I can't cry.* Frank repeated the words over and over again as he walked down the stairs and out onto the front stoop of the building. After a few moments outside taking in deep breaths of air to calm his nerves, the sound of sirens snapped Frank back to reality.

Frank directed the paramedics to the third floor and stayed outside with the ambulance. Fifteen minutes passed as Frank tried to clear his head. He felt so violated by the information Connor Gordon had collected. *How dare he write that crap? He has no right...*

Frank's thoughts trailed off as he tried to regain some semblance of balance.

"Frank, you okay?"

Frank heard the concern in Jasika's voice, but he didn't respond initially. Her voice was a hundred miles away, and he needed to use all his inner strength to pull himself toward it.

"Frank, do you want me to have officers posted to his room at the hospital and here at the apartment?" Aaron asked.

"Yeah, that sounds like a good idea," he said to Aaron. When Aaron walked away, Frank eyed Jasika, who was still staring at him with concern. "I'll be fine," he told her. But Frank wasn't entirely sure who he was trying to convince, Jasika or himself.

* * * *

By eight o'clock, Frank and the others had been back in the station for over an hour, and yet none of the details had led anywhere. The more information they gained, the less the scribbles on their whiteboard made sense. Frank combed through the files, desperately checking to see if they'd missed anything while Aaron reviewed the recent information from the geek twins in between phone calls with people at the BAU down in Quantico. He had faxed over his preliminary profile, and the other psychologists at the BAU were tweaking it and running the basic MO and signature through their database, Profiler, to see if anything jumped from other cases both nationally and internationally.

Jasika sat at her computer, filling out the paperwork necessary for a warrant to get information from Connor Gordon's web-hosting service. She had called and asked politely for information on who had accessed *holidayhorrors.com* but was quickly sent to legal, who had informed her that to receive any information, she would need a warrant, as the company refused to release anything private. Frank was proud of the effort she was making, regardless of the dead ends.

"Hey, Frank, I've finished the warrant application. Wanna take a look at it before we email it to the chief for final approval?"

"Sure, and while I'm looking at that, could you send a list of the different names on the website to dispatch? Let's get officers all over the city checking in on them. I want to know who is missing around town. If he keeps up with this MO, at least two people should pop as already missing."

"Sure thing," Jasika replied. "Hey, once I'm done with email, do you mind if I take off? My mom's been with Ginny, and I feel bad having her watch Ginny all day at her age. I don't want to leave, but…"

"Jas, go. I completely understand. You need time with your daughter. Bluntly, I need to get out of here as well. I feel like I keep seeing the same things over and over again."

"Well, the definition of insanity is doing the same thing repeatedly and expecting different results," Aaron quipped.

"Maybe we all should just call it a night. I mean, the board isn't changing. And maybe some distance will clear our heads," Frank suggested.

Jasika finished emailing dispatch with the list of names and addresses, grabbed her bag and coat, and headed out. Frank kept staring at the board, hoping something would finally jump out at him, but nothing gelled in his head. Aaron came up beside him and started staring at the board with him.

"Maybe we should go get something to eat," Aaron suggested. "Food always helps me focus."

"Sure, why not."

"Great."

"I know a cheap Chinese restaurant near the park. At this hour, we should be able to get a table with no wait." Frank grabbed his duffle bag and Aaron grabbed his briefcase before they set out into the winter air for the short walk to the restaurant.

* * * *

The restaurant was pretty empty that night, so they were seated in a booth away from any of the other patrons. Frank read the menu. *I don't know why I bother. I already know what I'm going to order.* Instead of putting the menu down, Frank peeked over the top of his to watch Aaron reading the menu. He noticed that Aaron's lips were moving as he read. *Well, that's fucking adorable. Mr. Perfect moves his lips when he reads.*

The server quickly approached, and Frank ordered his usual Cantonese roasted duck. Aaron ordered a chicken and broccoli dish. With their orders complete, they sat back and just stared off into space for a moment. Finally, Aaron broke the silence. "So, why did you become a cop?"

Frank started by explaining his background as the anticipated heir of Schultt Pharmaceuticals and how his family had disowned him after college. "I guess I was looking for something that seemed to bring justice to this world. I was so mad that my parents refused to accept me when I came out that I believed the universe needed to balance itself, and I was going to be the one who did it."

"How'd that work out for you?"

"I'll let you know when I figure it out myself. What about you? Why did you become an FBI agent?"

"Mom's a gynecologist and dad was a diplomat, so I spent most of my childhood at the US Embassy in London. I took a course in the history of crime when I was an undergrad at the University of Buckingham. Yeah, I didn't go to Mississippi."

"I kind of pieced that one together."

"That's right. Anyway, so after my undergraduate, I got a master's in Forensic Psychology from Middlesex University. By that point, my dad had left his post in London and the family had moved back to the States. They're all still in Omaha. I wasn't going to spend my life there, so I enrolled in the doc program in Forensic Psychology from CUNY John Jay College of Criminal Justice. I was recruited during my second year by the FBI when one of their behavior specialists caught a presentation I was giving at a convention—and the rest is history."

Soon their food arrived, and they dove in. "I didn't realize how hungry I was," Aaron remarked.

"Me neither," Frank agreed. "We had a busy day, and lunch was a protein bar on the go. Thankfully, I keep a stash of them in my desk, because there are way too many days like this one."

"I can only imagine," Aaron said between bites. "In my world, there are long periods where most of what we're doing is the hard game of paperwork tracing. As the saying goes, 'follow the money'. Thankfully, we have some amazing forensic accountants in the Bureau who can dig through shell company after shell company to figure out what's going on. The actual 'action' part of the job doesn't happen very often."

They sat in silence for a while, simply eating until Frank started, "Okay, I just need to get something off my chest about last night."

"No need. It was a heat of the moment thing."

"That's just it. It wasn't just the heat of the moment." Frank took a sip of his green tea before continuing. "Okay, so it was partly the heat of the moment. In reality, I suck at dating. I haven't dated anyone since... Well, I'm sure you've heard."

"I have," Aaron responded compassionately.

"Well, then you know I've had a rough few years. And I didn't know how to respond when you were hitting on me."

"I admittedly came on a bit too strong. I knew nothing about you other than I thought you were hot..."

"You think I'm hot?"

"Obviously."

"Well, the thought's mutual."

For the first time, Aaron watched Frank let down his guard. *God, he's hot like this. Don't push it, Aaron. Don't be your usual hard sell.* "I'm glad to hear that. I wasn't sure if you even liked me...especially after you hit me."

"I already apologized for that."

"I know. I know," Aaron responded. "But I wasn't sure what you thought. As easy as I find figuring out what's going on in the heads of criminals, I often can't figure out what's going on inside normal men's heads to save my life."

"God, I know the feeling."

After dinner, they split the check and left the warm restaurant into the wintry New York cold.

"Are we expecting snow?" Frank asked.

"I heard that it might cool off a bit more a little around midnight, so we may see snowfall by then."

"Where do you live?"

"I'm out in Tribeca. You?"

"Hell's Kitchen."

"Well, I'm either going to grab a cab or take the train. And this time of night, it's easier to find a cab than figure out which trains are running in that direction."

"What time is it?"

Aaron glanced down at his watch and replied, "A little after ten."

"Care to share a cab?"

"Sure," Aaron said, looking at Frank a little sheepishly.

Aaron watched Frank stand in the road waving down the first cab with its occupancy light off. Frank held the door open for Aaron, who slid across the fake leather seat to the other side. Once inside, Frank ordered the driver to head to Tribeca.

Did he really just ask the cabbie to go to Tribeca first, when Hell's Kitchen is only blocks away from here and Tribeca's on the other side of the fucking city? Aaron glanced over at Frank, studying his face. He tried to determine if Frank was making a move or just being polite. *Dammit, why can't I read minds?*

The slow ride across town became a little more complicated as the snow started falling around Fortieth Street, so the cabbie had to avoid a combination of both tourists milling around and other cabbies who hadn't yet realized that newly fallen snow was slicking up the roads.

Before long, the cab was pulling up in front of a high-rise apartment building on Warren Street. Aaron invited Frank up for a quick drink — and to his surprise, Frank agreed. Aaron stepped out onto the street in front of the Portman Towers, which was named after the billionaire who'd developed the building during the 1990s. Aaron walked over to the front of the building, where a doorman opened the door for him as he approached.

"Good evening, Mr. Massey. Please make sure you have your visitor sign in before going upstairs to your condo."

Once they were inside the building, Aaron showed Frank the sign-in log. Aaron noticed Frank glancing over the list. "Yes, there are a lot of famous people who live in this building, so we require everyone who brings a guest to sign in and sign out. Back after 9-11, they required all visitors to have a photo ID. Celebrities get a little freakish about their privacy and their security. I sit on the condo board, so I've listened to a variety of complaints about idiotic things."

After Frank finished signing the logbook, Aaron ushered him over to the elevator bay, and once inside, hit the button for the thirty-seventh floor of the building. Frank had to ask, "Okay, don't get me wrong, but how the hell do you afford to live in this place?"

"I was afraid you were going to ask me that question. As I'm sure you're well aware, I wrote a little book that did well on *The New York Times* Bestseller's list."

"Well, it was number one for almost two months on the nonfiction list!" Frank exclaimed.

"So, I wasn't the only one who did a little research when we met."

"Okay, I admit I checked you out. It wasn't difficult. I mean, just Google 'Aaron Massey' and you'll find out all about you. I've heard how you've been linked romantically to many closeted and openly gay movie, television and theater stars. Plus, I've seen pictures of you in a Speedo on the beaches in Spain."

"You what? I didn't even know about the last one."

"Yeah, well, I took most of it as gossip, but I checked you out."

"Well, Frank Schultt, you are full of surprises this evening."

"Don't get too full of yourself. I also checked out my next-door neighbor when he moved in, and even ran my primary care physician, just out of curiosity."

"But anyway," Aaron said overly dramatically, "the book helped me make the down payment on my condo, but I also had some help from my parents."

After a short ride in the elevator, they stepped off and walked down the hall to the last door on the floor. Aaron took out a keycard and slipped it into a door lock while sticking his thumb on a scanner.

"Biometric double security lock?"

"Yeah, the penthouses just have iris scanners, so my lock is on the lower end of the spectrum," Aaron said matter-of-factly. "Oh, and the key cards contain a microchip and not a magnetic stripe. As of yet, there isn't an easy way to duplicate a microchip key card, whereas magnetic strip cards can be duplicated by a portable magnetic strip reader and printer."

"Okay," Frank said as Aaron ushered him into the apartment.

"Please, make yourself at home," Aaron said as he motioned to an overstuffed leather couch in front of a large flat-screen television between two floor-to-ceiling bookshelves. Aaron walked into another part of the house. "Do you like a good Malbec?"

"Sure," Frank said, not knowing what a Malbec was.

"It's from the Don Miguel Gascón Malbec. I picked it up a couple of years ago in Argentina when I was doing press for the Spanish printing of *Blood Money*. I fell in love with it and had them ship back a case for me. The Malbec grape is one of only six allowed in the French Bordeaux wine," Aaron described from somewhere behind a wall.

While Aaron kept giving more detail on the history of the Malbec grape and the wine itself, Frank walked over to examine the two bookcases. He found two photographs with Aaron and a number of notable authors in and around the city. He took in a range of books on psychology and a handful of copies of *Blood Money*. He then looked at the second shelf, examining the pictures of various people Frank assumed were friends or family members. One picture showed Aaron and an older couple with two women, who Frank gathered was his immediate family. *That must be his sisters and parents. They even wore matching colors for the picture.*

On another shelf, Frank saw a picture of Aaron in a Speedo. *Damn! This pic of him looks even better than the one I found online.* "Hey, I didn't know you were a member of Team New York Aquatics?"

"Yeah, I played water polo throughout school, so I was excited when I found out about the gay water polo team in the city. Sadly, I had to stop playing when I was working on the Stapkovich case." Aaron came back into the room, carrying a bottle of wine and two wide-lipped wine glasses. He handed Frank one glass and poured the wine into it, then placed the bottle down on a side table next to the couch.

"Shall we toast?" Aaron asked.

"Yes, to catching this son-of-a-bitch."

"To catching the SOB and new friends," Aaron said as he clinked glasses with Frank. They sat down on the couch and talked about various things. Aaron admitted he was a huge fan of a trendy gay bar in Midtown called Therapy, whereas Frank admitted that he enjoyed going to The Eagle but had stopped going there over a year ago because he needed to escape 'the scene'.

Aaron studied Frank during the whole conversation and was transfixed by Frank's hazel eyes and his slender jawline. *God, his eyes are gorgeous. And look at that chest... He spends a decent amount of time in the gym.* Frank just kept talking, and Aaron was mentally undressing him while he spoke.

Aaron finished his glass of wine and watched as Frank did too. He grabbed Frank's glass and set it on the side table, brushing Frank's thigh while he moved. Frank reached out and grabbed Aaron's arm, pulling him onto his lap. Before he knew it, they were flicking their tongues in and out of each other's mouths. Frank pushed his pelvis into Aaron's, which caused a tiny moan to escape Aaron's lips.

When Frank moved to take off his shirt, Aaron leaned forward to help Frank lift it over his head. Immediately, his skin came alive as Frank lightly licked his way from Aaron's neck down to one of his nipples. Aaron's eyes rolled into the back of his head as Frank lightly grazed his nipple with his teeth before Frank flittered around the nipple with his tongue. After what felt like an eternity, Aaron looked down at Frank, who was staring up at him. Aaron reached out with both of his hands and lifted Frank's face toward his and they met in a deep kiss. For what seemed like forever, Aaron's lips never left Frank's. It was like the two were breathing as one.

Aaron reached down and pulled Frank's tie off, then started releasing each shirt button as he kissed Frank's chest all the way down. He stared up Frank's muscley torso, which had a thin layer of hair that was so different from his own thin and hairless body. As he released the last closure, he kissed Frank right above the buckle of his pants. Frank reached down, wrapping his arms around Aaron, lifting him back up from his crotch and bringing their naked torsos together.

Frank thrilled to the pounding of Aaron's heart against his chest as they embraced, and he stared into Aaron's deep-blue eyes. Aaron had the body of a swimmer. All his muscles were tight, but not bulky. His body was smooth, but naturally so—not like the Chelsea boys who spent hours each week having hair removed with lasers.

Frank leaned forward once again to kiss the nape of Aaron's neck, and Aaron threw his head back, letting out a slight moan of encouragement. Frank ran his hand down Aaron's chest, feeling each of his muscles underneath his fingertips. Then he pushed Aaron backward on the couch, lying down on top of him, tracing the steps down Aaron's muscles with his tongue that his fingertips had just taken. Then he nibbled on one of Aaron's nipples, garnering yet another slight groan. Frank looked up to see the pure ecstasy across Aaron's face.

Aaron touched Frank's stomach before dropping his hand southward and gently stroking his growing crotch. As he did, Frank reached forward to unbutton Aaron's pants, then grabbed the zipper to open them. At that moment, Frank stared into Aaron's eyes and Aaron smiled in return, encouraging him to continue. While gazing down at an eager Aaron, Frank saw Adam's smile. *What the hell am I doing?*

Frank gently pushed Aaron aside, quickly sitting up. He looked at Aaron, who had a confused look on his face, grabbed his shirt and shoes then rushed toward the door.

"I'm so sorry. I just can't do this," Frank explained as he grabbed his discarded clothes and left the condo and slid the door quietly shut behind him. It wasn't until Frank was in the hallway that he realized he was still half-naked, so he quickly put on his shirt, shoved his tie into his pocket and headed toward the elevator.

As Frank exited the building, the doorman said, "Leaving so soon, Detective Schultt?"

Frank didn't respond. He just walked.

Chapter Eleven

December 19, 12 a.m.

The snow was still falling, and there was a crunching sound of the freshly fallen snow beneath his feet. Frank was reeling with thoughts of what had almost transpired back in Aaron's condo. *I need to talk to someone. Jasika? No, totally the wrong person. Logan? Yes, I need to speak with Logan.* Frank reached into his pocket for his AirPods and shoved them into his ears, telling his phone to call Logan.

The phone rang three times before a voice on the other end of the phone picked up. "Hello?"

"Logan?"

"No, this is Ben. Frank?"

"I need to speak with Logan."

Frank heard Ben wake Logan up. "It's Frank, and something's seriously off."

"Frank, what's wrong?" Logan asked, his voice groggy.

Without skipping a beat, Frank unloaded everything in a blow-by-blow description, from the Malbec to Frank's sudden freak-out, when he'd looked down at Aaron and seen Adam staring back at him.

"God, Frank. Are you okay?"

"Does it sound like I'm okay? I'm losing it here."

"Frank, where are you?"

Frank stopped dead in his tracks and surveyed the area around him. "I'm somewhere in Tribeca near Federal Plaza."

"That's like five miles from your apartment."

"I need fresh air. I can walk. I need to walk," Frank said as he choked back tears.

"Let me send my car for you. It can be there in ten minutes."

"Logan, I'll be fine. I just need to walk. I need to let myself think."

"Aaron opened a flood-gate that's been closed for five years. You need to talk to someone. If not me, please talk to your psychologist."

"I promise I'll call her in the morning."

"Now, if you need to talk, if you need me to come get you, if you need anything, Frank, you call me back. I don't care what time of day it is. I'm here for you."

"Thanks. I promise I will." Frank hung up the phone, put his AirPods back in his pocket and started walking back to Hell's Kitchen. It took him an hour and a half to make it to his apartment, but Frank's mind with memories of Adam and what he'd just done with Aaron, so he barely noticed the time fly by.

* * * *

The next morning, Frank hit the gym then made his way to the precinct. *God, I really don't want to see Aaron this morning*, he thought as he walked up the steps. He made his way to the bullpen, seeing Jasika already at her desk. "Anything new to report?" Frank asked.

"Nope, still waiting on the complete forensics work-up from yesterday afternoon."

"Great." Frank sat down at his computer and opened his email. He scanned through it to see if there was anything important to read. He had one that caught his attention because it was from the FBI. He opened the email and read the message, which was from Aaron.

I don't know what happened last night. I thought things were going well. Clearly, you're not ready, so I'm sorry if I pushed you into a situation where you were uncomfortable. I don't want to have an awkward conversation when I see you, so I wanted to get this off my chest before coming into the precinct later this morning. I think you're a great detective, Frank. But we're clearly in very different places right now. So, I look forward to continuing to work with you on this case.

Sincerely,
Aaron Massey, Supervisory Special Agent

Frank read the message a couple of times. He noticed how the email was purposefully vague. *Well, I guess that's all I'll get on this one.* Frank began to compose a response but wasn't quite sure what to say. He opted for something short and to the point.

Supervisory Special Agent Massey:
Thank you for the email. I'll brief you on any case updates when you get to the precinct.
Detective Schultt

Frank hit the send button and kept going through his inbox, reading and responding to important emails and deleting ones that weren't.

* * * *

The next four days passed in a hurried frenzy of new cases. As more and more bodies started mounting, the resources devoted to the individual cases quickly escalated. Frank was still kept as the lead detective, but he was given individual detective teams to assess possible suspects for each of the different victims. The time and work that was being devoted to the Twelve-Day Killer was unlike anything seen by the NYPD since the Son of Sam cases back in the late 1970s, when David Berkowitz had terrorized New York City over the course of a year.

On the twenty-first, Jenny Mace ran a one-hour prime-time news special about the case and had a series of experts from around the globe discussing its details. The mayor even arranged for a candid interview with both Detective Schultt and Agent Massey to appear in the special. Frank could tell that the mayor was feeling pressure from every direction, so she was making sure that all the shit ran right downhill. The daily screaming matches between the mayor and Chief Hays were becoming as routine as morning coffee. Those heated discussions were followed by the chief's own yelling at his detectives, especially Frank. On more than one occasion, Jasika had taken the brunt of these dressings-down and was threatened to have her detective shield removed and have her sent back to vice. Jasika, being a good little soldier, would sit there and take the abuse, then mutter a string of profanity when the chief left.

The stress was mounting, and with it, everyone's last nerve was fried. Frank hadn't had a chance to have a real talk with Aaron, not that he wanted to deal with Aaron personally. Ever since the incident in Aaron's condo, both of them had kept their relationship as impersonal as humanly possible. At crime scenes, they each did their own investigations then relayed their information to Jasika, who would pass it on to the other.

Jasika had caught on to the tension between him and Aaron, but she wouldn't pry, and Frank didn't want to go into the drama. Instead, she played the part of Switzerland, passing information back and forth.

With each new body, the clues mounted, the possible unsubs tripled and the case came no closer to being solved. Even the *holidayhorrors.com* lead ended up being a bust. After getting the search warrant approved by a local judge, the firm that hosted the website had informed the police they didn't keep logs of IP addresses that pinged their sites because the amount of data would be astronomical, lead to system slowdowns and collecting IP addresses would give them problems with the European Union's General Data Protection Regulations. Although the firm kept data for a week, they didn't keep the information longer than seven days. The cybercrime unit had scrolled through what they firm provided, but nothing had popped and no one on their suspect list had ever visited the website. With each new body and set of possible suspects, they ran the list over and over, but nothing ever appeared.

As for Connor Gordon, he'd built the site after a friend of his had made a lot of money on a website that displayed tacky Christmas light displays from around the country. *Christmasdisplaydisasters.com* had become so wildly popular that Gordon's friend had retired at age thirty and lived off the advertising revenues the website was bringing in daily. In fact, Gordon was already in discussions with a couple of marketing firms that were looking at making his website go viral. He hoped to be making six figures by the following Christmas. After a little cajoling, he'd even promised to make sure that Frank's name never appeared on the site.

* * * *

On December nineteenth, Kyle Tucker's legs were found at Macy's Santa Village, dressed up and displayed like two giant candy canes. He learned that Kyle Tucker had been a Macy's accountant for fifteen years before he was caught embezzling funds. He'd spent ten years at the Edgecombe Correctional Facility in Harlem and had been released a little over a year before. At first, this victim didn't seem to match the usual MO of the Twelve-Day Killer. That was until they looked at the original files of his case and noticed that his arrest warrant had come down on Christmas Eve.

On December twentieth, Peter Smith was found at Madame Tussauds dressed as Santa. This time the Twelve-Day Killer had given Frank and his team an entire body stuffed into a Santa outfit and displayed right in public. At first, no one had noticed that Tussauds' Santa had been replaced. But as the day went along, the frozen Santa had melted, and one arm had drooped right in front of a child getting his picture taken with the 'lifelike' Santa. The screaming of both the child and the parent had set off alarm bells, so one of the security guards had come just as Santa's head tipped to one side. Sadly, the entire incident had been caught on multiple smartphones and had gone viral before the cops had even been called in.

Upon investigation, Frank learned that the victim had been a Santa stand-in all over New York City, but seven years before, he had been accused of inappropriately touching a kid. Although the kid had eventually admitted he was lying, Smith had never reclaimed his life.

As this was the first complete body to be displayed, the profile was altered slightly and Aaron informed everyone, especially Frank, that the killer was escalating. Aaron predicted from that point forward, the killer didn't want the police to delay in identifying the body. Aaron surmised that the killer wanted information about each of his crimes broadcast into everyone's home in an effort to make his crimes more widely known and seen across the entire area.

On the twenty-first, Frank got the call that famed former figure skater Hey Yuan Xuan had been found at Rockefeller Center dressed as one of the Trumpeting Angels on display. Hey Yuan Xuan was a nationally ranked figure skater who often trained at the famed Rockefeller Center ice rink early in the morning. She'd told the press several times that she enjoyed being able to be outside honing her craft. One day, she'd been in the middle of her practice and had just executed a triple toe loop. Everything until her landing had gone perfectly. When she'd landed, her skate had caught a sticky substance on the ice rink and sent her sprawling across the surface and slamming into the side wall. She'd broken her neck and both of her ankles in the incident. While she hadn't been paralyzed, she'd been informed that she could never perform jumps again.

The murder on the twenty-second was the first one to happen before a live audience, which, as Aaron explained to Frank and the rest of the team, was another clear indication that the killer was escalating toward some kind of clear conclusion on December twenty-fifth.

Joe DePadua had been a first tenor and had performed with the New York Philharmonic for many years before he'd come down with laryngeal cancer eight years prior. After two surgeries and a very intense bout of chemotherapy, Joe had kept his life but lost his ability to speak. Once heralded as the NYC voice of Handel's *Messiah*, Joe had become a recluse after losing his voice. His body had been found dangling from the rafters after having been shoved off a catwalk over the New York Philharmonic during a production of *Messiah*. The killer had waited until the famed 'Hallelujah Chorus' to dump the body. Of course, the mayor, a state senator, a federal congressman and half of the major money in NYC had been in attendance when DePadua's body had been suspended over the stage.

Aaron continued his repetitive speech that the unsub was escalating. Everyone looked to him for more information, but he seemed as directionless as the rest of them. Thankfully, Mariella had noticed something very different about DePadua. His body hadn't been frozen. According to DePadua's liver temperature, he had been killed less than three hours before he had been hung from the rafters. Aaron believed the killer was speeding up his timeline, but the card found on Hey Yuan Xuan had DePadua's fingerprint. The only problem was that DePadua had been seen having a fairly public fight with another opera singer the night before. DePadua had sucker-punched a former colleague of his at a Lincoln Center Benefit. DePadua had been taken into custody, fingerprinted, charged with disorderly conduct then released on the morning of the twenty-second.

By early afternoon on December twenty-third, the frustration around the precinct was clear. Everyone felt the political pressure to get the case solved mounting from every corner to get the case solved. "So, tell me again why DePadua's print wasn't in the system?" Frank asked into the phone.

Frank heard Richardson jot something down on a notepad before he spoke. "Okay, so here's what I think happened. Now, I'm not completely sure about this timeline, but here's my best guess. We scanned the fingerprint of Hey Yuan Xuan in the afternoon on the twenty-first, so it's in the system. DePadua was booked into the Twentieth Precinct over on the West Eighty-Second around eleven p.m. The Twentieth Precinct's biometric scanner was down, so they printed him the good, old-fashioned way."

"Okay…"

"DePadua's lawyer had him out pretty quickly thereafter. The system had no priors for DePadua and apparently his lawyer had a judge release him shortly after midnight. Go, night court. All in all, DePadua was in the system just under two hours. Ultimately, the manual prints were sent to the Office of Forensic Services, where they are still waiting to be processed. OFS is behind because, ironically, they're processing evidence from the Twelve-Day Killer crime scenes."

"So, we had a window when we should have been able to prevent this murder?"

"Looks like it."

"Fuck me! If this gets out, we'll all be crucified."

"Tell me about it," Nasab started. "It makes the entire NYPD forensics system look completely inept. In reality, it was the perfect storm of problems."

"The poor son-of-a-bitch didn't even know that he'd already been marked for death almost twenty-four hours before meeting his maker," Frank said after he'd hung up the phone and told Jasika and Aaron what he'd learned from the ME. Frank and Aaron had at least started speaking again, but there was an air of distance that still hovered between them. "So, Mr. FBI, any ideas?"

"Just a second, Frank." Aaron had taken a call on his cell while Frank had been on the line with the geek twins. "Another one? Are you fucking kidding me?" Aaron motioned to Frank to hand him a pad and pen while quietly whispering, "We have another body already." Aaron continued to get the details and jotted them on the pad Frank had handed him. Frank and Jasika were already picking up their coats and getting ready to leave the station when Aaron finished. Shrugging into his, Aaron said, "Apparently, this new body has led to a few hundred phone calls on the tip line in the last five minutes alone."

"What?" Jasika questioned. "How have we not heard about this yet?"

Aaron replied, "Because the calls just started a couple of minutes ago."

"Where are we heading?" Frank asked.

"Radio City Music Hall."

* * * *

On the way to Radio City Musical Hall, Frank listened as Aaron caught him and Jasika up on what he'd learned from Mariella.

"So, Aaron, what are your thoughts?" Jasika asked from the backseat when Aaron finished relaying the information.

"Well, at least the killer is sticking to his original signature. He was giving us twenty-four-hours to find the victims, but that just changed. I questioned in the past if the delay expressed remorse or a desire to be caught, but now I think he's merely toying with us. He wants us to know he's smarter than we are."

Frank found a parking space between Fifth and Sixth avenues on Fifty-First Street, and they made their way to the stage entrance of Radio City Music Hall. A patrolman noticed them approaching and immediately opened the door.

Inside the lobby Frank quickly divvied up the tasks. "I'll check in with Mariella. Jas see if they have identified the victim yet. Aaron, why don't you see what's going on in the theater itself."

Aaron and Jasika nodded their heads in agreement and set about their jobs while Frank went to find Mariella.

Aaron stopped a woman with a clipboard in the hall and asked for directions to the stage. She pointed in a general direction and said he couldn't miss it. He followed the hall and finally found a side entrance that was ajar with the words 'stage left' printed in blocky letters. The stage door opened into a small hallway, and Aaron followed the voices until he found himself standing center stage. Various cast members from the afternoon's show were out in the seats, and two uniformed officers were already taking witness statements from the cast and crew. Aaron went to check in with the officers to see if they'd learned anything helpful. He searched for a way to get off the stage and had to walk the full length of the curved proscenium to a set of side stairs before he stepped down to the orchestra seating of one of the largest theaters in NYC.

Aaron hadn't seen the Rockette Christmas Spectacular since he'd been a kid. He took a second to marvel at the facility's immenseness. It had four levels of seating. He wondered how the people on the third mezzanine could even see anything happening on the stage from that height. While he was taking in the theater, an officer walked up to him.

"Agent Massey? I'm Officer McLaurin, Debbie McLaurin. We've segregated all the stage and crew down here," the officer began as she ushered Aaron toward the center section of the orchestra seating. "We took the liberty of starting the interviews, and thus far, the descriptions of what happened are all pretty much the same."

Aaron then heard an overview of the typical day at Radio City Music Hall. The Rockette Christmas Spectacular had four shows scheduled that day at eleven, two, five and eight. The eleven o'clock show had gone without a hitch, and the two o'clock show seemed to run as scheduled. At the beginning, there was a huge opening with Santa on a giant screen, and the audience members wore 3D glasses to get the full effect. Once the video was over, a full-sized Santa sleigh was supposed to fly over the audience's heads and land on the stage, where Santa would be escorted out of the sleigh by Rockettes. The sleigh would be taken off stage, and the crew would ultimately take the sleigh back to its starting point after the first show and get it set up for the second.

The crew working on the sleigh said they'd seen nothing abnormal or strange when they set up the sleigh after the first show. It had started, the stage manager had called places and the actor playing Santa had made his way back to his starting point, gotten into the sleigh and been ready for his big appearance. Unfortunately, when Santa's sleigh had started flying over the audience, a woman's body had been trailing behind it.

Aaron asked Officer McLaurin to show him to the head stagehand on the show. She pointed out a scruffy-looking woman wearing a black knit shirt and jeans. Her hair was pulled back in a neat ponytail. As Aaron approached, he noticed the woman tightened up a bit, which wasn't uncommon when witnesses were interviewed.

"Hi, I'm FBI Special Agent Aaron Massey, and you are?"

"Melanie Smithers. I'm the chief stagehand or lead on this show."

"Great," Aaron said as he wrote the woman's name in his notebook, "Now, were you responsible for checking the sleigh before the beginning of the show?"

"Yes. Forty minutes before curtain, I run through all the major pieces to make sure everything is ready to go on and off stage. I have a checklist that's five pages long for pre-show."

"Okay, and where did the sleigh fall on that list?"

"The sleigh was first because it comes in from the back of the house. Everything else is on stage and comes up from below, down from above or in from one of the wings."

"So, the sleigh was checked off your list around one-fifteen and not seen by anyone on the crew or cast until one-fifty-five?"

"I would guess that's right. I'm not sure when Benny—the guy who plays Santa—got to the sleigh. You'd have to ask the stage manager about that one."

"So, Benny doesn't need anyone's help getting in the sleigh?"

"In previous years, he would need a team of two, but we automated some parts we used to have stagehands do, which was a huge contention with the IATSE, I might add."

"Who?"

"IATSE, the International Alliance of Theatrical Stage Employees, the union that covers those of us who are never seen or heard by the audience—assuming we do our jobs right."

"Okay, thanks for the information." Aaron turned and headed away from the group. He pulled out his cell phone to call Frank, and Frank picked up on the second ring. "It's Aaron. I talked to the chief stagehand down here. There was a window of about forty minutes where the killer could have placed the body."

"Thanks," Frank said as he looked back to Mariella. "That was Aaron. He talked to a stagehand and got a rough timeframe for when the body was placed. Have you figured out the time of death?"

"Well, from what I can tell, the victim has been dead for almost three hours. So, that places the time of death around twelve-thirty."

"The killer killed the victim at twelve-thirty and placed the body between an hour and an hour and twenty minutes later," Frank said, more to himself than anyone else.

Jasika approached Frank. "Hey, we have a positive ID."

"Already?"

"Yeah, apparently, the head usher got a glimpse of the victim's face when the geek twins rolled the body."

"And?"

"Her name is Donna Pinkerton. She's a former member of this cast. She was a Rockette."

"Huh?"

"Last year, she was performing on this stage when someone in the audience thought it would be funny to shine one of those blasted laser pointers at her eyes during the performance. She was dancing very close to the pit where the orchestra was located. She lost vision for a second and fell in before she'd known what happened. She broke her leg in two places. And while the break was clean and she recovered nicely, she couldn't put her body through the strain of the Rockettes' training and intense schedule."

"Ouch," Mariella exclaimed. "It sucks to lose your job like that."

Jasika shook her head reading from her notes, "Nope, she didn't lose her job. Madison Square Garden Entertainment, the parent company of the Radio City Rockettes, retained her. She's been working in the corporate office for the past year in public relations."

"So, do you think she was killed here?" Frank asked.

"Not according to the head usher. She'd talked to Donna before the doors opened for the eleven o'clock show. Donna was just checking in before heading back to the corporate offices."

"How far are those offices from here?"

"Madison Square Garden," Jasika replied.

Frank pulled out his cell phone and called Aaron. He explained what he had just learned and that he wanted to leave Jasika at Radio City and have the two of them head over to the corporate offices. Aaron agreed and said he'd meet him in the lobby. After they hung up, Frank turned to Jasika. "Go grab me a geek and tell him to get an evidence kit."

Jasika walked over to where the geek twins were located and grabbed Richardson, who quickly exited the building. Frank met up with Aaron in the lobby, and the two of them went out to find Richardson.

Aaron and Frank followed Colin to his van. He had already opened the van and was inside, taking out a duffle bag, which he opened. "This isn't fully equipped like the big bags we carry, so let me throw in what we may need just in case." Aaron watched Richardson toss in a handful of extra evidence bags of various sizes, shoe coverings, gloves and a few things Aaron couldn't see.

"Okay, where to?" Richardson asked.

"Frank went up the block to find the car, so he should be back in a few minutes." Richardson got out of the van, closing the door and they stood in silence, waiting for Frank to get the car. Frank and the car approached, and Aaron began walking toward the vehicle as it pulled up to the curb. Unexpectedly, Frank exited and motioned for Aaron to come over to him.

"Agent Massey…" Frank seemed a bit more frazzled than Aaron had seen before. "I have an appointment that I must keep at five. I just noticed that it's already four-fifteen, so I'll be unable to go with you to Madison Square Garden. Can you and Richardson handle it?"

"Umm-m," Aaron started, not really sure what to say. "I guess so. Can you postpone the meeting, though? I mean, it's hardly protocol to jet during an active investigation."

"Let's just say that this meeting takes priority in the eyes of the chief and the commissioner."

"All right, whatever... I guess I'll see you tomorrow," Aaron said.

Aaron walked around to the driver's side of the sedan. He motioned for Richardson to put his bag in the back seat as they headed over to Madison Square Garden.

"Frank's not coming with us?"

"He has an appointment."

"Ahh, yes, his appointment," Richardson said cryptically, clearly knowing the appointment Aaron was referring to.

Aaron steered the car west, heading toward The Garden. Aaron drove in silence as he headed to Two Penn Plaza, where the executive suites were located. The burning question finally broke through his lips. "What appointment is Frank keeping?"

"Umm, you don't know?"

"Clearly not. If I did, I wouldn't be asking."

"Not sure if it's my place to tell you," Richardson said hesitantly, but continued chatting like a high school girl with a fresh piece of gossip. "Frank has been ordered to attend weekly sessions with the NYPD shrink."

"Because of Adam's death? That was like five years ago."

"No, there was a shooting incident about six or eight months ago."

"What shooting?" Aaron questioned, but without skipping a beat, he remembered what Richardson was talking about. "Oh, *that* shooting."

"Yeah, that shooting. Frank agreed to undergo shrinking, and the commissioner and chief agreed to let him keep his job."

"Ahh, now it makes sense," Aaron said loudly.

"What does?"

"Umm...why Frank can't go with us today," Aaron responded, probably not too convincingly. *How did I not put this together? He's never dealt with Adam's death, which is obvious because of the shooting incident. How I hadn't linked those two in my head is beyond me. Then I try to pressure him sexually, and he just flips out because all this is still way too raw for him. God, I hope that therapy helps him, because he still has a lot of room for growth.*

Aaron drove around the block a couple of times before finally finding a parking space near Madison Square Garden. They found the side entrance and headed up to the fourteenth floor, where the executive offices were located. At the reception desk, Aaron asked to speak to Donna Pinkerton's boss. At first, the receptionist didn't understand the request and informed Aaron that Donna Pinkerton wasn't in her office.

"I'm sorry, Miss. I think you misunderstood my request. I'm not looking for Donna Pinkerton. I'm looking for her boss." As he said this, he took out his FBI identification badge and shield. "It's an urgent issue." The receptionist glanced at the shield and quickly paged Mona Generosa to the front reception.

Mona was an older woman, probably in her early sixties, but with the amount of facial work she'd obviously had done, she could easily be in her late seventies. She had silver hair that framed her face. *God, the amount of hairspray needed to keep it in place is enough to cause a new hole in the ozone layer!* As she introduced herself, her Long Island accent came through her thin lips.

"How can I help you, Agent...?"

"Massey, Supervisory Special Agent Massey, and this is Colin Richardson with the NYPD crime lab." The woman looked bored and unimpressed, so Aaron continued, "Is there somewhere we can talk privately?"

Mona Generosa glanced from Aaron to Richardson, then back to Aaron, and finally said, "I suppose." She turned on her Manolo Blahnik heels without saying a word, opened a glass door and kept walking. She never turned to see if they were following.

She walked down a long hallway with offices on either side. The entire area was made of glass, giving no one any real privacy, like a giant fishbowl. She finally came to the end of the hall to an office that had frosted glass walls. *So, she's the only allowed any privacy in this place.*

Entering her office, Aaron took in the layout as he put together a mini-profile of Mona Generosa herself. The room was smartly decorated, with a lot of empty space. Her desk was tall and made of acid-etched glass. She sat behind it and motioned for him and Richardson to sit in two chairs. The chairs were shorter than Generosa's chair, which forced most people to stare up at her. *Wow, she is definitely ensuring that people look up to her. But I guess you don't become head of Madison Square Garden Entertainment without forcing people to respect you.*

She thinks she's in charge, so I will have to throw her off her game and get her to play mine.

"Ms. Generosa," Aaron started, "Donna Pinkerton was murdered this afternoon and hung behind Santa's sleigh at the Rockette show at two p.m. We believe she was abducted from here and have reason to believe someone here may have been involved."

"What? Did the show go off without any problems? Why didn't they call me? Dear God, that's a small fortune in lost revenue today," the woman exclaimed. Unfortunately, the latest round of Botox hid any other signs of actual emotion, assuming she had any.

"Well then, you'll be sorry to hear that we'll be canceling all the shows today and possibly tomorrow."

"You can't do that. Tomorrow is Christmas Eve, and I get premium prices for those seats. At the eight o'clock show tomorrow, we'll clear just under a million dollars easily. You're killing my budget. In my world, that makes you the murderer."

"So, I take it you and Pinkerton were not exactly friends?"

"She worked here—nothing more, nothing less."

"Cold-hearted bitch," Colin muttered under his breath.

And this is why we don't bring the geeks to an interview.

"Yes, young man, I am a cold-hearted bitch. But I'm a wealthy cold-hearted bitch with connections and phone numbers, who could have both of your badges without a second thought."

She let the threat sink in. Aaron didn't doubt the woman wouldn't give a flying fuck about either of them and that ruining their careers wouldn't be an issue.

"Now, I want my shows open. I'll give you today, but if my shows are not open by tomorrow at eleven, you'll be hearing from my lawyers. And I'll also make sure that the mayor and Chief of Police also get a call from me directly. Do I make myself clear?"

"Actually, no," Aaron replied. "You just broke a federal law." Aaron smirked. "It is illegal to attempt to influence, impede or threaten a federal agent. You may have the NYPD wrapped around your finger, but I'm a supervisory special agent of the Federal Bureau of Investigation, and your offense generally has a mandatory sentence of six to eight years in a federal penitentiary. Not even the governor of this state could stop that one from happening."

"Well, I..." Generosa huffed, seeming a little shell-shocked about being dressed down in that manner.

"Now that we've played 'whose cock is larger' today, I have an investigation to run, and you're either going to fully cooperate or I'm going to perp-walk you right from this building in handcuffs. Or, I may even tell someone to call the media. How would that look? One of your employees gets murdered and you on the six o'clock news being walked out of here in handcuffs? Trust me... It's amazing how fast all those friends you think you have disappear when they have to stick their necks out for you."

Aaron watched as Ms. Generosa shrank. While he couldn't tell what she was thinking from her facial expressions, her shoulders relaxed ever so slightly, showing that she was finally giving in.

"Fine... Do what you need to do. I will tell you that my lawyers will have the theater opened by tomorrow at eleven, but I'll make sure you have access to anything you need here."

"Great. It's amazing how it works when we all play nice. Now, we need to see Ms. Pinkerton's office."

Aaron watched as Mona Generosa pushed a button on her phone, requesting that someone from public relations come to her office immediately. Within thirty seconds, a young woman in her early- to mid-twenties, wearing a holiday sweater, was knocking on the door.

"This is…"

"Abigail Kelly," the young woman responded.

"Abigail Kelly," Generosa repeated, as if Kelly hadn't just told her. "She'll help you in any way you need."

Aaron stood, shook the woman's hand and introduced both himself and Colin.

"Oh, and Ms. Kelly, I thought the memo I sent out about not wearing holiday garments in my workplace was very clear."

"Ms. Generosa…" The girl looked devastated as she spoke to Generosa, not making eye contact. She then shakily added, "You sent out another memo allowing us to wear holiday clothing during the party."

"Oh, is that today?" Generosa said, tilting her head slightly to the side. "I didn't notice." She looked down at her desk, picked up a stack of papers and glanced up at the three. "I have work. You all may leave." She waved them away with a shooing motion, like one might do to a pesky dog.

Aaron wanted to pick another fight with the woman, but there was no point. *God, she's a piece of work. She really needs to be knocked down a couple of pegs. Not my job, but someone should do it.* They all left the room, and Colin shut the door behind them. *Well, more slammed than shut.* Aaron swung his head toward Colin, who just smiled, shrugged and mouthed, "Oops." Aaron had to smile a little himself.

"So, Agent Massey, what can I do for you?" Kelly asked.

Aaron then proceeded to tell Abigail what had happened at the two o'clock show.

"Oh my God! How did we not hear?"

"Well, you said something about a party?"

"We've all been at the office holiday party up in the penthouse most of the afternoon. I just came downstairs to get my purse when Ms. Generosa's call for a PR person came to the office. As you can see, when Ms. Generosa beckons, we come running."

Abigail led the way through a maze of hallways to a large open room with a series of cubicle areas. She showed them to Donna Pinkerton's desk.

Colin pulled his duffle bag off his shoulder, unzipped it, put on a pair of gloves and set about examining Pinkerton's workspace. Aaron motioned for Abigail to sit at a nearby workstation while he grabbed a rolling chair from another and sat, staring at the woman. He could tell the news of Pinkerton's death was just now starting to hit Abigail.

"I-I really didn't know her. We worked on different projects. I work less on the Rockettes than I do on concerts. During Christmas time, it's pretty much all-hands-on-deck for the Christmas Spectacular. But the rest of the year, we worked in different divisions, even though my cubicle is just over there." Abigail pointed to an area on the other side of the room. "She seemed like a nice person, but I didn't know her. God, why didn't I know her? To be honest, I didn't even notice she wasn't at the party upstairs."

"Did she have a lot of friends in the office?"

"Not...not that I know of. I mean, she may have had friends here, but I have no clue. About all I know is that she had been a Rockette, which is why she got the job in the first place. The rumor was the company faced a huge lawsuit, so they put her here to prevent it. Again, this may be rumor, but it was one that sure got passed around a lot."

"Well, thanks for your candor, Ms. Kelly. Why don't you go back up to the party? I'll be up shortly. Please, don't let anyone leave until I get there." Abigail went over to her desk, grabbed her purse and headed out of the office.

When she was out of earshot, Colin finally said, "I have hair and blood. The killer may have tried to clean up in here, but they didn't do a great job. I'm confident that unless Pinkerton had bloody noses daily, this is probably the primary crime scene."

"Thanks, go ahead and call in a full team. I'll get more help to secure this floor and the one where the party is located." Aaron pulled out his cell phone, dialed the number for dispatch and informed them of the news. Dispatch said it would take at least thirty minutes, but Aaron told them that they needed uniformed officers there in less than ten.

Aaron then called Jasika to let her know what was going on and left a message on Frank's cell phone. Aaron glanced down at his watch, noticing that it was already past five. He didn't try calling again.

Chapter Twelve

December 23, 5 p.m.

Frank hated the very idea of therapy. He didn't like opening himself up to a complete stranger, let alone one paid for by the NYPD. He always worried that Dr. Weintraub was reporting back to his superiors about him. Although Dr. Weintraub had ensured Frank would have his confidentiality, it still didn't completely alleviate the skepticism that Frank felt, sitting on the floral print couch while she sat in a high-backed chair with that damned legal pad in her lap.

Dr. Weintraub started the session by asking how his week had gone, so Frank talked a little about the case and the problems it was causing him. He then talked about not getting to the gym as often as he'd like because the early mornings and later nights were keeping him from making it. As usual, Dr. Weintraub just nodded and said a few "uh-huhs" or "hmms" as Frank kept talking about nothing of any importance. After about ten minutes of idle chit-chat, Weintraub put her pen down and stared Frank in the eyes. Frank noticed the change in her demeanor and knew what was coming next.

"So, at the end of our last session, I asked you if you were ready to talk about Adam. Are you?"

"Wow, no pussy-footing around today."

"Frank, we've played this game for seven months and have gone nowhere. I think it's time we deal with the biggest issue in the room so we can move forward."

Frank took a deep breath, closed his eyes and stretched his head toward the ceiling. As he lowered his head and opened his eyes, he said, "What do you want to know?"

"I don't *want* to know anything," she started, "but I think we have to talk about you, Adam, your feelings, everything. Let's face it. You're here because you've never dealt with your feelings about Adam's death."

Frank started trying to defend himself and talked about how he'd grieved for an appropriate amount of time then moved on with his life. He explained that he'd tried to find love again in a variety of different ways.

"Really? Where were you searching for love, Frank?"

"Bars, clubs, the occasional bathhouse or the steam room at the gym," Frank said. But as soon as the words slipped out of his mouth, he recognized his own words had defied his stance.

"And how did finding 'love' go for you in those locations?"

"Well, I got laid a lot," Frank said sheepishly, not even allowing himself to make eye contact with the doctor.

"Come on, Frank," Weintraub started. "If you can't even be honest with yourself in here, how are you ever going to be honest in a real, adult relationship?" She stared at Frank for a few moments before she continued, "Frank, I don't normally do this, but if you're not going to be honest with me, I'll just let you go. I'll sign the appropriate paperwork releasing you from our sessions and be done with you. Then, in another year or so when you find yourself back under an IA investigation, you'll be right back in here if you're lucky, although they'll probably just terminate you next time. Hell, they almost did it this time, thinking you were a loose cannon."

"What?"

"Oh, I guess they probably didn't tell you about that, did they? There was an intense discussion in IA about whether the shooting was so overkill that it warranted firing you. Sure, you were justified, but you unloaded your entire clip into the perp. Let's face it. That's overkill by anyone's definition." She paused, and Frank watched her trying to gauge his reaction. "I've seen the video. The first shot you took disabled the guy. The other shots were unnecessary. So, before you answer my next question, you might want to think about what got you here and whether you want the help that's being offered — or do you want to play games? Are you ready to talk about Adam?"

Frank was speechless. After seven months of weekly therapy sessions, she'd never talked down to him, she'd never talked about what had gotten him there in the first place and she'd never raised her voice. Frank sat in silence for a couple of minutes, hoping she would take it back and they could keep talking about inconsequential topics.

"I miss him... God, I miss him." Frank wasn't even sure if he was speaking, as the words came out of his mouth in a whisper. He lowered his head and gently swung it from side to side as tears started flowing down his cheeks. "It just wasn't fair. It just wasn't fair." The next sound that came out of Frank was something he'd never heard before. It was guttural, primal. It wasn't a scream. It wasn't a cry. His whole body convulsed during the sobs that followed.

Dr. Weintraub sat and waited. When Frank had calmed down slightly, she reached over, grabbed a box of Kleenex and handed it to him. Tears kept streaming down his face.

"I never cried," Frank said, breaking the eerie silence that permeated the room. "I didn't cry at the crime scene. I didn't cry at the funeral. I just let myself get lost in my own self-destruction. I think I wanted to be fired."

"Huh?" Dr. Weintraub asked, seemingly not sure what Frank was referring to.

"The shooting that landed me here... I wanted to be fired. I couldn't protect the one man I loved more than this job, more than myself, more than anything. When I pulled that trigger, I just kept pulling. Everything that I had avoided came to the surface—my inability to protect Adam, my failings as a man. I just kept shooting." Frank took a deep breath and wiped a tear away from his eye. "I knew what I was doing. A voice inside my head was screaming for me to stop, but I just kept shooting. It's not like I took pleasure in killing the perp, because I didn't. At that moment, I just couldn't stop."

"Frank, you've got to forgive yourself for Adam. There was nothing—and I do mean nothing—you could have done."

"I could have gone with him to the store. I could have told him that the eggnog was fine without bourbon. We could have had Christmas alone. I could have never met him. He'd still be alive if he'd never met me."

"Frank, you have no way of knowing that. Hindsight is always twenty-twenty. We can always create a long list of things we should've done or shouldn't have done, but we don't know what would or would not have happened. We can't. What happened that night to both you and Adam was tragic, it was unnecessary, it was the worst of what it means to be a human, but you did nothing wrong. You can never move on with your life until you learn to forgive yourself."

"But I should have. I should have protected him."

"How? Tell me how and I'll drop this completely. Give me one shred of logical evidence that leads you to the conclusion that you could have done anything different beyond a bunch of platitudes about changing a past that's unchangeable."

Frank sat in silence for a few minutes, trying to come up with one good reason to give Weintraub, one fact that vindicated his self-pity and need to punish himself somehow for Adam's death, but he didn't have one. There was no justification for his stance. All his self-loathing was leading him nowhere except toward self-destruction, and he knew it.

"I almost feel like I deserve to be punished, deserve to have my life taken from me, to have my career destroyed."

"Why?"

"Because I'm still here." Frank shook his head as he watched Weintraub. "I just miss him. I miss him so much."

"Frank, we will always miss our loved ones who've died. How do you think Adam would respond if he saw you right now? Five years later?"

Frank thought about it for a second and chuckled. "First, he'd smack me. He loved life. He loved living life. So, he'd see the wreck that I've become and smack me silly. He'd be disappointed in me. God, would he be disappointed in me."

"Why do you think he'd be disappointed?"

"Well, I have an unbelievably hot guy vying for my attention, and all I keep doing is pushing him away." Frank went on to explain his 'date' with Aaron and what had happened in his condo afterward—how Frank had freaked out and pushed Aaron away because when he'd looked down, he'd seen Adam smiling at him.

"Could it be you saw Adam smiling because he was telling you it was okay? It's all right to move on with Aaron? Have you talked about any of this with Aaron?"

"No, God, no. We really haven't talked much since then. We just do our jobs and keep everything a hundred percent professional. He may even hate me by this point. Hell, I'd hate me. I don't deserve him."

"Whoa," Weintraub started. "You don't deserve him? Why would you say that?"

"Look at me... I'm a bumbling fucking mess. I can't even get my own head screwed on straight. Why would anyone in their right mind want to be with me?"

"Why does anyone in their right mind want to be with anyone? You've got to lighten up on yourself. I know it's hard to believe, Frank, but the weight of the world really doesn't rest solely on your shoulders. Aaron's a big boy. If he wants to be with you, let him, if that's what you want. You can only decide what *you* want out of life. Let

Aaron make that decision for himself. And from what you've said, that decision is you. Why sabotage something because you're scared it won't be perfect? Nothing in life is perfect. That's just life."

Frank pursed his lips and blew out a gust of air, looking nowhere in particular. "God, I am an idiot, aren't I?"

"You're not an idiot, Frank. You're just scared. You're in mourning. You're still grieving. But at some point, you've got to move beyond grieving to living. If you don't, you'll spend the rest of your life in this hurtful, self-destructive cycle you've created for yourself." She glanced down at her watch. "Dear God, we went over this week. I hope I didn't keep you from something, but this was the most productive session we've had, so it was definitely worth it."

"Nah, I have no plans for tonight. I'm just going home."

"Frank, be gentle with yourself this week. I know how hard the anniversary of Adam's death can be. Just remember to take care of yourself. Love yourself. And maybe, just maybe, you'll find that you can open yourself up to Aaron's love. And if not Aaron, some other equally amazing guy. Trust me... All things considered, you're a catch, so don't forget it. Same time next week?"

* * * *

Frank's heart was pounding. The world was utterly silent except for the *boom boom* beat from the music he had playing on his iPhone. For the first time in days, Frank was enjoying a good morning run. Club H was practically dead due to the intense snowstorm raging through Manhattan. The National Weather Service was predicting that the city could get ten to sixteen inches by midday before the snow stopped falling. *Gotta love twenty-four-hour gyms.*

Suddenly, *Latin Girls* by the Black-Eyed Peas rang through the club-mix he was listening to. Frank glanced down at his iPhone, seeing Jasika's face on the small screen. Normally, he wouldn't answer the phone because of gym etiquette, but he glanced around and noticed no one was even near his bank of treadmills, so he hit the green answer button.

"Hey, Jas, jogging here. What's up?"

"Fucking Aaron Massey!" Jasika shouted into the phone.

"Whoa, what the hell, Jas?"

"And fuck you too for not answering your phone last night!"

"Whoa, calm the fuck down," Frank said between breaths. "What are you so worked up about?"

"Well, if you'd answer your phone ever, you'd know what was going on and the shit storm that is heading our way."

"Sorry, Jas. I got home around eight and just passed out after eating takeout from the deli under my building. This morning I got up at five to get to Club H. I haven't even looked at my phone other than to turn on my gym playlist."

There was a slight pause. "Fuck, it's running again. You near a TV? Turn to WNTV."

Frank reached down and clicked the remote control attached to his treadmill that immediately turned on the small television screen in front of him. He went through the channels until he got to WNTV. Currently, a commercial was playing.

"Okay, on that channel. Now what?"

"Just wait," Jasika said. "Just wait."

After another commercial for some kind of dishwashing soap Frank had never heard of, a television anchor's face filled the screen. "Once again, good morning, New York. The time is six-fifty-five. As promised, we have new information about the Twelve-Day Killer from our very own Jenny Mace, Jenny." Suddenly, the immaculately groomed Jenny Mace was staring at Frank through the television screen. *Aw, fuck!*

"Good morning, New York. As reported last night, the hunt for the Twelve-Day Killer is still very much underway at this hour. After numerous calls to the mayor's office demanding an answer as to why the NYPD has been inept handling the case, Mayor Rinehart promised a shake-up this morning. We're just moments away from the breaking news." She tilted her head and raised one of her fingers to her right ear, as though trying to hear what someone was saying through a monitor in her ear, "We now go to Gracie Mansion for a live press conference."

An outside shot of Gracie Mansion's historic yellow siding suddenly filled the screen. Mayor LaGuardia had officially made the mansion his place of residence in 1942, and ever since, it had been the primary residence of all NYC mayors.

An interior shot of Gracie Mansion's famous foyer filled the screen. The painted trompe l'oeil flooring shown like black-and-white marble before a grandiose staircase that came down and curved to someplace beyond the reach of the television camera. At the bottom of the staircase, a large podium with the seal of New York City emblazoned against the dark cherry wood stood waiting for the mayor to make her announcement. The podium had a dozen different microphones connected to the top, and numerous reporters and television cameras were gathered, waiting for the entrance of the mayor, despite the early hour of the press conference.

In a matter of seconds, the mayor, a smartly dressed Olivia Rinehart, came down the stairs with a couple of people following on her heels. Frank couldn't make out the people behind her. The mayor reached the bottom of the staircase and started her address to the city.

"My beloved New York City residents... I address you this early morning because dark days have come upon our city as a madman has taken it upon himself to destroy our way of life. The NYPD has valiantly tried capturing him, but the killer has remained just out of reach. After serious consultation between myself, the Director of the FBI and the FBI's NYC Bureau Chief," the mayor said, nodding to the woman standing next to her, "we've decided that we need to bring in a team of experts who are adept at handling this specific type of crisis. From this moment on, the investigation is being taken over by the FBI. Chief Barling..."

Temperance Barling moved to the set of microphones, and the camera zoomed in on her face. Frank could see the other person standing behind her now, but his face wasn't in the picture. Even without seeing it, Frank recognized his suit. *Aaron?*

"For those of you who do not know me, my name is Temperance Barling, and I am a twenty-year veteran of the FBI. We welcome the opportunity to work with the NYPD on this case to ensure that all New Yorkers are safe and secure this Christmas. As requested by both Mayor Rinehart and NYPD Commissioner Diaz, we are providing field support from the Behavioral Analysis

Unit located at Quantico, to be spearheaded by Supervisory Special Agent Aaron Massey. Massey has been helping the NYPD on a consulting basis. Still, we are sure that his taking over of the day-to-day functions of the case will ensure a speedy capture of the animal that is behind these murders."

The camera panned up, and Aaron stood somberly against the backdrop of the staircase. *That fuck! He just threw us under the bus!*

Aaron was then asked to say a few words. "For obvious reasons, I cannot comment on the specifics of the case, but we do have a working criminal profile that will be faxed to all media outlets by noon today. We suspect that the unknown subject is probably planning another murder today and a larger, more public spectacle tomorrow. Although I do not want to cause panic in the city, we want everyone to be safe. For this reason, take some important steps during the next few days. First, do not answer the door for anyone you do not know. If you are expecting repair or delivery people, please make sure you seek proper identification before unlocking your door and letting a stranger into your house."

Aaron kept talking, but Frank had stopped listening, as the only thing he could hear was the rage running through his veins. For a second, he totally forgot Jasika was still on the phone until her voice snapped him back to reality.

"As I said, that *fuck!*"

"Did you know this was coming?"

"Yeah, he called me last night to give me the heads-up. I was already asleep, but he left a message on my cell phone this morning. He said to call him, but when I saw that the mayor was making a press conference, I knew what was going down and had to call you immediately," Jasika bitterly responded.

"Well, I guess there's no need to hurry into the office this morning," Frank said, his voice heavy between breaths. "I'll see you there around nine-thirty. Don't want to see the Aaron Massey Spectacle that is sure to happen at nine when the shift change occurs."

"You know what? Fuck it. I'll walk Ginny to school for a change and get there late too. How about we meet up at Viva La Coffee at nine and go in together?"

"Now that sounds like a plan," Frank said. Frank turned off the television and kept running for another ten minutes. With each step hitting the treadmill's belt, he noticed himself getting angrier at Aaron. *How could I let myself trust that asshole? The second I think about letting him in, he turns around and stabs me in the back. What the fuck?* As Frank let his anger course through his body, he finished his morning run, hit the showers and began his walk through the raging blizzard.

* * * *

At nine o'clock, Frank showed up at Viva La Coffee to find the place practically deserted. Besides the two baristas, only one other patron was in the coffee shop. Frank stomped off the snow he had accumulated on the mat as he stood in the entryway. He walked up to the barista and ordered a large dark-roast coffee. The barista poured the cup, and Frank paid for the coffee and walked over to one of the many unoccupied tables.

Sitting on the table next to him was an unattended copy of *The New York Times*, so Frank picked it up and glanced at the headline—*Mayor Shakes Things Up at NYPD*.

Fuck. Frank read the accompanying story about how the NYPD was letting the ball drop, and the mayor was promising to step in and had scheduled a six a.m. press conference to discuss changes she was making. He stopped reading halfway through the article. *Well, there goes my career. I'll probably be stuck at a desk for a year, assuming they don't use the old IA investigation to fire me.*

The jingle of bells over the front door caused Frank to glance up and see Jasika striding in. She smiled at Frank and headed straight for the barista.

"One Café Americano and vodka if you have it," she joked with the woman.

"I'm sorry, miss. This is a 'bring your own alcohol establishment' today," she joked back. The other barista quickly set about making the drink, seeming glad to have something to do. After receiving her order, Jasika came to sit down with Frank.

"So, be honest with me, Frank. What's the likelihood I'm losing my shield today?"

"Honestly, fifty-fifty. Hays may just place all the blame on me. I'll try to protect you if I can, but at this point, I'm not sure what's going to happen."

They sat in silence, drinking their warm, caffeinated beverages. After a few minutes, Frank finally suggested they head off to see what the day would bring. They bundled up, grabbed their coffees and set back out into the continuing blizzard.

The snow was like tiny pinpricks across Frank's exposed face. With each step, the ferocity of the cold, wind and snow bit at him, which made him only want to walk faster. He continued walking at a slow pace anyway, so Jasika could keep up and because he wasn't looking forward to the inevitable showdown he knew was coming when he arrived at the precinct. They turned the corner to see a series of black SUVs parked up and down the street.

"Guess the Feds got here, despite the snow," Frank commented, more to himself than Jasika.

"Fun times," Jasika responded.

They trudged on while Frank contemplated calling in sick and running back to his warm apartment, where he could get hammered and ring in Christmas his own special way. At the base of the steps, Frank looked at Jasika, then back at the main door, kind of hoping she would recommend fleeing. She only shrugged, and they walked up the stairs into the building.

The precinct was eerily quiet as Frank and Jasika walked through the front door. He expected to see lots of people running around in circles like chickens with their heads cut off. They walked over to their desks and took off their coats. Finally, an FBI agent walked past their desks.

"Detectives Schultt and Torv?"

"Yes," they replied in unison, though a little hesitantly.

"Supervisory Special Agent Massey asked me to stay with you until his briefing is completed."

"Okay," Frank said. *What? We need a babysitter now? What a smug prick.*

Frank sat down at his desk and booted up his computer. He glanced over and saw Jasika doing the same thing. The agent sat on the corner of a nearby desk, watching the two of them like a live version of *Big Brother. Dear God, is he afraid we'll somehow contaminate the evidence?* "Am I allowed to look at my email?" Frank questioned.

"Of course, detective. Despite what you may think, I'm not here to babysit or guard you."

"Really?" Jasika questioned sarcastically.

"I promise. Agent Massey just wanted to make sure that you two didn't take off before he had a chance to talk to you both," the agent responded.

Frank tried not to stare at the agent but kept him in the corner of his eye. Frank opened his email and noticed the image files from both Two Penn Plaza and the Radio City Music Hall were sitting in his inbox. *Better not look at them, just in case.* He glanced through the other emails. One was from Logan that morning, marked 'urgent'. He double-clicked and found it was just a message from Logan asking if he was all right. Apparently, Ben had been watching the news since his rehearsal had likely been canceled due to poor weather.

Frank took out his cell phone and found a couple of dozen texts and phone messages starting at six o'clock the previous evening. Most of them were from Aaron and said things like, *We need to talk. Where are you?* and *Come on. We've got to talk.* After reading half of them, Frank deleted the rest and turned back to his email. He composed a quick message to Logan, reassuring him that the situation hadn't sent him off the deep end and promised to call after work.

Almost immediately, Logan emailed him back, telling him what an evil, horrible, no-good bastard Aaron was for doing this to him. Frank smiled. *It's nice to know that your true friends always have your back.* Frank read through the other emails, but none of them seemed all that pressing or important.

"Jas, anything interesting in your inbox?"

"Nothing really. I had a few emails from friends checking on me."

"Me too."

"Logan?"

"But of course. Ben probably has the day off because of the snow, so he caught the press conference. Let the drama ensue."

Jasika chuckled as the squad room filled with a mixture of uniformed cops, detectives and men and women in suits. *The suits have gotta be the Feds. No self-respecting detective would dress that uncomfortably.* A few detectives were people Frank knew, and most of them averted their eyes, refusing to look at either Frank or Jasika. *Great, they're already treating us like lepers.*

"Agent Albarracin, thank you for waiting for Detectives Schultt and Torv for me," Aaron said as he approached the group. Frank immediately noticed that Aaron was back in the Armani suit. *I guess he owns more than the off-the-rack Brooks Brothers.* "Agent Moczek has your assignment for you," Aaron continued saying as he turned toward Frank and Jasika. "You two, come with me."

"What makes you think I'm going anywhere with — "

"Frank, for once, just shut up and do what you're told." The urgency in Aaron's voice showed that it was in Frank's best interest to do what he'd said. So, he did. Aaron led the way back to the conference room. Once they were inside, Aaron closed the door.

"For Christ's sake, do either of you ever answer your fucking phones?" Aaron exclaimed. "I spent half the night trying to get ahold of you two to give you the heads-up on what was coming down this morning. I left the Rockettes' headquarters a little after six o'clock and had a message on my cellphone to call my boss, Chief Barling. She told me they were about to throw both of you under the bus and that the FBI was taking control."

"Which is exactly what you did," Frank said.

"Not really. If you had called me back at any point in the last fifteen hours, you would have known what was going on."

"Do tell," Frank said flatly, not trusting Aaron.

Aaron took a deep breath and started in on the rest of the story. Aaron had apparently been told by Chief Barling that he was to report to the mayor's office by six-thirty, so he'd hightailed it over to the other side of town. He'd gotten there and found the mayor, Chief Hays, the Director of the FBI and his Bureau Chief all waiting for him. The mayor had then explained that the case wasn't being solved fast enough.

"I tried to explain to them the problem with the evidence. How the killer had purposefully left little details that couldn't be followed forensically, but she couldn't have cared less. She just wanted it over. I tried to plead with the director, but he and the mayor go way back, so he just kept telling me to 'make it work', like some kind of law enforcement version of Tim Gunn."

"Who?" Frank asked.

"Are you're sure you're gay?" Jasika jokingly questioned.

Frank looked at Jasika, confused, but Aaron continued, "Not really important. Anyway, the conversation continued, and the mayor laid out the plans for sidelining both of you, if not suspending the two of you for negligence." Aaron went on to explain how the mayor and chief were going to release a statement blaming both Jasika and Frank for the mishandling of the case. For Jasika, they were going to explain that she was young and inexperienced and had probably been promoted through the ranks too quickly because of a flaw in the promotion system.

"The mayor has been looking for a way to get rid of the policy allowing someone to become eligible to make detective after working for two years in an investigative unit. She wants to get the 'shield clause' removed from NYPD's contracts in the next round of negotiations. She figured this case might just give her the political leverage to go after the union with public support," Aaron explained. "As for Frank, the mayor planned on releasing the video of you and the burglary store shooting. They also planned on leaking some information to Jenny Mace about your drug history and some of your sexual exploits they've heard about over the past five years. They were going to paint you as some kind of drug-filled, oversexed psychopath with a badge and gun. The mayor figured public opinion against you would skyrocket, and the union would back off and let them fire you for cause, even though the IA report came back in your favor. Although your Chief was not in favor of this, he sat there like a good little soldier, hoping no one would pay close attention to what they were doing. They'd pass all the blame onto the two of you while the FBI came riding in to save the day."

"And why are you telling us this?" Jasika asked, looking at Aaron squarely. Her fists were clenched, and the words barely escaped her clenched jaw.

"I'm telling you this because that was what they wanted to do, not what is happening."

"What do you mean?" Frank asked, eyeing Aaron with skepticism.

Aaron let out an exasperated sigh. "This is what I was afraid of," he said as he ran his hands through his hair and watched them. "I agreed to become the face of this case because that was the only way I could save the two of you. Well, that, and I also threatened to release some information I'd gathered about Rinehart's financials through some friends at Interpol."

"Wait! You have dirt on the mayor?" Frank questioned.

"Not exactly, but you don't get to be a mayor of one of the largest cities in the world without a little dirt in your background. Combine her own sense of fear and my notoriety as a forensic psychologist who has closed one of the largest financial cases internationally, and she took the bait."

"So, our careers came down to you bluffing the mayor?" Jasika asked, sounding bewildered.

"I could tell instantly that I'd hit a nerve. One benefit of being an internationally recognized author is that people just assume I have the dirt."

"So, where does this leave us?" Jasika wondered.

"We're still a team. Technically, I'm no longer a member of the BAU. I had to make the concession to Director Price. He's wanted me out of there ever since the book was published. For all intents and purposes, I'm now the public affairs liaison officer for the FBI in New York. Although this is a demotion within the Bureau, it's technically seen as a promotion in both rank and salary. But after the case, I'm officially benched."

"You killed your career for us?" Frank asked, astonished by what he was hearing.

"Well, my days of fieldwork were already numbered. I may never get the chance to work in the field like I do right now, but I'll still work for the FBI. Besides, I've been offered a job as a faculty member for the John Jay College of Criminal Justice. I'll liaison by day and teach by night. All in all, it won't suck completely."

"Talk about pulling the wind out of our sails," Frank started. "We were ready to crucify you this morning."

"I figured as much when neither of you were here for the morning briefing. I assumed that you watched the press conference and took it the wrong way. That's why I had Agent Albarracin wait for you near your desk. I agreed to a comprehensive multi-agency briefing at nine. When you didn't show, I didn't want you coming in and taking off without my knowing about it."

"Yeah, but what would have happened if we had left?" Jasika questioned sarcastically.

"I gave him permission to taser the two of you," Aaron responded with a grin. "So, what do you say we all get back to work?"

"I say, let's. But first, I need more coffee," replied Frank, gesturing toward his empty cup. "Aaron, Jasika, either of you need more?

"Nah, I'm still good," Jasika responded.

"I could definitely use a cup and some fresh air for a few minutes. Want to take a quick walk?" Aaron asked.

* * * *

"Dear God, it's freezing outside. I feel like I just lived through the blizzard scene in *Frozen*," Aaron said as they entered Viva La Coffee. The coffee shop was still pretty empty. *Guess most people don't want to be out walking around in this mess*, Aaron thought.

Frank shook off the snow that had accumulated on his jacket when he replied, "Did you just make a Disney cartoon reference?"

"Maybe..."

"Okay, then."

"Hey, I have nieces and nephews. Trust me... I've seen both movies way too many times when I've visited the family on vacations in Omaha."

"Sure... Let's stick with that story," Frank joked. They quickly ordered and Aaron suggested they warm up before heading back outside into the snow. They found a table in the corner of the room away from the other two patrons.

"Again, I really am sorry for how things went down last night and today. If I could have thought of a better way out of this situation that protected all of us, trust me, I would have done it." Aaron watched Frank's face for a few seconds, waiting to see how Frank would react.

Frank took a sip of his coffee, then set it back on the table and responded, "I'm sorry too. I'm sorry for a lot of things. I'm sorry about assuming the worst. I'm sorry about the other night..." The silence hung between them.

Okay, so maybe he is ready to have this conversation. Aaron could tell that Frank needed to talk, so he said nothing, letting the silence continue unabated.

"I don't know how much of my life you know about," Frank continued, "but it's been a very rough five years."

Aaron listened to Frank's retelling of everything from the previous five years — from Adam's murder to his spiral into drugs and sex, to the shooting that had landed him in therapy. At some point during the story, Aaron had put his hand on top of Frank's. Frank didn't seem to notice, so Aaron kept it there, running his thumb gently over the back of Frank's hand.

"So, that's everything." Frank sighed audibly. "I guess you now know what a fucking mess I am. I'm glad we can work professionally, but I just wanted you to know that the other night had nothing to do with you."

"But it does, Frank," Aaron started. "Despite everything you've just told me and everything I've seen, I still think you're a great guy. As I said in my email, I'm to blame too. I should have known better. I knew some of your story, not everything, but enough to know that my pushiness was probably not a good idea. And yet I did it — and I kept doing it."

They just stared at each other for what seemed like minutes before Frank pulled his hand away after squeezing Aaron's hand gently. "Well, I guess we should get back to the precinct. Jasika's going to put an APB in on two missing persons if we don't return soon," Frank said, likely attempting to bring some levity back to the conversation.

* * * *

He, Frank and Jasika brought three laptops in from one of the SUVs outside the precinct to set up a strategic command center. Two agents brought in an electric whiteboard system, copied all the information from the old dry-erase board and converted it to e-form. By doing that, Aaron explained, it allowed them to see how information cross-checked not only in their own minds but also with the information they could gather through the various databases available to the FBI.

The Midtown Precinct had been tasked to solve this one case, so all other open cases were farmed out to the other precincts in the area. More and more information kept getting placed onto the digital board, and soon a clear picture of everything seemed impossible. Unfortunately, as had often been Aaron's experience, as even more information came in—not only about the individual crime scenes but about the victims—the board went from something slightly organized and promising to a chaotic maze. Periodically, Aaron would ask the tech assigned to the case to run a pattern search to see if anything jumped. As of yet, the board was a jumble of people, places, motives and possible unsubs.

By noon, they were at an impasse, and Aaron suggested that they take a break to clear their heads. The FBI had ordered food to be brought in for the precinct to make it easier for everyone to stay focused. Prepared boxes containing a sandwich, pasta salad, a soft drink, an apple and a cupcake were scattered around a large table. Frank took a turkey sandwich while Aaron and Jasika both went for the tuna salad. They then sat at Frank's and Jasika's desks and started tossing around possible new ways to approach the case.

"We've been spending way too much time on victimology. We know why they are being targeted. And I bet looking for motives among possible suspects is causing too much information," Frank suggested.

"Okay, I can see your point," Aaron replied. "But what do you suggest we do? Just not follow the suspects?"

"Not necessarily, but I don't think our time is best used when we end up with so much information. I almost wonder if the unsub is toying with us again by giving us too much."

"All right," Aaron said as he took a second to process the idea. "Where would you have us look, then?"

"Well, let's say that by chance, the unsub knew one or even two of the victims, which is unlikely."

"Well, even the basic profile of an organized serial murderer would suggest that the unsub probably doesn't know his victims, especially since this unsub is killing for a very specific reason and targeting very specific people," Aaron acknowledged.

"If we keep adding numerous suspects to our board, wouldn't that prevent your computer from seeing possible relationships? From what I understand about your system, the more information that is programmed in, the better. But doesn't there come the point when a computer is too saturated with useful information and it all begins having a negative effect instead of the intended positive one?"

"You know, you may have a point. I've never run into a case that had the sheer quantity of data we're accumulating. Most serial murderers stick to one subtype of victim...like blonde women between twenty-one and twenty-eight, or middle-aged Black men who are truckers. Whatever the case, the signature is generally very clear. In this case, we have someone killing for the purpose of destroying Christmas — or at least having a clear negative impact on how people are living Christmas in New York."

"What about the website?" Jasika asked.

"You mean *holidayhorrors.com*?" Aaron asked. Jasika nodded. "Well, thus far, most people who have been victims have been on the list. The last victim..." Forgetting the woman's name, Aaron picked up his notepad and read off it. "Donna Pinkerton was the first one to break free from the website. Maybe the unsub heard that we knew about the site, so he decided it was best if he found a possible victim on his own."

"Donna's name might not have been on the published website, but was her name anywhere in Connor Gordon's other files?" Frank chimed in.

Aaron turned to Jasika and asked, "Can you pull up the files on your computer and see if there is one for either a Donna or a Pinkerton?"

Aaron watched as Jasika flew her fingers over the keyboard before she responded, "Nope. Nothing." Aaron could practically see the gears in Jasika's mind whirring before she added, "Let me try one more thing." Once again, Jasika went to work. "There is a folder called 'Research'. But it looks like the Rockettes did a good job of keeping this one out of the news. I'm just not finding anything in here. Sorry."

Aaron nodded. "It was worth a shot."

Aaron picked up his sandwich and took a bite when someone yelled, "Aaron Massey?" There was a courier wearing a bright orange bubble jacket taking off his hat and gloves.

"Over here," Aaron yelled and motioned for the messenger.

"I'm sorry, I was told by the sender to make sure I ask for your badge and ID before I delivered the folder. Apparently, the information in the package is sensitive," the courier informed the group.

Aaron pulled out his badge and ID, and once the courier was satisfied, he handed over the package and left. Aaron then opened it to see what was so urgent and secretive.

Inside he found a plain manila envelope marked 'Agent Massey' on the outside, and he opened the folder. "Hey, it's the forensic evidence from Madison Square Garden." He glanced through the report before handing it over to Frank.

"Give me the quick version," Frank said, putting the folder down on the desk.

"The forensic techs found blood evidence, as suspected, and it definitely came from Donna Pinkerton. So, we can be pretty sure that the primary crime scene was her desk."

"Somehow the killer snuck into the office, killed her, left with her body and no one noticed?" Jasika questioned.

"The only person in the office at the time was the receptionist and the vile fucktwit executive, Mona Generosa. There could have been a shoot-out, and as long as it didn't cost her money, Generosa probably wouldn't have noticed or cared," Aaron added. Aaron watched Frank ruminate on the new information for a second.

"So, somehow the killer murdered Pinkerton with no one noticing, got her back to Radio City Music Hall and had time to string her up behind Santa's sleigh. The killer has some method to gain access to these locations in a way no one notices him coming or going?"

"Yep, even the receptionist had no idea someone had gotten by her," Aaron agreed.

They all stared at each other for a few moments, and Aaron took a bite of his sandwich, not sure where to go next. He finished it, opted to bypass the pasta salad and went straight for the cupcake. He lifted the dessert and noticed that it looked familiar. "Holy Fuck!" he exclaimed.

"What?" Jasika and Frank said in unison.

"How can we be that stupid? How can we not see what's right in front of our faces?"

"What?" Frank asked, alone this time.

"Look who catered this lunch." They stared at the boxes and noticed the logo for Delicious Delights. Without waiting for a response, Aaron got up and ran into the conference room with Frank and Jasika on his heels. The tech was eating his lunch. Aaron noticed he appeared to have startled the man. "Pull up the photos from the Christmas Party yesterday at Two Penn Plaza."

The tech brought up a folder and hit a few keys until the screen was reflected on the electronic whiteboard. He clicked through some pictures before Aaron found what he was searching for. "There, right there. Can you zoom in?" The picture contained a group of revelers in a conference room, celebrating the holidays. On a table in the picture's background was a series of white boxes. When the tech zoomed in where Aaron had indicated, the logo for Delicious Delights filled the whole board.

Chapter Thirteen

December 24, 1 p.m.

Aaron was behind the wheel of the police sedan as he pulled out of the station garage and started driving south toward Washington Square. The snow had let up, but only a few people were actively driving around the city besides police and taxis. Jasika sat in the back seat, calling representatives for Madison Square Garden's Entertainment and Radio City Music Hall.

Frank and Aaron sat in silence as the car's police radio squawked, "10-53H at Broadway and Forty-Second Street."

Frank explained that the radio signal code meant someone had been hit at that location, so he recommended going up to Fifth Avenue to avoid the emergency personnel.

Aaron took it easy driving toward Greenwich Village. The streets hadn't been completely plowed, so they were a sea of white, compacted ice. After passing East Fourteenth Street, Jasika hung up her phone, and for the first time since getting into the car, she started talking to them.

"Okay, I finally got the building supervisor at Radio City Music Hall on the line. According to him, Delicious Delights catered the cast and crew's lunch yesterday prior to the second show."

"How did we not know this?" Frank questioned.

"Apparently, they used a conference room that was very removed from the rest of the theater for lunch, so we had no reason to go near there. In fact, the building supervisor was quite taken aback that we would want to know about catering. He had to find the stage manager to even find out who they'd used."

"But we still have a basic problem with all this," Aaron said while keeping his eyes on the road. "We've already ruled out everyone at Delicious Delights as suspects. Sure, we have another connection, but this may be a huge coincidence. And trust me, I don't believe in coincidences, but I just don't know if this is a break or another red herring."

"Well, we've got to follow every lead we get," Frank noted.

Aaron remembered the side driveway to the underground parking lot where they had pursued Geraldo Salvador the previous week, so he pointed his car down the incline into the small garage. A short, heavyset man who had been sitting in the attendance booth approached the car, yelling, "Hey! This is a private parking lot. You can't park here." Frank yanked out his shield and pressed it against the side window. "Oh, sorry, officers," the man said, motioning the car forward.

Aaron noticed the man return to his perch and pick up the phone. *Probably letting Ms. Clegg know we're here.*

Aaron guided the car into a parking space next to one of the white vans and put it in park. The three reached for their door handles and exited the vehicle almost in unison. The garage was surprisingly warm, so Aaron took off his trench coat and laid it over the back of the driver's seat.

"Jasika, talk to the attendant. See what you can learn from him," Aaron said. Jasika turned and headed in the short man's direction. Aaron then heard a door opening on the other side of the garage. Instinctively, Aaron swiveled in the direction of the open door as he reached toward the Glock 23 in his concealed holster.

"I'm unarmed," came the surprised voice of Alexi Clegg. After turning toward the open door, Aaron watched Ms. Clegg take a step down toward them, showing that she had nothing in her hands.

"Sorry, ma'am. The quickness of the open door kind of threw us off. Better safe than sorry," Aaron said, relaxing.

"So, I'm going to guess this isn't a social call?" Alexi said, looking at them. "I'm in the middle of preparing several major catering events that all have to get pulled off this evening. I practically have one in each borough. So, I hate to be rude, but can we skip the small talk and you just tell me how I can help you?"

Aaron sensed that Alexi wasn't being rude but was just overstressed by the frenzied life that holiday catering caused. *I bet the blizzard isn't helping her nerves, either.* He looked at her for a second and weighed his options but decided that a direct approach was for the best. "Ms. Clegg, we believe the continuing rash of murders in this city is related to your catering business."

"I gave you the files on everyone who works here last week. I thought everything checked out. When I talked to Chief Hays — "

"Wait! You talked to Chief Hays?" Frank questioned.

"Yeah, I called last week to see if you needed anything else and I was transferred to him."

Aaron looked at Frank, "Did you know about this?"

"Nope," Frank said, shooting Aaron a quick look.

Aaron could tell Frank's wheels were spinning, but he seemingly couldn't come up with a clear meaning for this bit of information. "What else did Chief Hays tell you?"

"Umm, he told me he'd let me know if you guys needed anything. Oh, he's also a big fan of my cupcakes. I catered a party he attended at The Whitney earlier this month." Alexi looked at Aaron and Frank and added, "So, I'm guessing you're not here on a cupcake run."

"Oh yeah," Frank muttered, "We...umm-m...have reason to believe... Well, it's more than just a reason — "

"Your catering company was peripherally associated with another killing," Aaron started. "This time, the murderer killed in one place and transported the victim to another. Based on the time of death and the fact that your company catered events in both locations, we think someone may have used your business as a cover for the murder — or at least used access through your company to kill and transfer the body from one location to the other."

"What?" A look of pure shock and terror came over Alexi's face. Suddenly, a small voice came out of her as she muttered, "I'll be ruined by this, won't I?"

"Excuse me," Frank interjected. "Ruined by what?"

"It's just like what happened to Katie Simmons. Getting myself wrapped up in one of these media circus events will kill my business. Guilty. Innocent. It doesn't matter. If word of this gets out, I'm screwed either way."

"Ma'am," Aaron started.

"Don't 'ma'am' me. This town is fucking fickle. The media love to elevate the underdog but love tearing someone down just as much."

"Ms. Clegg, I understand that you are distraught—"

"I'm not distraught. I'm screwed." She took a deep breath and leveled her eyes toward Frank and Aaron. "I'm sorry. I shouldn't be freaking out in this way. It's just that I had a conversation with my fiancé last night about Katie Simmons. You know she was one of the Twelve-Day Killer's victims… Of course you do. Dear God, I'm rambling."

"Ms. Clegg," Frank started, "maybe we should go inside and sit down."

Without saying a word, she walked back up the stairs, opened the door into the bakery and motioned for Aaron and Frank to follow her. She led them back to the small conference room where they had initially talked. She closed the door and sat down, then immediately started apologizing again for her sudden outburst.

"You see, the catering business is stressing me out. Any wrong move at this point could make or break me. I shouldn't be worried about myself. I mean, this fucker killed an old friend of mine, but this season really takes a toll. Half the time I'm handling complaints from clients who are upset that their caviar wasn't 'cooked' right. Or they're freaked out because they didn't remember to tell me that Uncle Sal is on a special diet and can't have gluten, yeast or sugar, so can I make another couple of dozen cupcakes." With each sentence, her voice became more manic. "Argh! And the two of you come in here telling me that my catering company is being implicated as an accessory to one of the worst killing sprees in the city's history." At that, she hit the table with both palms and let out a sigh.

As a trained clinical psychologist, Aaron realized Clegg's emotional state was on the verge of unraveling, so he had to tread carefully to ensure the woman didn't have a complete breakdown before she was able to provide them with any information.

"Alexi," Aaron started in the calmest voice he could muster, "I cannot imagine the stress all this is putting on you." He let the sound of his voice start to soothe her before he continued. "Please know that we have no desire to hurt you or your business. But there may be someone who works here who is doing horrible things to people. We need you to help us find this person before he or she can do any more harm."

Alexi took a deep breath in and looked up at Aaron before muttering, "Tell me what I can do."

Aaron leaned forward, grabbed one of the woman's hands and held it while he laid out what had happened the day before. He explained that the evidence pointed to Donna Pinkerton being murdered at Madison Square Garden, then how Pinkerton had been transported to Radio City Music Hall. Upon finishing, Alexi stood, opened the door and walked over to her office. She came back about thirty seconds later carrying a large notebook.

"This notebook is the real heart of this place. It has all the jobs for the entire month. Every detail of every job, down to the delivery person and catering team assigned to each one, is listed in here." She opened the book and found the sections of the book where the two jobs for the Rockettes were listed. "According to this, both jobs were simple drop-offs. Umm, Hernando Alvarez delivered to both locations." Aaron studied Alexi's face when a sudden look of dread flashed across the woman's face.

"What was that?" Aaron quickly questioned.

"What?"

"You just had a thought." Alexi looked blankly at Aaron, so he pressed on. "When you mentioned Hernando Alvarez, your face suddenly flashed fear. Are you scared of this man?"

"Hernando? No," Alexi responded quickly. "It's just—"

"It's just what?" Frank joined in.

"It's just that Hernando wasn't here yesterday. He's been out for a couple of days with the flu."

"Then who covered those deliveries?" Aaron questioned.

"My fiancé."

Suddenly, Aaron realized why the look of fear had come over her. "Does your fiancé do delivery jobs for you often?"

"He's a schoolteacher at the Borough of Manhattan Community College, so he has time off at Christmas."

"What does he teach?" Aaron asked.

"He teaches physical sciences. I know he's taught biology and anatomy. But generally, he teaches whatever the school tells him to teach."

"Where does your fiancé live?" Aaron asked.

"This is going to sound weird," Alexi said hesitantly. "I've never actually been to his place. He generally stays with me because it's closer to both of our jobs."

"So, you don't know where he lives?" Frank questioned.

Alexi let out an audible sigh before continuing. "I said it was going to sound weird. I've never been there, but I can give you the address." Alexi reached into her pocket and removed her iPhone. She scrolled through a few menus before handing the phone to Aaron, who pulled out a pad of paper and jotted down the address.

The three of them sat in the room, silently looking at each other for a minute, before Frank finally said, "Ms. Clegg, we need to see the delivery van your fiancé used yesterday."

"Sure, but—" Suddenly, a look of absolute dread washed over Alexi.

"What is it?" Aaron questioned, noticing her sudden change in demeanor.

"He washed the van last night. He said that a container of soup had spilled. I thought nothing of it because these types of accidents and cleanups happen daily around here. You don't think? Did he? Dear God."

Alexi's face fell as the realization that her fiancé was the Twelve-Day Killer took hold. Aaron could tell from her expression that somewhere, deep inside her, Alexi likely knew that her fiancé was capable of murder. The next sound out of Alexi's mouth was guttural. Aaron's heart broke for her as he listened to the sound of a woman whose life was being destroyed both personally and professionally.

* * * *

Once Alexi showed Frank and Aaron which van had been used by her fiancé the previous afternoon, Frank didn't waste any time calling Nasab and Richardson to the scene. By three-fifteen, Nasab and Richardson had confirmed that the van definitely had trace amounts of both blood and hair. Furthermore, a small scrap of clothing under one of the catering racks might be a match to one of the victims.

"Of course, all this is circumstantial at this point. We need to run a fiber comparison and wait for DNA results to get back to be completely sure," Nasab said hesitantly.

"Okay, I get it. You can't be a hundred percent sure yet. But what does your gut tell you?"

"Well, Frank, my gut says we've probably found our transport vehicle."

That was all Frank needed to know. He looked at Aaron, who was busy talking to Richardson about speeding up the DNA comparison on the FBI's end. Frank looked around to find Jasika. She was sitting at the base of the garage's stairs, going over paperwork with Alexi. He watched Alexi put her head in her hands, audibly crying. Jasika patted her on the shoulder before standing up and walking over to Frank.

"We just compared her fiancé's van usage with the dates of the crimes. He definitely catered or at least set up catering the night before in all the locations. That's why it didn't trigger the first time. On the first two catering jobs, her fiancé" — glancing down at her notes, she continued — "Thomas Hecht, went the night before to set up tables with her or one of her assistants. He shouldn't have had access to the other areas, but it appears he figured out a way around that."

"Good job, Detective Torv. We may get you your second-grade shield yet."

Jasika beamed with pride.

A sudden vibrating sensation from Frank's pants caught his attention. He shot his hand instinctively into his right front pocket, pulling out his cell phone. He glanced at the caller-ID, which read ME.

"Hey, gorgeous, what's happening on your end this fine snowy afternoon?" Frank asked.

"I should be in bed with hot cocoa and you, but alas, I'm at the ballet—and God knows I hate the ballet," Mariella Ramos replied.

"Ballet...auditioning, I hope. I think you'd look great in a tutu and tights."

"You wish, you big pervert. But alas, we've got another one. Well, two." Mariella went on to explain what had happened. That afternoon, during the two o'clock performance, two of the dancers had been dressed as giant rats. They had come on stage during their battle scene with the nutcracker. Everything was going as it should, but then both dancers had started weaving. One collapsed on stage, and the other had fallen into the orchestra pit. Things had looked a little hinky, so they called me over. I would have come with my usual team, but someone had already stole my geeks."

"Yeah, we think we have a lead on the unsub. Dear God, did I really just say that? Aaron must be rubbing off on me."

Mariella let out a laugh on the other end of the line before saying, "Hmm, at this rate, maybe I'll have two hot gay lovers to contend with. Be still my heart," using her best attempt at a Scarlet O'Hara accent.

"Well, I wouldn't go that far," Frank said with a definite hint in his voice that he didn't want to have that conversation. "So, which geek do you want?"

"Hmm...good looking Middle Eastern or skinny, pasty-white American? You know I like all flavors, Frank. Send me whichever one has the hottest ass today."

Instead of taking the bait, Frank yelled loud enough for Mariella to hear through the phone, "Hey, Mariella needs a geek at the NYC Ballet. She said to send whoever has the best ass today."

Richardson, without hesitation, piped up, "I think it would have to be Nasab. I really don't have an ass," which led to a round of hysterics among those in the garage.

Frank turned his attention back to Mariella after laughing. "Well, I guess you have your answer. I'll send Nasab over, and I'll call dispatch to send another set of detectives to your location. Right now, we have a suspect we need to bring in — and fast." Frank hung up the phone, found a uniformed officer and asked her to drive Nasab over to the Lincoln Center. She agreed, and he grabbed his spare kit out of the forensic van and was on his way.

Frank walked over to Aaron and informed him of everything he'd found out from Mariella. Aaron then went over to Alexi, who had pulled herself together. "Ms. Clegg, did you have a catering event at the NYC Ballet today?"

"Uhh... Umm-m," she said, muttering as she tried to focus her thoughts. "I had... Oh God... Thomas delivered food this morning to the NYC Ballet at Lincoln Center before heading to Midtown to complete some last-minute Christmas shopping. Afterward he was supposed to return to the Bronx."

Frank immediately called dispatch. Upon pickup, Frank didn't hesitate. "This is Detective Schultt."

"Yes, Detective," an operator's voice responded, and she sounded slightly taken aback.

"I have a series of codes."

"Ready when you are."

"We have a level four mobilization."

"Ten-five?" the operator responded, indicating that he needed Frank to repeat himself.

"I repeat, we have a level four mobilization."

"I'm sorry, Detective, but you're not allowed to make that level of authorization."

"Just a second." Frank rolled his eyes and handed Aaron the phone, who then repeated the message, but in his capacity as Supervisory Special Agent.

"Yes, Agent Massey. I have you down as having the authority to instruct a level four mobilization. Ten-four."

Aaron handed the phone back to Frank. "Okay, now that that's cleared up, level four mobilization on suspect Thomas Hecht. I'm going to need a level three mobilization from the Washington Heights precinct." Frank then read the address of Thomas' apartment that they'd gotten from Alexi and turned to Aaron, who was already heading toward their car. "Jasika, stay here and cover the scene," Frank barked over his shoulder.

"Got it, boss," Jasika responded.

While Aaron drove, Frank spent most of the ride coordinating efforts with the Bronx Borough Precinct. By the time Aaron and Frank made it across Manhattan to Washington Heights, the borough precinct had already established a perimeter and a staging location one block over from Hecht's apartment. Frank ordered men on roofs in four locations to ensure every line of sight was completely under surveillance.

Uniformed police had already placed blockades, so as they approached the staging area, a uniformed police officer stopped their car. Aaron rolled down his window, and both Frank and Aaron held up their shields. The officers moved the barrier to let the sedan through the snowy street. They found a parking spot near the hotspot of activity and got out of the car. Aaron grabbed his coat and slipped on his gloves. An older female officer approached the two of them.

"Dalia Washington, Emergency Service Unit. I'm the field command agent from ESS-3 covering the Western Bronx. And you are?"

"Detective Schultt, NYPD."

"Supervisory Special Agent Aaron Massey, FBI."

After she shook both of their hands, she led them to a small trailer brought in for administrative purposes. Inside the trailer, two Emergency Service Squad guys were already poring over a pair of maps. She introduced them and continued telling Aaron and Frank her plan.

"We tried to get eyes in the apartment, but the blinds are closed and we don't know if he's there or not. We want to evacuate the building before we infiltrate. We've already got four-point tactical on the adjacent roofs to ensure that we've cast as wide a safety net as possible. According to these blueprints" – she then turned a laptop toward Frank and Aaron. The laptop contained a schematic of the building where Thomas Hecht lived – "the only way in and out is through one of three exits, and all of them are covered. We're good to go on your command."

Aaron checked a couple of details with Washington and consented to the take-down. Washington then grabbed a walkie-talkie from the table and said firmly, "We're a go in ninety seconds."

Aaron and Frank were able to watch the entire mobilization effort from several video cameras mounted on the ESS members' helmets. Washington explained that the videos were some of the best training tools and great for proving a suspect had resisted arrest or that the officers involved in a take-down were within the limits of the law.

Surprisingly, the whole affair took less than fifteen minutes. The building was evacuated quickly and quietly. Once the building was emptied, a team of three approached Hecht's door and slipped a small video device under it that resembled a bendy straw. The video swept the room, looking for any signs of life. "Switch to thermal," Washington ordered. The place was cold. No one was in the apartment. Hecht wasn't there.

Officers breached then swept the place. Once the location had been secured, Washington led Aaron and Frank to the apartment. Groups of residents were being given blankets as they stood out in the snow. An ambulance had been called to help an elderly woman who needed more support than the officers could supply. All-in-all, the evacuation and breach had been handled quickly and efficiently. *If only all police work was this easy and clean.*

Frank, along with Aaron and Washington, climbed the stairs toward the fourth floor of the building where Hecht's apartment was located. ESS members were still milling outside the apartment as Frank and Aaron approached. They walked into the room and came face-to-face with a devilish version of Christmas. A Christmas tree was hung in the corner, upside down. In a rocking chair in the living sat a stuffed Santa, but the stomach had been slashed and the stuffing was coming out of its midsection like it had been disemboweled. A box of Christmas cookies was molding in the corner of the living room. The whole apartment looked like Christmas had gone to hell.

"God, and I thought Tim Burton's *The Nightmare Before Christmas* was a little ghoulish," Aaron muttered to himself.

"Washington, you've got to see this," an ESS member yelled from a back room.

They followed the sound of the voice and found a locked door that had been previously busted open by the ESS members. When the door opened, the slightest sound of hissing occurred, followed by a blast of freezing cold. Staring across the threshold, Aaron and Frank bore witness to the devil's workshop.

Thomas Hecht had converted his spare room into a walk-in freezer. On one corner, they found industrial steel shelving with various saws and other tools. In the corner, on a peg, hung a leather apron and a pair of goggles. A box of large-size surgical gloves lay on a stool. In the center of the room was a metal table, still stained by blood and grime. On the farthest wall, hung from meat hooks, were the remains of the first six bodies. Frank wanted to throw up, but he was able to keep himself in check as he looked around the demented playground.

"Call Mariella," Aaron suddenly said. "Dear God, it's going to take a team of scientists days to comb over everything in this room...let alone the whole apartment."

Frank took out his cell phone but couldn't get a signal. He stepped out of the spare room and walked toward one of the outside windows. He found a signal and called Mariella. "Hey Mariella, we've got an all-hands-on-deck situation." Frank then proceeded to tell Mariella about what they'd found in Hecht's apartment.

When Frank was done talking, Mariella also had some news. "Thankfully, ballerinas don't eat much. The food that was brought to the women's dressing room was laced with cyanide. Nasab ran a test on the food. I talked to one of the other girls and found out that the two who died were known bulimics and were known for pigging out in private then barfing it back up. That way they got to eat their food and continue looking like sticks."

"Wow, that could have been much worse. I guess it's a good thing those women don't like to eat and dance, or we could have lost half the company. Anyway, get over here as soon as possible."

"That may be a while. I'm waiting for a return on a phone call. Well, not to me, to one of the techs. One tech had been sent to help me worked on what we thought was an unrelated burglary at a chemical storehouse last week, but he remembers that one chemical on the list was potassium cyanide, so that theft may be related to this case. We may close two cases at once."

"When the pieces fit together, the pieces fit together." A beep suddenly sounded in Frank's ear. He looked at the caller ID and saw that Richardson was calling him. "Hey, Mariella, I've got Richardson on the other line."

"Okay, I'll be there soon."

Frank clicked over. "Richardson, tell me you have something good."

"As a matter of fact, I collected some hair and blood samples the killer missed. Furthermore, I dusted part of the van and found a print that matched Donna Pinkerton."

"How'd you get that so fast?"

"Easy, Aaron left me the FBI tech guy's number and I called him for a quick turnaround on it. He just had me send him a picture of the fingerprint using my cell phone, and he was able to run it off that. Gotta love technology!"

"Richardson, thanks for the heads-up. Just as an FYI, we found the killer's place and torture chamber. Try to get over here as soon as you can. We're going to need everyone to process this." Then Frank gave him the address.

"Gotcha. Will do."

Frank hung up the phone and stared out of the mini blinds for a second. Then he pulled the cord and opened them completely. As he did, he noticed a faint reflection of green light in the window. *What is that?* Frank tried to recreate the conditions and once again saw the pinpoint of green light. He looked around the room to trace the light's origin.

He found the device that was emitting the mysterious light. He walked over and squatted down to see something plugged into the wall behind the upside-down tree. The light was directed toward the front door, but one ornament hanging from the tree had redirected some light toward the window. Frank looked at the device. *Ah fuck, a cellular-based alarm system.*

"Aaron, we've got a problem!" Frank bellowed. Aaron came running into the room, and Frank showed him the piece of equipment.

"What is it?"

"It's a laser device set up to catch its own reflection. See that strip at the bottom of the front door?" Frank said as he pointed to a thin mirror-looking piece. "As long as that device is making contact with that strip, the circuit isn't broken. As soon as the circuit is broken, it sends out an emergency signal that someone has broken into the house."

"We broke the circuit and sent Hecht a notification, letting him know we were here. Fuck! We might as well have sent him an engraved invitation to his own arrest."

"The notification is probably either monitored or routed through the host company, Cell Security, so we can try to track that down, but it may be a dead end." Frank located the company's phone number, called Cell Security's toll-free number and got someone on the line. After some wrangling, Frank got a manager who would help them with no questions asked. Thankfully, the call center was located in New Jersey, and the guy had heard of Frank because of the case.

"You know, I shouldn't be doing this, because it violates everything, but if it helps your investigation, Detective Schultt, let's do it. I need the serial number off the base of the unit." Frank then provided the requested information. "Okay, it's a 914 number, so it's definitely a city area code," the manager informed Frank and gave him the rest of the phone number.

"Thanks," Frank said. "Your assistance may help bring this bastard in." Frank hung up the phone. "Aaron, I need you to run down a number for me."

"Why me?"

"Easy... You guys in the FBI have better toys than we do."

"Fair enough."

Frank gave Aaron the number and Aaron called it in, asking for an immediate GPS trace. In about thirty seconds, Frank noticed Aaron was talking to someone. But from Aaron's expression, it didn't look promising. Aaron hung up.

"Well, we know Thomas was in Midtown until about thirty minutes ago, when he received a call from Cellular Security, then the GPS and cell phone fell off the grid. Our best chance of finding him just disappeared."

"So, we're now looking for a needle in a haystack with nine million pieces of hay."

Chapter Fourteen

December 24, 7 p.m.

After spending two hours hanging out at Hecht's house, Frank and Aaron were relieved by a team of NYPD and FBI criminalists, so the two headed back to the precinct. When they got back, Jasika was already sitting at her desk.

"We impounded the van," Jasika noted, barely looking up from her computer as she entered something. In a couple of seconds, Jasika started printing a color picture from her computer. She then placed it on the original whiteboard. "There we go. Meet Thomas Hecht."

On the board in front of them was an average-looking guy with brown eyes and brown hair. On the surface, he was utterly unremarkable. *You could pass right by him on the street and not even think twice*, Frank thought.

"What all have you learned about this guy?" Aaron asked.

"Surprisingly, very little," Jasika started. "As suspected, he'd had two run-ins with the law when he had been a teenager and had been institutionalized during his late teens. But after that, he fell off the grid. Well, at least our grid. Not even as much as a jay-walking ticket."

"Find anything linking him to Christmas?" Frank questioned.

"As a matter of fact, I found out something fairly curious. When he was ten — he's twenty-six now — his parents were killed by a drunk driver coming home from a Christmas Eve party. The driver served five years and was then released, and he's been a model citizen ever since."

"We have a possible motive," Frank started, "But what was the trigger? I seriously doubt he's been hanging out for fifteen years plotting this."

"Sorry, Frank. Google isn't that great with finding motives," Jasika replied.

"But, hey, look... I've been in charge for less than twenty-four hours and we already have a suspect," Aaron joked. In response, Jasika picked up a rubber ball she kept on her desk and threw it at him. "Hey, don't shoot the messenger. I was just pointing out the obvious."

"Go fuck yourself, Aaron," Frank said flatly, with a hint of sarcasm.

"Anyway," Jasika began, "I should be getting back to Queens. It's Christmas Eve and I should be at home with the family. There's a city-wide manhunt for him. As long as he's still around here, it's just a matter of time before someone spots him and we bring him in. Until that happens, there's not much else we can do but sit on our asses and twiddle our thumbs. I can do that at home with Ginny and my mother."

"Not a problem," Aaron replied. "If we need anything, I can always send a vehicle for you. I totally understand the need to be near one's family at the holidays."

Jasika gathered her belongings and looked back at Frank, giving him a quick hug and whispering, "Merry Christmas," in his ear.

With Jasika gone, Aaron headed into the precinct conference room to find the FBI computer specialist assigned to the case packing up for the day.

"Hey, before you take off, can you upload the information from Detective Torv about Thomas Hecht to the shared drive?"

"Yeah, sure. Not a problem. I'm staying at the Belvedere over on Forty-Eighth, so if you need anything, just call there and ask for Agent Rummy. I'll get some takeout and go back to the hotel. I'm going to go to the hotel gym, but other than that, I really don't plan on being out of my room. I'll be back whenever you come in tomorrow morning."

"Well, until we have a sighting of Thomas Hecht, we're kind of at a standstill. The whole city is looking for this guy, but he's definitely gone to ground, so who knows when we'll need to move. But I'll definitely call if we need you."

Frank walked in at the end of Aaron speaking, and he quickly informed Frank that Agent Rummy was going to be leaving for the evening. "Oh, hey, thanks for helping Officer Richardson with the fingerprint earlier," Frank said.

"Not a problem. Glad I could be of service." Rummy finished picking up his gear and headed out. "Detective Schultt, here's my business card with my cell phone number, just in case you need to get a hold of me and Agent Massey isn't around."

"Thanks," Frank said as he accepted the man's card and put it in a jacket pocket.

Aaron watched the exchange as he sat down at the computer terminal and pulled up everything Jasika had found about Hecht. Aaron started sifting through a variety of folders. At some point, Frank had come up from behind him and started looking over his shoulder. Aaron stopped briefly and perused the file on Hecht's financials. Right after the cell phone had gone off, he'd withdrawn five hundred dollars from his bank account.

"Probably the maximum daily allowance from the debit machine," Aaron muttered to himself.

"I doubt he'll use any of them again, but put a trace on all his cards. Don't freeze them, but just trace them," Frank said.

"Detective Schultt, this isn't my first time to the party," Aaron replied as he hit a number of keystrokes at the terminal. "Done and done."

Aaron noticed Frank glancing down at his watch. "Got somewhere to be?" he questioned.

"Nah, I'm probably just going to hang out here this evening and wait for information to pour in. You?"

"I'm meeting my best friend for dinner, and we're heading to the midnight mass at St. Patrick's Cathedral. It's our little tradition."

"Oh, that's cool. I used to have traditions — back in the day."

God, I wish I knew what to say to him, Aaron thought, staring at the computer screen and refusing to make eye contact with Frank. *He looks like a hurt puppy dog.*

Aaron looked at a few more files and showed Frank how to navigate the system. He opened one control panel and explained how every call to the tip line was being logged and updated for their perusal. He also showed Frank how to hit a couple of keys and mobilize half the NYPD and FBI in under thirty minutes.

"We really do make a good team," Frank said, more to himself than to Aaron.

"Yeah, we do. You know, Frank, I originally accepted this position when Mayor Rinehart asked me because I wanted to get to know you better."

"I wondered as much."

"I mean, I didn't want it to seem like I was stalking you, but fate kind of led me to this point," Aaron said as he turned around in his swivel chair and found Frank's face inches from his own. *God, his hazel eyes are so intense. I wish he would just lean in and kiss me. I'm not going to make the first move again, though. It's on him this time.*

After an awkward moment, Frank stood. "Aaron, I have to be honest with you. I think you're amazing. You're fucking gorgeous, you're smart and in another life, I would gladly swim to the ends of the world to kiss you again."

"Then, why don't you?"

"You—you already know that I'm still not over Adam. I don't know if I ever will be."

Aaron kept staring at Frank. *I can't let myself make the first move, even if that's what Frank wants right now. He has to be the one to do it.*

"I mean—" Frank started.

He's going to do it. Fuck, right here he's going to open up to me. God, I wish I knew what was going on inside that head of his. Wait a second, what was that look he just had? Dammit!

"I mean—" Frank continued, "I really want to be friends, and maybe, at some point in the future…" Frank let his voice end before finishing the thought.

Well, fuck! He's staring at me waiting for a response. What the fuck do I say? "I get it, Frank. Like I said earlier today, I really do get it." Aaron swiveled back around and stared at the computer screen, blinking away a tear that was starting to form in the corner of his eye. "Well, I—ummm, I need to be going. Judi, my friend, won't wait for me long, so I better catch a cab back to my place and get ready. I'm meeting her at Pectopah for dinner."

"That Russian place?"

"Exactly. They have an authentic Russian Christmas dinner tonight. A lot of people go there before heading over to the mass. Kind of ironic, when you think about it…"

"What is?"

"Going to a Russian restaurant then going to a Roman Catholic mass."

"I guess, in a strange way, it is, Agent Massey."

"That's Supervisory Special Agent Massey to you," Aaron said with a wink as he swiveled back around to look at Frank once more. "Well, I best be going. I'll be on my cell, so if you need anything, let me know."

"Will do, Aaron."

Aaron packed up his belongings in the conference room, then they both headed out of the room toward the bullpen. Aaron strolled toward the front door, and Frank went to sit at his desk. As Aaron reached the door, he stopped, turned and said, "Frank, take care of yourself. Have a happy Christmas."

Before Frank could respond, Aaron was through it and outside in the snow. Instead of calling a cab and going home to change, Aaron looked down at what he was wearing and thought, *This'll do.* He spent the next hour walking around town as a light snow began to fall.

Frank got up as Aaron left the station, traversing the steps following him then moving out of sight. He turned around and mumbled a holiday greeting to the sergeant sitting at the front desk then went back into the bullpen. *God, this place is quiet tonight. Between the snow and Christmas Eve, it's like a mausoleum.*

Frank let out a loud sigh and went to check his email. Nothing new had come in from either the NYPD or FBI criminalists. *Probably won't see anything new until the twenty-sixth. Even if crime doesn't take a holiday, things sure slow down around here.* Frank busied himself for a few minutes with paperwork, until his stomach growled audibly. *I haven't had anything to eat since sometime this morning. Not quite sure what's open that I can grab quickly, but I'm sure there's something around here.* Frank grabbed his coat and headed out into the snow to find something for dinner. The snow had tapered off from the intensity of the previous day, and there wasn't any wind that evening to speak of, so Frank didn't bother buttoning his coat. Thankfully, there was always a deli or street vendor out and about. He walked a few blocks, trying to decide what he wanted to eat before finding the Halal Guys still open at Fifty-Third and Sixth Avenue.

During Frank's walk, the snow had once again started to fall. Not much, just enough to make things seem a little serene as a he waited in line to order. Thankfully, the line was pretty quick. "What can I get you, officer?" the man in his mid-twenties asked, his focus flicking to the holstered gun inside Frank's jacket.

"I want a combination platter, a side of baba ganouj and a piece of baklava." The young man quickly took Frank's money, and a minute later Frank was carrying the yellow takeout bag with red lettering back to the station.

God, this city is gorgeous when it snows. And right now, it's just me, my thoughts, the snow, the empty sidewalk and the city. Frank smiled to himself, taking in a deep breath of cold air. *And it only partially smells like piss tonight.* He leisurely made his way back to the station. Thankfully, most of Midtown was only twenty to thirty minutes on foot in almost any direction.

Frank got back to the station and once again nodded hello to the sergeant before heading to his desk, where he opened the bag and pulled out his dinner. Frank enjoyed it and was finally diving into the baklava when he heard the vibration of his iPhone on the desk, letting him know he had a new message. He pulled it out and noticed a text from Logan.

Just saw the nine o'clock news. Jenny Mace says you have a suspect? Is that true? Ben wants to know.

Logan, tell Ben I'm not allowed to comment on an ongoing investigation.

Really? It's us!

Really. But…

I knew there would be a but —

But we do have someone we think is good for the murders. Unfortunately, we don't have anyone in custody yet.

Frank looked down at his iPhone, thinking about what he should tell his friend next.

Logan, I fucking blew it with Aaron again today.

What do you mean? I thought we were hating him for trying to fire you.

Wow, you did miss a lot today. I'll call you in a few minutes.

Frank put in his AirPods, grabbed the rest of his baklava and headed into the conference room. The FBI's equipment was still piled around the room. Even though the precinct was practically empty, Frank closed the door to give himself a little privacy before dialing Logan.

"So, what the hell happened today?" Logan asked as soon as he picked up the phone.

Frank heard holiday music in the background, along with a few voices, so he asked, "Where are you?"

"Christmas Eve get-together with the co-op board."

"I'm sorry. I didn't mean to take you away from the party."

"Trust me… I'm grateful." A door was shut before the sound was suddenly muffled. "I'm hiding in the bathroom. I only came because Ben thought it would be a good idea. I hate these things. Thankfully, it's going to be over by eleven because a few of the partygoers are attending midnight mass somewhere."

"Midnight mass... That's what Aaron's doing tonight."

"Ahh... good Catholic boy?"

"Honestly, Logan, I don't know. We really haven't talked about religion."

"So, what happened today with Federal Agent Hotness?"

"God, not you, too."

"Sorry... Ben got me calling him that around the house."

Frank groaned a little before diving into everything that had occurred over the past fourteen hours. "So, there he was, inches from my face. I could tell he wanted me to lean in and kiss him—and I froze. I fucking froze. I swear I'm fucking relationship-impaired."

"Frank, don't be so hard on yourself."

"Why not? I know I'm interested. I know he's interested. And I know that he knows that I'm interested. And yet, I was there, inches from his face, and just stood up as if nothing happened. And the moment was just...gone."

"I'm sure it wasn't as bad you think it was."

"Trust me... It was that fucking awkward. He couldn't wait to get out of here. He barely looked at me as he packed up and went to have dinner with his best friend."

"For fuck's sake. Do you like this guy, Frank?

"Yes."

"Could you see yourself with him?"

"Yes."

"Then the next time you see him, just tell him."

"But—"

"No buts, Frank. Just tell him. You already said that you know he's into you and you're into him, so the hard part's already out of the way. It's not like you're trying to figure out if your schoolyard crush likes you back."

Frank let out a quick sigh. "You're right. I know you're right."

Suddenly someone was knocking on the door and he heard Ben ask, "Logan, is everything okay in there?"

"I'm fine, Ben. Just talking to Frank."

"Is he dating Agent McHotness yet?"

"Not yet."

"Well, tell him to hurry the fuck up!"

Frank laughed at that. "Well, on that note, Logan, I should probably let you go."

"You probably should," Logan replied. A few seconds of silence passed before Logan asked, "So what are you going to do?"

"I'm going to tell him. I don't know when and I don't know how, but I'm going to tell him."

"Good for you. You deserve to be happy."

"I'm just starting to realize that."

"On that note, Merry Christmas, Frank."

"Merry Christmas, Logan." The words slipped off Frank's tongue with ease.

* * * *

"Aaaarroonn!" Judi cried, when she saw him walking up the street. She ran toward him and threw her arms around him. "So, any news on the man front?"

"Oh God, let's not talk about it."

"What happened?"

"Let's just say that ship has beyond sunk."

"Ouch, sorry to hear that."

"Ehh, shit happens. We are at least talking civilly to each other, but he's not ready, and I now get that. Maybe one day...but that day isn't today."

"Well, tonight we'll drink and be festive—and try to forget about men."

"Sounds like a plan to me," Aaron said, but he was still thinking about Frank. He opened the door to the Russian restaurant and stepped inside. A coat check person took their coats and showed them to a waiting area.

"Supervisory Special Agent Massey? Imagine seeing you here," came a high, squealing voice Aaron knew all too well.

"Jennifer Mace. Interesting to see you," he said as he turned to find the woman working her way toward him through the crowd.

Instead of shaking his hand, Jenny leaned in for a quick kiss, as if they were best friends, separated at birth. "So, I hear through the grapevine that you found a suspect. Good for you. I knew putting you in charge would speed things up. I mean, that's exactly what I told Rinehart she should do yesterday."

"Excuse me... *You* told Rinehart?" Aaron questioned.

"Of course. You know she and I go way back."

"Oh, really," Aaron said. He'd heard rumors that Jenny and the mayor had had an affair, but those rumors had always been discussed in the past tense.

"So, can I get a quote from my favorite sexy FBI agent?"

"Oh, Jenny, you know I can't share anything with you."

A tall blond man suddenly appeared at Jenny's side. "Oh, Aaron, this is Donald Bankert of the Wall Street firm Bankert Associates. Donald, honey, this is Aaron Massey, the FBI agent I was telling you about."

"Nice to meet you," Bankert said as he extended his hand.

"Oh, and who is your friend, Aaron?" Jenny asked.

"Oh, umm, Judi Wright, meet the notorious Jenny Mace."

Judi gave Aaron the eye before extending her hand. "Nice to meet you, Ms. Mace."

"Ms. Mace, oh so formal. I guess they teach you that in children's publishing. Gotta teach our kids good morals."

"Oh, you've heard of me?" Judi questioned.

"Honey, I know more about Supervisory Special Agent Aaron Massey than he probably knows about himself. That's my job, you know, as an investigative reporter."

"Oh, really?" Judi said with a clear sense of sarcasm in her voice that went completely unnoticed by the Macinator.

"So, Aaron, dear, are you and Detective Dreamy an item or what?"

"Uhh, what?" Aaron was surprised by the sudden change in questioning.

"Oh please. What? You didn't think I'd notice how you slipped your arm around him while you two were at Bloomingdale's?"

"I, uhm —"

"Bankert, party of two," a voice suddenly broke through the crowd. "Bankert, party of two, your table is ready."

"Oh well, Aaron, dear, I must get all the juicy details from you later."

Aaron ignored that as Jenny leaned in and kissed him on both cheeks before turning away.

"Dear fucking God, I hate that woman!" Judi said as soon as Jenny was out of earshot.

"That makes two of us."

"Why do you pretend to like that bitch?" Judi questioned.

"She's a necessary evil in this town. You either play nice with her, or you get run over by her. And I, for one, have no desire to be her next target."

"Massey? Massey, party of two?"

The maître d' led them to a small table next to a window toward the back of the restaurant. Aaron examined the area, spotted Jenny flirting with her date on the other side of the room and gave a deep sigh of relief.

While they were eating, Judi finally broached the topic of Frank. "So, tell me what happened tonight."

"What do you mean?"

"Aaron, I'm your best friend. I'm not an idiot. Something has you preoccupied. It's written all over your face." Judi stared at Aaron with a clear look of concern.

Aaron took a deep breath and relayed the conversation he'd had with Frank before Aaron had left the precinct.

"So, do you think he said that because he wants you gone or to see if you'll go?" Judi questioned.

"I really don't know. I wish I did, but I just don't."

Instead of pressing Aaron further, Judi looked down at her watch, exclaiming, "Oh God, it's almost eleven. We probably should get moving if we're going to make it to midnight mass. You know, St. Patrick's fills so quickly for this service."

Aaron signaled for the server and got their check. After paying, they picked up their coats and headed out into the cold. Judi took Aaron by the arm as they headed down the street. She talked the whole time, but Aaron was still thinking about Frank.

* * * *

At around a quarter till eleven, Frank decided it was time for a caffeine run. Sadly, Viva La Coffee wasn't open, but there was a deli around the corner that at least had a hot substance that resembled coffee. He asked around the bullpen to see if he could get anything for the handful of offers still there before leaving, but no one needed a refill yet.

The trip was uneventful, and Frank was back in under fifteen minutes. The snow had started coming down a bit harder than it had a couple of hours before, so Frank was glad when he climbed back up the short set of stairs into the precinct. At eleven at night on Christmas Eve, the building was virtually empty. As Frank entered, he shook off the snow from his coat. "Detective Schultt," the desk sergeant started, "a guy from the FBI just delivered a box to your desk."

"Hey, George, thanks for the heads up," Frank said as he walked to the bullpen. He noticed the medium-sized white box with a bow on top and reached into his desk to find a pair of scissors to help him open the box. *That fucking Aaron. Can't believe he messengered over a Christmas present.* Frank opened the box and found a wooden nutcracker. He took the nutcracker out of the box and set it on the table. *Why the fuck did he send me this?* He looked at the nutcracker for a minute before noticing something glossy white sticking out from the base. *Must be the card.* He flipped over the nutcracker to see the final postcard in the series — Twelve Drummers Drumming. Frank snatched the postcard off the base and flipped it over. *My masterpiece is complete,* was written on the back in a dried reddish-brown ink Frank knew was blood.

Frank put the nutcracker back into the box. He looked around the bullpen, but no one was there. He picked up the desk phone and called the front lobby.

"NYPD Manhattan Precinct, Officer Kaminsky."

"George, it's Frank. Did you get a good look at the delivery person?"

"Average-looking guy, nothing too remarkable."

"Don't move. I need you to look at a picture." Frank hung up and grabbed Hecht's photo from the whiteboard Jasika had stuck on it earlier and ran out to the front lobby. "George, look at this photo. Was this the delivery man?"

Officer Kaminsky looked at the picture for a second, "Could be. The guy had darker hair and a mustache." Frank picked up a pen on Kaminsky's desk, drew a quick mustache on the picture and showed it again to George. "Yep, that's definitely the guy. Who is he?"

"George, you just let the Twelve-Day Killer deliver a package to my desk." Frank picked up his cell phone and called Aaron's, but it went immediately to voice mail. He walked back into the bullpen, not even acknowledging the look on George's face or his immediate series of ranting apologies. Frank called Jasika and told her what had happened, and that he was sending a car to Queens. He then called dispatch

241

and had a car sent to get Jasika and bring her back ASAP.

Back at his desk, Frank pulled out the card Agent Rummy had given him. He turned it over and noticed the cell number scrawled on the back. He plugged the number into his phone and hit dial.

The voice that greeted Frank wasn't exactly awake. "This is Rummy."

"Agent Rummy, Frank Schultt, I need you here *now*. The Twelve-Day Killer just entered the precinct and left a package for me on my desk."

While waiting for Rummy to get to the station, Frank called Aaron's cell twice more, then called Mariella. She had still been working at her desk at the medical examiner's office but was preparing to head out. She informed Frank that she'd keep her cell phone with her and on, just in case.

Frank then called the geek twins and got a hold of Nasab, who was still there. Nasab said he'd get a van and come over to assist Rummy in any way he could. He informed Frank that Richardson was with his wife and kids, so unless everyone was needed, he'd prefer not to call him.

"Don't worry about bothering him, Nasab. If we need more eyes and hands, we can always keep him in our back pocket. Are you on duty tonight?"

"Yeah, I'm a Muslim, so it's not exactly my holiday. It works for me."

"I would think so," Frank said, noticing Rummy had entered the building. "Okay, get over here as soon as you can. Rummy just got here."

Rummy walked over to Frank, reached into his coat jacket, removed a pair of latex gloves and began putting them on. "Anyone touch the box?"

"I did. I thought it was a present from a colleague," Frank said, purposefully leaving out whom he thought the colleague was.

Rummy picked up the box and its contents and headed into the conference room. "I have a criminalist toolbox in here, just in case," Rummy said. He quickly pulled out what looked like an oversized tackle box. "Fuck, I don't have any fingerprint dust in here. Where's your copy machine?"

"It's in the main room."

"Show me." Frank escorted Rummy to the copier. Rummy opened the machine, pulled out the toner cartridge and opened the container. He created a small funnel using a piece of paper and poured some toner into a small jar. He then shook the jar, Frank supposed to make sure that the toner was sticking to the sides. He was proven right when Rummy said, "Perfect," then walked back into the conference room, spread out a piece of *The New York Times* on the table and set about dusting the box.

"Do me a favor and start by dusting the card. If history remains the same, that card will be the key to this."

"Sure thing, Detective." Rummy picked up the notecard, held it in the light and twisted it to examine from various angles. He found the single fingerprint and dusted it. He then took out his cellphone, took a picture of the print and sent it to the FBI mainframe for analysis. "Should take less than ten minutes for a return."

"Can I just say, that is so fucking cool."

"Thanks, it's a system I designed while I was in graduate school. I have a master's degree in biometrics from Cornell. When I created the cell phone scan to

AIFIS compatibility, the FBI recruited me before I was even finished with school. We're still pilot-testing the interface, but thus far, it's working really well."

Beep, beep.

Rummy looked down at his cell phone. "We have a match. The system should be sending me the file right now."

Rummy sat down at the computer screen and opened an email attachment while projecting his screen to the virtual whiteboard in the conference room. The email attachment contained one name, a set of prints and a picture of Aaron Massey.

Chapter Fifteen

December 24, just before midnight

Frank took out his cellphone and called Jasika. She picked up on the first ring. "Frank, I'm almost there. What's up?"

"The print…" Frank's voice wavered for a second as a swell of emotion almost overtook him. He took a deep breath and continued, "We printed the card. It came back as Aaron's."

"Oh my God!"

"I've tried calling him, but it just keeps going to voice mail. Rummy's trying to rectify that."

"Got it," Rummy responded. "I was able to remotely ping his cell phone's GPS. The phone is off, but the power source is still inside, so we should get a location. I'm triangulating his location now."

Frank looked down at his watch and noticed that the time was just shy of midnight. He then suddenly realized where Aaron was. "St. Patrick's Cathedral."

"Huh?" Rummy asked.

"Aaron was going to midnight mass at St. Patrick's Cathedral."

Rummy looked at the screen and the triangulation pinpointed Aaron blocks away. "The cell phone is at St. Patrick's Cathedral. You're right."

Frank told Jasika to direct her car to St. Patrick's and he'd meet her there. Frank headed back to the bullpen when George came running in from the front lobby. "There's been a bomb threat at St. Patrick's Cathedral. At least one person's been shot."

"Rummy," Frank barked, "Aaron said we could mobilize the NYPD and FBI in less than fifteen minutes... Do it *now!*"

Frank grabbed his coat, put his AirPods in his ears and called the Chief. Chief Hays' wife picked up the phone, woken from sleep. She got her husband on.

"This better be fucking important," Hays muttered.

"Chief, he's at St. Patrick Cathedral and phone calls are already coming in that he's killed one person and has a bomb."

"Whoa, Frank, slow down. What the fuck?"

Frank exited the precinct, walked out into the snow and started jogging toward St. Patrick's. He hung up with Hays, who was going to call the mayor and let her know what was going on. As he rounded the corner near St. Patrick's, he saw the mayhem erupting around the front of the church. People were screaming and wailing, seemingly not sure what to do or where to go. Some were hanging out on the church steps while others were standing across the street.

The first group of squad cars began to arrive, and uniformed patrols started unloading, awaiting orders. Frank stopped and took in the whole situation before barking directions to the officers on the scene.

"Establish a perimeter. There's a bomb in there. Get everyone back!"

An NYPD utility van emerged down the street, and a group of officers began setting up a roadblock around the church. A couple of minutes later, a mobile command officer was on the scene. Frank recognized the Brooklyn ESU field agent he'd met earlier that day.

"Detective Schultt," Dalia Washington called as she stepped out of the van when it came to a stop in front of the church, "what do you know?"

"I was in the precinct when the call came in. The emergency hotline suddenly lit up like a Christmas tree as people sitting in the church for mass witnessed a man pull out a gun, kill someone and scream that he had a bomb," Frank explained.

"Okay, we know that he's still inside the church with at least a handful of hostages. We don't know who's in there yet. I will get snipers set up on the surrounding buildings and get some infrared for a general idea of what's going on inside. I don't know how useful the information will be, but I'm hopeful we'll have a clear picture in about ten minutes," Washington told him.

"Perfect. Handle tactical but keep me in the loop," Frank said.

"Will do."

"Frank!"

Frank spun around to see Jasika making her way toward him. She was wearing a heavy coat, and her shield hung around her neck on a silver chain.

"What's going on?" she asked.

Frank filled her in on what he'd learned from Washington. He was finishing his conversation when he once again heard his name being yelled out from somewhere in the crowd. Finally, Frank spotted a woman calling his name from the other side of the newly erected police barricade. He walked over to her.

"Frank, he's got Aaron!"

"What? Who are you?"

"I'm Judith Wright — Aaron Massey's best friend."

Upon hearing those words, Frank motioned for the officer to let her through the barricade. She hesitated but came over when Frank motioned for her to follow him. "Tell me everything you know," he said as he led her toward the main command station. Frank opened the door and ushered Judi into the command vehicle.

"What are you doing in here? This is for police personnel only," Washington said before seeing Frank following Judi.

"Officer Washington, this is Judith Wright. She was in the church and has information," Frank said.

Judi looked at Frank, who motioned for her to tell her story. Judi started hesitantly but then explained, "After dinner at Pectopah, we walked over here to get a good seat. Right after the bishop stood up and started the mass, a man in the aisle behind us tapped Aaron on the shoulder. Aaron turned around and the man shoved a syringe into his neck and injected him with something. Aaron just collapsed. He was still breathing, but he just slumped. The woman next to us started screaming and the guy pulled out a gun and shot her. At that point, I'm not even sure how I got out of there. Someone grabbed me and started pushing me toward the exit. I remember someone falling in front of me and people were walking on him as they tried to escape. The whole thing happened so fast."

"Judi, I don't know how, but this motherfucker is going down," Frank said, emotion welling up inside him.

Frank had an officer escort Judi out of the van and take her to a patrol car. Frank instructed the officer not to leave her side. He then turned back to Washington and asked for an update.

"We just had a phone call from a burner phone go through our central system. The man claimed to be Thomas Hecht, and he says he's holding the mayor, a councilman, a congressman and Agent Massey hostage inside the cathedral. I have officers checking on these claims, but I have no reason to believe that it's not Hecht or that he has the hostages in question."

"Fuck!" Frank exclaimed.

"Oh, and one more thing... He will only negotiate with you."

Chapter Sixteen

December 25, 12:30 a.m.

"He *what*?" Frank asked with a hint of skepticism in his voice.

"He only will negotiate with you, and he wants you in person."

"Why?"

"I don't really know. And at this point, we really don't care. Come here. We can replay the phone call for you." Washington leaned over a computer terminal and handed Frank a headset. Frank put it on, and immediately a voice started speaking.

"My name is Thomas Hecht. Please let Detective François Schultt know that I have Agent Massey, Mayor Rinehart and her husband, Congressman Sias, Councilman Sandvik and a few other choice guests still inside the cathedral. I will only speak to Detective Schultt. Once this phone call is over, I'm destroying the phone, so he'll have to come talk to me in person."

"Dear God, he's really been planning this whole thing," Frank said to himself. "I mean, we knew he had a big showcase for December twenty-fifth, but we never would have guessed this would be his goal." Frank lost himself as he tried to think of an easy way to end the situation. *He's got Aaron. But why does he have Aaron? How did he even know where Aaron was going to be?* The thoughts swam around Frank's head like a feeding frenzy at the Bronx Zoo.

"Detective?" Washington's voice yanked him from his maze of wayward thoughts. "Detective Schultt?"

"Oh...yeah...sorry. Suggestions?"

"As a matter of fact, we've had a hostage plan in place for St. Patrick's Cathedral for a few years. After 9-11, we created contingencies for a range of terrorist situations for most of the major monuments in the city." She hit a few keys on the computer, and immediately an internal blueprint of St. Patrick's Cathedral came onto the screen. "The major entrances and exits are on Fifth Avenue, Fiftieth and Fifty-Second Streets. There's also an underground entrance into the crypt that leads up to the high altar. Once we have infrared, we'll be able to decide on which place to proceed. I've already sent a SWAT member to the church to cut a precision hole into a pane of glass and insert a camera. We're hoping to get a general idea of what we're seeing. Speak of the devil—"

The computer screen flickered as an image suddenly appeared, showing the inside of St. Patrick's Cathedral. The nave of the church was virtually empty. The camera strained to see the rest of the area but couldn't quite make anything out. "Moving to secondary camera position," a voice said over the radio.

"Is that frequency secure?" Frank asked.

"Don't worry. It's a special frequency for emergency responders that was created after 9-11. It's the most secure form of communication we have in these situations," Washington assured him.

Frank and Washington stayed transfixed to the screen. While they were waiting, Jasika came into the mobile command unit and let them know that the block was completely secure. Frank filled her in on the progress that was being made and the hostage rescue plan the NYPD had created. A new image suddenly appeared, and this one was much closer to the high altar. Frank could see a group of people who'd been tied together sitting in front of it. The bronze baldachin loomed in the background. A briefcase was sitting on top of the altar, which Frank assumed was the bomb the fleeing churchgoers had talked about. Walking in front of the altar was Thomas Hecht. In the center of the raised platform, Frank could see Aaron Massey, still unconscious, tied down to an oversized, hand-carved wooden chair. *Okay, he's not awake yet.*

"The crypt entrance is officially off the table. We'd make entirely too much noise trying to come up that way," Washington said matter-of-factly.

"Recommendations?" Frank asked.

"Our best bet is to get a sharpshooter into the tower and hope for a clear shot. This is, of course, assuming that Hecht hasn't barricaded himself into the building and booby-trapped the tower doors. We should know in a minute."

Frank turned his attention back to the monitor as simultaneous cameras appeared in a dark area and immediately switched to infrared. Washington started narrating the video feed. "We can see that both doors have been padlocked shut, but that's fairly easy to get through. As far as I can see from these images, there are no improvised explosive devices or alarms attached to the doors. Our best bet is a simultaneous distraction as both doors are breached."

"I can provide the distraction," Frank said.

"How?" Washington countered.

"Send me in. It's me he wants, so it's me he'll get."

"Officially, your involvement at this point goes against all the clear codes of conduct for a hostage negotiation."

"And?"

"Unofficially, I agree that you're probably the best distraction. You can enter and make enough noise to allow us to breach the building. There's just one problem."

"What?"

"I only have one sharpshooter. I will pull a secondary, but that could take an hour if not longer."

"You have two," Jasika offered.

"Huh?" Washington replied, confused.

"Check my scores at the academy. I scored top in my class for sharpshooting there. I was recruited for ESS but wanted to be a detective, so I went to vice instead. I'm certified by the American Sniper Association."

"I'm not quite sure if you're qualified..."

"Trust me," Frank replied. "I've seen her shoot. She's amazing. Right now, time is of the essence. If Detective Torv thinks she can take the shot, she can take the shot."

"Fuck it," Washington replied. "None of this was part of the original scenario." She turned and looked at Jasika. "You only take the shot after I've given the go-ahead, and only after the primary shooter says he can't get it. Is that understood?"

"Yes, ma'am."

In minutes, Frank, Jasika and another ESS member were outfitted and ready to breach the three entrances to St. Patrick Cathedral.

The breach was borderline textbook. Frank entered the building through the front door as Jasika and the other officers entered the two towers from the east and west tower doors. Frank started yelling as he entered the building to catch Hecht's attention.

"Thomas Hecht! It's Detective Frank Schultt. I'm told you want to talk to me," Frank called out as he made his way through the cathedral's foyer into the back of the nave. Frank listened as he did so but didn't hear a sound coming from either side of him. He kept walking toward the altar.

Hecht seemed to be taken aback by his brazen entrance and quickly put himself between Aaron and the other people tied to the altar.

"So, Mr. Hecht, what is it you wanted to talk about?" Frank asked as he took an aisle seat halfway down the nave.

"What are you doing?" Hecht's raspy voice asked as Frank sat down.

"Well, according to your phone call, you'd only talk to me—so here I am," Frank said, stretching his arms across the back of the pew he'd sat down in.

"Come closer!" Hecht practically screamed down the aisle at him.

"Nah. For the moment, I'll stay where I am."

"If you don't come closer, I'll start killing people."

"If you were going to start killing people, you'd have already done it. The way I look at it, you've waited to get into a room with me, so here I am," Frank said, eyeing Hecht and hoping that his diversion was giving

Jasika and the SWAT officer enough time to get into position. "Oh, and thanks for the Christmas present."

"You got it? Good." Hecht's demeanor quickly changed, clearly showing that he was proud of himself. "I couldn't believe that guard was so dumb. I planned on just shooting him, but he made it so fucking easy. He let me walk right in and place it on your desk. If it had been a bomb, you'd have blown up before you even knew I'd been there."

"Yeah, apparently you have a thing for bombs," Frank noted as he motioned toward the briefcase.

"They're crude devices, but they're definitely effective. Nice to know that my New York education is being put to such good use," Hecht replied.

"So, how'd you get Massey's fingerprint for my last postcard?" Frank figured he might as well keep the suspect talking.

"Oh, that?" Hecht started, "Easy. I walked right into your precinct earlier in the day and got it from him. You were standing right next to him. Don't you remember?"

Frank thought about it for a second. *How the hell did this guy get into the precinct during the middle of the day? Fuck! The FBI had our lunch catered-in to help speed up the investigative process.* "I didn't even realize that Delicious Delights had catered our lunch."

"So, you do remember. When the call came in that morning, dear Alexi was so busy that I helped handle the entire order without it ever going into her precious notebook. Some surprises are just fun to keep until the end of the story, wouldn't you say?"

"Yeah, love her cupcakes. That should have triggered my sensory memory. Oh well." Frank stood and walked a couple of more pews forward to test Hecht's reaction.

"Stop right there, Detective," Hecht said flatly. "In fact, take off your jacket." Frank complied and even spun around to show Hecht that he wasn't carrying a gun. Of course, Frank had a small-caliber one located in a concealment undershirt beneath his bulletproof vest, just in case. "Lift your pant legs." Frank once again followed Hecht's instructions.

"I would let you give me a full-body cavity search, but you'd have to buy me dinner first," Frank joked. He turned and smiled at Hecht, who eyed him questioningly. Frank noticed a slight movement from Aaron, who was sitting in front of him. *Hurry up, Aaron. I need you awake for this to work.*

"So, you have me here. I don't have a gun. Why don't you tell me why you're doing this? All of this."

"You haven't figured it out yet?"

"Nope. I have some pieces to your puzzle. We know about the drunk driver when you were ten, the foster homes and being institutionalized. Still, those happen to lots of kids who don't kill over a dozen innocent people."

"Maybe I'm just fucking insane. Maybe mother dearest raped me — or one of my myriad foster fathers beat me. Does it really matter why?" Hecht countered.

"Nah, but I'm sure Agent Massey will want to know. You know, when he writes his next bestseller all about you."

"Trust me... He won't be able to write that book," Hecht said as he pulled out a small device that Frank immediately surmised was the detonator.

"Hey, let's play this cool. There's no need for anyone else to get hurt. What do you want?"

"Justice."

"Justice. For what?"

"Everyone knows that this holiday sucks and makes people feel and act badly. Just look at you."

"What about me?" Frank questioned.

"Please… We both know how much you hate this holiday. And I get it, I really do. If my husband had been shot on Christmas, I'd hate it too. So, why should everyone be allowed to rub our faces in it?"

"Huh?"

"Come on. Everything about this holiday shoves your past into your face — every light, every decoration, every holiday jingle just a reminder of the worst day of your life."

"I won't deny it. I hate this fucking holiday."

"See? We're on the same side."

"How so?"

"We hate the holiday and what it's done to us and others. The only difference is that I help people out of their misery. I release them."

Frank took a moment, looking Hecht in the eyes. Then, glancing down at Aaron, Frank noticed his eyes were partially open for the first time. *He's awake.* Not wanting to give anything away, Frank decided to go bold.

"Well, I may have hated this holiday. I may *still* hate this holiday, but it's also given me something new."

"Something new?" Hecht asked.

"Sure, it's given me the amazing man sitting in that chair. In fact, I can say that I think I may love that man. Trust me… I've done my damndest to push him as hard and as far away as humanly possible, but he's still here —"

"I seriously doubt it's love, Detective," Hecht replied, cutting Frank off. "Lust, maybe, but not love.

You two haven't known each other long enough for it to be love — assuming love even exists."

"I disagree. Trust me... I haven't felt this way about anyone since my husband died. Hell, I didn't even let myself admit it until I saw him tied up unconscious there. I would do anything to trade places with him right now. And isn't the desire to sacrifice oneself for another person the ultimate sign of love?"

"Maybe, but this conversation bores me." Hecht raised the remote control for the bomb. "Merry Christmas to all, and to all, a good nigh — "

Aaron swung his weight to one side, causing the wooden chair to topple over. The arm of the chair shattered in a splintering crack, freeing one of Aaron's arms in the process. The look of sudden shock on Hecht's face was obscured only by the subsequent red hole appearing in the center of his temple. The detonator fell out of his hands as he crumpled. Aaron, still moving, lurched to catch the detonator before it hit the floor. Frank catapulted himself over the pews to make sure Hecht was dead.

Frank threw off his bulletproof vest, revealing his concealment undershirt, and immediately withdrew a walkie-talkie and a Swiss Army knife. "Suspect is down!" Frank said energetically into the walkie-talkie. "I repeat, suspect is down. We need emergency personnel in here immediately." Frank set about releasing the hostages one by one.

The mayor's husband took Frank's hand and shook it vigorously, saying that he was forever in his debt. The mayor threw her arms around Frank's neck and kissed him on the cheek. She looked absolutely mesmerized, probably because the whole ordeal had ended so quickly. *You were just kidnapped and tied to an altar, but you're still a fucking politician,* Frank thought as he smiled back at the city leader.

After releasing the other victims, Frank turned to Aaron. "Thank God you woke up when you did." Just after showing Hecht that he wasn't carrying a gun under his pants legs and at the moment he'd noticed that Aaron was resuming consciousness, he had made a gesture to the left and Aaron had blinked twice, acknowledging what he had to do. When Frank had given him the nod, Aaron had thrown his weight in the direction Frank had pointed.

Frank released Aaron and threw his arms around him. "I almost lost you, Aaron Massey. Fuck you for making me care about you! Fuck you." Frank brought Aaron closer and kissed him deeply. He pulled Aaron as tight as he could, shedding a tear, but not because he was grieving. He was crying because he was happy.

Epilogue

January 15, 8 p.m.

"Frank, we're going to be late!" Aaron said, gently pushing Frank off him. "We have to help Logan console Ben for that horrific disaster that was *Moose Murders*."

Much like the original production, the critics had panned the revival. They'd said that *"Benjamin Hiller should stick to soap operas and let real actors do the acting."* The producers closed the show two days later when only twenty tickets had been sold, and those people were either out-of-towners who hadn't shown up to TKTS early enough to get tickets to *Phantom* or people who'd mocked the play. To help Ben deal with his humiliation, Logan had organized a small get-together at La Bella's to help console him.

Frank, decked out in a winter sweater and jeans, forced himself back on top of Aaron, bent down and kissed him before resting his head on Aaron's chest. For the first time in years, Frank was at home with himself and with someone else. Although Frank hadn't moved in with Aaron, they were practically inseparable.

Frank was proud of Aaron because he'd decided to fully resign from the FBI and had taken a job at John Jay College teaching Forensic Psychology, but Frank doubted the FBI was going to let Aaron go that easy. Aaron was already pounding away at his new book based on the Twelve-Day Killer, with his proud and dutiful boyfriend as the star attraction.

Jasika and Frank had both received commendations from the mayor for bravery and had been touted across the nation as heroes. Jasika had even earned her second-grade shield, so there was no more knocking her back down to vice.

Mariella and the geek twins had spent a week finishing out the case and making sure that all the body parts were returned to family members for burial or cremation. The geek twins were already working on a paper together dealing with some finer aspects of the forensic science of the case. Mariella had expressed her disappoint that she'd have to share her affections for Frank with 'another woman', as she referred to Aaron.

An anonymous donor in the city had provided financial support to all the families to ensure their loved ones were properly buried. Frank couldn't prove who the benefactor was, but he suspected that it was Aaron. After practically moving in with him, Frank had quickly come to realize that dating an international bestselling author provided a few perks he hadn't expected. And although Frank had never seen Aaron's financials, he was positive that Aaron was living far below his actual means. In fact, after moving some of his own clothing into Aaron's closet, he'd noticed that the rich version of Aaron he'd met at FAO Schwarz just a month earlier was more Aaron's usual style than the nose-to-the-grindstone everyman that Aaron had portrayed during the case—but that didn't matter to Frank.

Frank pulled his head up just slightly that was still nestled right below Aaron's chin, and stared into his deep blue eyes. "God, I love you."

"I know you do," Aaron replied. "And it sure took you long enough to realize it." Aaron bent down, kissed Frank on the forehead and squeezed him tightly as their hearts beat in sync.

"Now, get off me. We don't want to be late."

Want to see more from this author?
Here's a taster for you to enjoy!

Till Death Do Us Wed
Jason Wrench

Coming February 2022

Excerpt

Frank stared around the pink office, wondering if a bottle of Pepto Bismol had accidentally spilled. He watched the perky blonde woman sitting in front of him, doing his best to pay attention. It wasn't exactly how Frank liked to spend his Saturday mornings. But it was Aaron's big day, so he'd promised to grin and bear it.

"With Central Park wedding locations, we are definitely somewhat limited. For example, the Bow Bridge only allows for ten guests and the Belvedere Castle Terrace only allows thirty. The North Garden, Southern Garden, Wisteria Pergola and Cherry Hill each allow for up to one hundred. What size are you two thinking?"

"Eloping," Frank muttered.

"Twenty-five to fifty," Aaron said, shooting Frank a sideways glance.

"I'm joking," Frank reassured, patting Aaron's leg and giving it a squeeze before turning to the woman. "Whatever Aaron wants, I want him to have."

NYPD Detective Frank Schultt and FBI Special Agent Aaron Massey had met the previous year during a serial murder spree. The Twelve-Day Killer, as dubbed by the media, had terrorized NYC over the holidays. Aaron and Frank had put their lives and careers on the line hunting the bastard down. In the process, they had found each other.

Frank glanced over at the man he loved. *God, where would I be without him?* He reached up and rubbed the back of Aaron's neck gently. From the top of Aaron's head with his dark brown quaff haircut and his Caribbean ocean-blue eyes, to his lithe but fit body, Frank took in this man sitting beside him who was going to be his husband. Frank was still stunned at his good fortune in landing the affection of such an amazingly intelligent and gorgeous man.

Realizing his thoughts had drifted, Frank brought his attention back to the woman sitting in front of him, who was rattling on about Central Park weddings. He glanced down at her nameplate, '*Amber Wethersfield*'. The woman was in her late twenties. And judging by the giant diamond on her wedding ring, her husband was definitely wealthy. Frank glanced across the pink office looking for personal items and was surprised by the lack of photos. *For a woman who sells marriage, where are the pictures of her happy day?*

"So, do you have an officiant for your wedding lined up? If not, I have a list of great people who work with LGBTQIA+ people."

"Huh?" Frank blurted before he could catch himself.

"Officiant...the person who will oversee the ceremony and the exchange of your vows," Amber offered.

"No, you listed off a bunch of letters," Frank said.

"Oh." Amber perked up. "Lesbian, gay, bisexual, transgender, queer-questioning, intersexed, asexual and others."

Dear God, that sounds like a gay BLT. Frank was about to make the snide comment, but a quick glance from Aaron told him that he'd better hold his tongue. Instead, Frank just nodded his head and gave a thin-lipped smile.

"Actually, we have a few people in mind," Aaron noted. "Frank knows a judge who volunteered her services, and we have a couple of other names in the hopper as well."

"Oh, good," Amber said. "You'd be amazed at how many people totally forget the officiant until the last minute. I even have a license I got from an online church because I've had to step in at the eleventh hour when something went horribly wrong. I just don't enjoy being in the wedding party, because it makes it harder for me to run things behind the scenes."

Frank leaned back in the chair and watched as Aaron and Amber discussed the wedding. This wasn't Frank's first. He'd been married, but his husband had been murdered in a liquor store robbery on Christmas Eve over six years ago. As much as Frank loved Aaron, there was still a vast hole in his heart that had been left by Adam's death. But Frank loved Aaron and was going to make sure their wedding day was every bit of glitz and glamour that Aaron desired.

"Well, if you have questions," Amber said, bringing Frank's attention back once again, "just let me know. You have my email, cell phone, home phone and office phone numbers, so never hesitate to reach out. I look forward to working with both of you on your big day."

Amber stood up from her desk to usher the couple out of her office. She pushed herself up, exposing her pregnant belly.

"When's the due date?" Aaron asked.

"Mid-March. But I swear she's ready to come out any day."

Frank stared at her belly and just thought, *Are you sure there's only one in there?* But once again, he held his tongue.

"Don't worry. I won't miss your big day. When I'm out on maternity leave, my assistant will take over the day-to-day preparations, and he'll be in constant contact with me. When I had my first baby, we were texting right up until they told me to push."

"Well, it was really was nice meeting you," Frank said.

"Likewise. And I just have to say, you two make such a cute couple."

"Thank you," Aaron said. "I think he's a keeper." Aaron gave Amber a little wink before turning to leave.

As Frank followed suit, Aaron's hand rested in the small of Frank's back. Frank leaned into Aaron in response.

"Earth to Frank!" Aaron said as they exited onto the sidewalk. The February chill immediately caught Aaron off guard, and he lifted the collar on the trench coat to protect his neck.

"Huh, what?"

"I said, "*Earth to Frank.*" What's going on inside that head of yours?"

"Overwhelmed, I guess."

"How so?"

"The whole wedding planning is just bringing up some memories."

Aaron squeezed Frank. "I hadn't thought about that. I forget that you've done this before."

"Yeah," Frank said, scrunching his forehead. "It's surreal. Don't get me wrong, I'm excited to be marrying you. I hope you know that. It's just that it brings up memories of Adam."

"I get it," Aaron said. "I would be surprised if it didn't, to be honest." Aaron hesitated for a second before adding, "Just know...I will never try to replace Adam. I know what you two had was special—"

"What we have is special too."

"I know," Aaron acknowledged. "I just want you to know that I love you and would never try to change you...warts and all."

"God, I hope I don't have any warts."

"We all have warts. Some have them physically and others have them metaphorically."

"Sure thing, professor," Frank teased.

After dealing with the Twelve-Day Killer, Aaron had taken a teaching position part-time with the John Jay School of Criminal Justice. He was technically still on the FBI's payroll, but his utility as an undercover agent had taken a hit after the amount of press the Twelve-Day Killer had received. And with the forthcoming publication of his new book about the case, Aaron and Frank both knew a fresh round of press attention was right around the corner.

"So, we didn't have breakfast after the gym this morning," Aaron said. "Shall we have a quick brunch before heading back to the apartment to get ready?"

"Do we have time?" Frank asked, glancing down at his watch. "It's already ten a.m. What time is the car picking us up for the reading?"

"The reading's at two o'clock, so the car is scheduled to pick us up about one-fifteen."

"I guess we have plenty of time. Any suggestions on where we should eat?"

"How about 9Ten?" Aaron asked, referring to one of their favorite diners.

"Lead the way."

* * * *

Frank ordered the 9Ten Tsoureki French Toast, a Greek sweetbread topped with powdered sugar and maple syrup, and Aaron ordered the Topped-Out Waffle with organic scrambled eggs and Black Forest ham. At ten a.m., the diner had slowed from the early morning rush, but it was still a bustling establishment. It sat on Seventh Avenue between Fifty-Seventh and Fifty-Eighth, so it wasn't exactly in a high-traffic tourist part of Midtown, which was one reason Frank and Aaron enjoyed going there.

"So, are you ready for your reading this afternoon?" Frank asked.

"As ready as I'm going to be, I guess."

Aaron's new book, *The Twelve-Day Killer*, his follow-up to the international bestseller *Blood Money*, was coming out the next week, so his agent and publisher had scheduled a reading at Barnes & Noble to build buzz — not that the book needed it. The book was already sitting atop several bestseller lists, based on preorders alone.

"Decided which part of the book you're going to read?"

"I'm still debating, but I'm definitely leaning toward how we met."

Frank and Aaron had met at a crime scene. Frank had found Aaron's demeanor extremely suspicious, so Aaron had catapulted to the top of the list of Frank's suspects. Frank had later found out that Aaron's suspicious behavior resulted from his being undercover on a human-trafficking case for the FBI. At first, Frank had loathed Special Agent Aaron Massey, but Frank and Aaron had quickly realized that they liked each other and had eventually fallen in love during the case.

The waiter, a very attractive Greek man in his mid-twenties, approached the table and set down their breakfast. *Damn! He could be a model*, Frank thought. Frank caught the slight uptick at the corner of the man's mouth as he set Aaron's plate down in front of him.

"Flirt much?" Frank said under his breath as the waiter left the table.

"I beg your pardon," Aaron said, stabbing a piece of waffle into his mouth.

"Not you," Frank reassured. "The waiter. He was practically drooling on you."

"Frank," Aaron said with a bit of an exasperated sigh, "he wasn't flirting. Besides, I don't think he's even gay."

Frank narrowed his eyes skeptically but decided not to pursue that line of thought any further. *Keep it together, Frank! Jealousy is not sexy.*

Frank quickly changed topics, "So, how are things in your class?"

With a new topic on the table, Aaron spent the rest of their breakfast talking about his new group of students and how much he was enjoying teaching. Frank wolfed down his French toast, smiling and nodding his head at appropriate times. The couple of more times when the waiter approached the table, Frank did his best to keep it together, but he instinctively wanted to growl at the man and tell him to back off.

About the Author

Jason Wrench is a professor in the Department of Communication at SUNY New Paltz and has authored/edited 15+ books and over 35 academic research articles. He is also an avid reader and regularly reviews books for publishers in a wide number of genres. This book marks his first full-length work of fiction.

Jason loves to hear from readers. You can find his contact information, website details and author profile page at https://www.pride-publishing.com

PUBLISHING

Sign up for our newsletter and find out about all our
romance book releases, eBook sales and promotions,
sneak peeks and FREE romance books!

www.ingramcontent.com/pod-product-compliance
Lightning Source LLC
Chambersburg PA
CBHW031451260626
47154CB00016B/746